BRIGIT'S BOW

Chronicles of Eirgalon: Book 3

By

Joel Kreger

ISBN 978-0-9889514-8-8

Dedication

To Kathy, the one who has always been by my side
with her love and support

Table of Contents

Prologue

By mere tendrils of thoughts do the gods speak, ere so slightly, to the choices of a young woman, and so is altered the course of human history.

In realms which lay beyond domains of humankind, exist such beings called by mortals: "the gods." Be they gods or demons in human thoughts matters little; for truth be told, to some they may be gods and to some they may be demons. Be that as it may, at times they touch the human world, and in their touching they move and turn that world into different outcomes and alternate timelines.

One of these beings was known as Gluskabi. The people of Eirgalon viewed him as a benevolent spirit who delighted in the passion and pathos of the people of the land. It was his touching of human history that resulted in the timeline of a mixed society of people descended from the first inhabitants of the land, and the immigrants from eastern Celtic and Nordic lands.

His alter-ego was a spirit called Lox. Lox's malevolence toward the human migrants from the east was palpable. So much so, that Lox manifested his evil intentions into the dream of a chosen one of the Haudenoshonee - Deganawida - and corrupted him to become Malsum. The Great Creator had intended Deganawida to be a great peacemaker for the people of Eirgalon, but Lox had twisted this man's vision quest to evil ways. The new High King of Eirgalon and the legendary Ayenwatha, leader of the Mohak, had thwarted these designs. Together they had worked to join all the people of the land - Celtic, Norse, Wabanaki, Lenape, and Haudenoshonee - into one society. They had defeated and banished Malsum.

However, while Lox was stymied; he was not destroyed. Malsum, his human incarnation, now set his sights upon the bearer of the Loon's Necklace, the one who could seal into permanence the timeline Gluskabi had intended. Brigit became his target. In time, he vowed to destroy her.

Born of blood, with the fire of life coursing through her veins, she had been entrusted with the power of the Loon's Necklace. Should she live and learn to use its power, the people would grow and prosper. Should she fall to Lox, the people's future would flounder.

Chapter 1 - The Necklace

Eighteen years have passed since the making of the Great Peace on the plain of New Alba. The world of Eirgalon has grown and prospered. Its domains now spread from the windswept northeast isles of Vinland down the Big Waters River into the western great interior lakes region, throughout the great Mahakentuck River valley, and southward along the coast to the lands of the Powhatans.

High King Skoth and his talented Queen Evlin have ruled the land with integrity, justice, and compassion. There have been challenges aplenty, and difficulties commonplace, but through it all the people and land have enjoyed the prosperity that comes with peace. Descendents of the settlers who came from Northern European lands and descendents from native cultures of the land have formed a society that blends the cultures and traditions of the various entities. The expanding economic association, called The Eirgalon League, rivals that of its European model, the Hanseatic League. Viking and German trade across the North Atlantic is bringing increasing prosperity to both continents, and the southern European nations are beginning to venture across the Atlantic, sending ships to the southern lands of the western continent.

However, there remains the threat of Malsum, and the nagging uneasiness of the unfulfilled completion of Skoth's quest. The Loon's Necklace has been found, and it has been bestowed upon Brigit, daughter of Skoth and Evlin; but no power has been observed within it.

And so it was that on a cool and misty morning of a spring day Evlin made her way to Nealhall, the academy for learning that had been built in the new capital of

Eirgalon. The construction and establishment of this institution had been a gift from Unaine, the former king of Fada Innis who was now the Headmaster of the academy.

Accompanying Evlin to the academy was Waneek, a wise woman of the Mohak, and Teite, one of the "three sisters" who had come from New Caledonia to visit her old friends.

As they made their way through the main entrance of Nealhall, a young druid noticed them and scurried off to alert Master Unaine of their visit. Within moments, a wizened and white-haired old man, appeared at a doorway and beckoned to them.

"Come in! Come in! What a pleasure to see the three of you. A delight to my old eyes you are! I don't see you often enough."

Teite responded, "Oh, Da! What a charmer you are. You saw all of us at the evening fire last night. Don't start going on as if you haven't seen us for ages!"

Unaine had to laugh at her gentle rebuke. "Ah, well. Sure enough I have, but at my age, one wants to appreciate a sight of beauty as often as possible, for one never knows how long one has to do so!"

Evlin chimed in, for Unaine was like a father to her and Skoth, and was like a grandfather to their Brigit. "Now, don't you be going and talking like that. You'll be around to enjoy many more days with those who love you."

"I do, indeed, hope so. But please come into my sitting room. Let us sit. Tell me what brings you to the academy on this fine spring day!"

They arranged themselves comfortably in the chairs around Unaine's conference table. Then Evlin reached into the bag she carried and pulled out a necklace made of alternating black and white moonstones. It was the famous Loon's Necklace. She placed it on the table and allowed them to gaze upon it before she spoke.

"Here it is, the object of Skoth's quest. For eighteen years I have held it in my possession - in trust for my daughter. As you know, we have examined it and tried to figure out its power and how it may be used. All to no avail. I have a sense about me that we may be called upon to use it in the near future." She paused and then, in response to raised eyebrows, went on, "Don't ask me how I know. I simply have a feeling. And I am troubled. How are we to use it when the time comes?"

Waneek sighed before speaking, "You have heard my thoughts on this. Perhaps its power vanished with its previous guardian, my sister. Perhaps we will have to find a different way to respond when the times comes."

Teite shook her head. "No. I don't think so. I still believe our future is linked to this necklace. It was after your sister was gone that Gluskabi communicated with us about the necklace. It must still have some power or use."

Evlin said, "It may, indeed. But how? All of our studies and efforts to use it have come to naught. And Brigit has demonstrated no power concerning it."

Unaine spoke up, "She is young. Give her time."

That wasn't something Evlin wanted to hear. "She is eighteen. She is in her womanhood. If it was possible, she should be able to connect with it by now."

Teite said, "I know this is a sensitive subject, but perhaps her power to touch it was extinguished when, as a babe, she stopped the attack of Senadondo. Since that time, she has shown no special gift, though many have tried to teach and tutor her."

Waneek nodded and Evlin grimaced at the thought.

The elder statesman said, "I still say, give her time. She is a smart and talented girl."

Evlin shook her head sadly, "Yes, she is quick-witted, athletic, and she does have a talent with the bow, but touching the powers of the spirit realm seems beyond her."

Unaine replied, "Given that she is the child of two powerfully gifted people, that seems strange. I say give her time."

Waneek sighed again and added, "Would that we could give her all the time in the world. But if Evlin is right that a moment of crisis is approaching, then we must make other plans."

Unaine asked, "And what other plans are you suggesting?"

Waneek smiled, "It is the men who make such decisions, but I think we might encourage Skoth and his councilors to make agreements with the Powhatans to our south and with the Anishanaabe to the north and west."

"My husband and his advisors have already done so. They have made entreaties toward both parties."

Unaine agreed. "Aye, they have. And wisely so. But as Waneek suggests, perhaps it would be wise to re-double such efforts."

Teite pointed to the necklace, and asked the group, "What of this? Do we just assume there is no power left within it? Do we just leave it lying on the table? Useless? What can we do with it? Should we, perhaps, give it back to Ayen, and suggest he try to find a way to its power?"

Waneek shook her head. "No. It is gone from the possession of the Mohak people. It has been entrusted to others."

"Others who can find no way to use it!"

"Be that as it may, once freely given away, its power has passed away from us - of this I am certain."

Unaine raised a hand and then slowly reached out to lift the necklace from the table. Turning it over in his hands wrinkled with age, he gazed upon it, "Then I suggest we entrust it fully into the hands of the one to whom it was given. As we have noted; she is of age. I say we give it to Brigit. No strings attached. No longer in our care, or under our control. She should be the one to possess it. The responsibility belongs to her."

He slowly looked around the room. As he made eye contact with each of them, they, in turn, nodded their heads in agreement.

Chapter 2 - The Bow

Brigit hefted the finely crafted bow that Erik had presented to her on her eighteenth birthday. It was made of fine hickory and had perfect balance for her slender and athletic frame. She stood between Erik and her father as they nocked their arrows for the final shot in their friendly competition. Skoth was an accomplished archer, but already on most days Brigit could best him. Erik, however, was another matter. Though now into his seventies, he could still wield the bow with fluidity, and his accuracy was uncanny.

It was all of a hundred yards to the hand-sized bullseye on the target that stood on the far side of the archery practice range used by the king's men-at-arms. Skoth's arrow hit the target, but missed the bullseye. Brigit's arrow barely nicked the edge of the bullseye. But Erik's arrow plunged into its center.

"Now that is how it is done!" declared the elder warrior.

Skoth grinned as he replied, "No doubt you compensated for the fine mist in the air slightly more than I did."

Brigit chimed in, "And as for me, I'm still adjusting my shot to this beauty of a bow you gave me. But before long, I'll be splitting your arrows, sure enough!"

Erik's grin covered his face as he looked at his young protege. Her long wavy black hair was tied in the back by a simple leather thong. She had her father's hair, but she had her mother's features. She was attired in the brown leathers of a casual and functional huntsman's jerkin and breeches. She had every claim to the title of a princess, yet she was dressed as one of the common folks.

Erik teased, "Perhaps a wee bit of the magic that your parents possess will come out of you soon, and then you'll be able to match me."

A scowl crossed Brigit's face. She turned away from them and ran across the open field to retrieve their arrows.

High King Skoth, his face now beginning to crease with the lines of a middle-aged man and his hair showing the occasional grey hair, turned his worried face to Erik as he spoke, "I know you mean well by the teasing of her, but she is so touchy about not being able to develop any druidic skill. Perhaps you could ease off her a bit."

"Hmmmph. You know I'd not be doing anything that would hurt the lass. The sooner she is able to deal with her feelings about it, the sooner she'll be able to move on. If you know what I mean?"

Skoth sighed, "Yes, I reckon I do. But how long will it take?"

"The way I see it, it will be when she is ready to come to terms with who she is. She doesn't need to pretend to be you, or her mother, or one of her aunties. She is a talent and wonder in her own right. When she comes to totally accept and trust herself, and stops second guessing what others think she should be, then she will be just fine."

"Erik, I have never seen such a girl with the physical talents she has. Surely she knows how physically gifted she is."

"Aye, she does at that. But all her elders seem to have decided that she must also have the skills of a wise woman, or shaman. She seems to think we all look upon her as a failure because she demonstrates none of those gifts."

"So teasing her about it helps. Wouldn't it be better to just say that to her?"

"She's heard so from me. The rest of you seem to think that saying nothing of her lack of demonstrable mystical talents is best. As if ignoring it will make her feel better. The teasing is to keep it fresh enough in her mind that she is forced to think through it. I'll not give up on her. I believe the time will come."

They brought their conversation about her to an end, as she returned with the quiver of arrows they had used in their shooting contest. Brigit gave them a curious look.

"What were you two so deep in conversation about? And why did you stop when I returned?"

Erik grinned at her. "Aw, lassie, you always have your eye on us, don't you? I'm wondering about that bow of yours. Did I perhaps make a mistake with the balance? I know you are a good shot. You should be used to it by now."

"Oh, Uncle Erik. I'm used to it. I was just saying that as an excuse. I didn't really mean it. You won, fair and square! It is an awesome bow, and I do intend to be able to match you, arrow for arrow, some day."

"I have no doubt you will. You are talented, and you are persistent. That's one reason I chose hickory for the wood of your bow. I had other woods to choose from, but this seemed right for you. Hickory is a wood with strength and flexibility. Those are character traits that can get you through the hard times. You have these qualities. Your natural abilities will develop to their potential as they are used. Be persistent and you will succeed."

Her eyes narrowed slightly as she thought about what he was saying - and not saying - about her 'natural abilities.' Then she hefted her bow, looked at it with admiration, winked at Erik, and started walking toward the Great Hall of Tara.

With a lilt in her voice, she called back over her shoulder, "Well, these 'natural abilities' of mine need some nourishment. I'm famished and it is time for lunch. Are you two going to stand there jawing all day, or are you going to join me?"

Chapter 3 - Wulf

The women had returned to the Great Hall from their visit to the academy. Evlin looked to the kitchen staff and gave the order to ring the bell announcing the commencement of the King's Open Table. As monarchs of Tara, Evlin and Skoth had begun the custom of having an open table at the King's Great Hall every work day. All those at work around Tara who were within walking distance were welcome to come and partake. High King Skoth had found that any expense accrued by providing the meal was more than compensated for by the increased camaraderie, as well as by the productivity of the satisfied and well-fed workers.

Many of the men and women had finished their mid-day repast and were returning to their work when the horn sounded from the shipyard docks, announcing the arrival of a large vessel. Approaching the docks of Tara on the western bank of the Mahakentuck River was a large ocean-going ship similar to a Viking knarr. It was a single masted ship of more than eighty feet in length. Flying from the top of its mast was a red and white pendant.

As they were leaving the Great Hall, Brigit made her way over to Finn, the nephew of Erik and the king's master shipwright.

Brigit asked him, "What kind of ship is that?"

Finn replied, "Why that, my dear, is a Baltic trading cog. You'll notice that it is similar to one of our knarrs, but a wee bit wider in the beam and heavier in the water. Notice the pendant at the top of the mast. If I'm not mistaken it is a trading vessel out of the Hanseatic port of Hamburg, far across the sea. Let's go take a look at her as she berths."

They quickly made their way down the hill and through the bustling streets of Tara to the quays and wharves that lined the the riverbank. The local dockmasters were guiding the foreign ship in docking at one of the larger wharves where it would be moored.

When they neared the vessel, Finn said to Brigit, "Do you see the flag flying from the cabin on the deck? That white castle on the red flag is a symbol of the city of Hamburg. Sure enough, I was right about this being a trading vessel from there. And notice that she lies pretty deep in the water. I'll wager she has a full load of trade goods for us. I'll have to make sure the dockmasters send a messenger to our Grand Trading Master Notaku. I suspect he'll want to deal with this personally. If you'll excuse me, Princess, I'll be off."

Curious men, women, and children had gathered to see the unusual sight, for while Tara was a busy trading port, this ship from such a distant land was not exactly an everyday occurrence. Brigit stood in the midst of the crowd, dressed in the the attire of the common folk, as curious as the rest of them.

She noticed that the ship had a crew of more than a twenty men. As she watched them secure their vessel, her eyes were drawn to one of the men. He looked to be a young man of approximately her own age. She couldn't quite identify it, but there was some quality different about him. He was rather ordinary looking, with a slightly ruddy complexion and dark brown hair. He was well-muscled and a bit taller than most of the men, but he seemed slightly out of place as he tried to help the rest of the crew.

The young man was near the edge of the ship, when suddenly one of the crewmen accidentally bumped into him. The young man lost his balance and went tumbling off the side of the ship into the water.

The watching crowd roared with laughter at the pratfall, but Brigit noticed that the young man was floundering in the water. She didn't hesitate, but leapt in to help him. As soon as she grabbed him, he stopped his struggling and allowed her to drag him to a ladder where the wharf met the quay.

When he had his hands on the ladder, and before he climbed it, he turned to her and whispered, "Danke."

It wasn't the Norse tongue that she was familiar with, but it was close enough for her to understand that he meant, "Thanks."

She climbed the ladder after him.

Awaiting them at the top of the ladder were Erik (she wondered where he had come from since she hadn't noticed him in the crowd) and a burly shaggy-bearded sailor from the ship.

The sailor grabbed the young man's arm as he reached the top of the ladder and said to him, "What are you doing, Wulf? This is no time to take a bath! What an impression you are making on our hosts!"

To which the young man stammered in reply, "But Uncle Walt, I didn't mean to. I was bumped off the ship."

"Ach. You're not much of a sailor. Why you even had to have this little girl jump in to rescue you."

By this time Brigit had also climbed up the ladder and stood next to them. She was not in any mood to have someone call her a little girl.

"I'm no little girl!" she declared, "and I'm sure he would have been just fine without me."

Wulf sheepishly said, "I wouldn't have been. I can't swim."

She turned and looked at him incredulously, "What? You are a sailor, and you can't swim? I thought you must have been stunned, or bumped your head and were disoriented. You really can't swim?"

Uncle Walt said, "Not a lick. And he's no real sailor either. He's my brother's boy that I agreed to bring along on this voyage. Though for the life of me, I don't know what possessed me to agree to it. Across the North Sea to Greenland, wintering there, and then this spring journey across the Greenland Sea to Eirgalon, and he is still no sailor. He never will be."

Brigit could see the pain in Wulf's eyes as his uncle spoke. Then the focus of her vision widened and she noticed that a large trading canoe from the north had pulled next to the wharf that lay beyond the Hamburg cog. Getting out of the canoe was one of the most striking young men she had ever seen: tall, muscular, flowing black hair, and when he turned to look at her the visage of a god.

She pulled her eyes and thoughts back to Wulf and said, "Well, that matters not. Tis a nice enough spring day, yet it is not one to be walking about in wet clothes. Since, in your humble opinion, he's not much of a seaman, then you'll not mind losing his help for a few minutes. I'll be taking him to the Hall and we'll get into some dry clothes!"

Not waiting for a response, she grabbed Wulf by the hand and dragged him off toward the Great Hall.

Uncle Walt stood there, mouth hanging wide open and saying nothing. Finally he stammered, "What? Who the name of Wodan was that?"

Erik, who had been silent to this point, stepped over to him and extended his hand to him. Trying not to smirk, he said, "Welcome to Tara. I'm Erik, Advisor to the High King, and that my friend, is Princess Brigit. You're blessed by the gods that she took it easy on you. I'd suggest you don't want to get on her bad side."

Chapter 4 - Maengun

The large trading canoe that had arrived nearly simultaneously with the Hamburg cog was filled with furs of animals that had been trapped in the northwoods during the winter months. They were a valued commodity, especially in the growing trade with the European nations.

The traders were from the Sunset Lakes area of the Haudenoshonee people, but the young man who accompanied them was a passenger from the lands of the Anishanaabe that lay even further to the north and west. The traders made arrangements with the dock workers to meet with the Tara Trademaster, and the young man took his gear and made his way away from the docks, disappearing into the streets of the city.

Erik had noticed Brigit's eyes flicker toward the young man during the incident at the dock. Though he continued his conversation with Captain Walt, hoping to learn news of distant places, he managed to keep the young Anishanaabe man in his sight for several moments. He noted which street he headed up and made a mental note to go that way on his return to the Great Hall.

Since Erik had revealed himself to be an advisor to High King Skoth, Captain Walter shared his desire to meet with the High King and his trademaster and discuss his hopes for establishing some sort of trading alliance. Thereupon, Erik invited the captain to join the High King at his table for the evening meal. He also suggested that after the captain's crew secured their ship, they would find agreeable lodging at the Riverside Inn.

Upon finishing his conversation with Captain Walt, Erik turned from the docks and started to amble his way back to the Great Hall. It wasn't that he needed the slow pace, but he wanted to think as he walked. He followed the path of the young Anishanaabe man as far as he had observed him. Then he opened his mind to seeing the sights of the city in the way that a young man seeing it for the first time would see it. He imagined what that young man would be thinking. He let those thoughts direct his path.

After a few minutes he turned and walked into a boarding house by the name of Tante's Table and Inn. He sauntered up to the counter and winked at the woman behind the bar. The buxom thirty-something woman hurried out from behind the bar and gave him a strong embrace.

Then, kissing him on the cheek, she said, "What a pleasure to see you, Uncle Erik. You don't stop in here often enough."

"True enough, my dear. But you know how it is. Doing the king's business and all. And keeping my eye on the young princess - why that would be job enough for any three men!"

The blonde haired women smiled and chuckled. "Aye, that it would!"

They exchanged pleasantries for a few minutes, for Marilla was family, of a sort, to Erik. She was an orphan who had been raised by Susie, of the original Tante's Table in New Caledonia. She had found her way to Tara to work in the kitchen of the Great Hall after Skoth had established his capital. A few years later she had married Erik's nephew, Finn, and then started Tante's Table and Inn of Tara. While Finn may have been the Master Shipwright of the High King, Marilla was master of this inn. She provided healthy, full meals for her customers and safe and clean rooms to bunk in.

25

Erik leaned in close to her and spoke softly so no one else could overhear them. He asked her to keep her eyes and ears open for the young Anishanaabe man. When Erik described him, her eyes opened wide and a grin spread across her face.

"Well, Uncle Erik, that'll be easy enough to do. The young fellow you describe is upstairs right now, settling into his room. He came in just minutes before you did. He gave his name as Maengun."

Erik smiled knowingly, "Then I must be off. I don't want him to see me here. Send word to me of any information about him that you think might be important to me. Thank you, Marilla."

Erik gave her a quick hug and then departed. It was only minutes later that young Maengun came downstairs. He politely asked what time the evening meal would be served, promised to return for it, and then left the inn. Marilla noted to herself that Maengun spoke the mixed language of Eirgalon with fluency, though with a slight northern accent.

Throughout the afternoon Maengun wandered the streets and shops of Tara. Occasionally he would stop to strike up a conversation with a local shopkeeper. Although he asked questions concerning the city and the people, they seemed innocent enough questions. The locals were accustomed to strangers coming to their city and making inquiries of all sorts.

Whenever he was asked where he came from or what he was doing in the city, he adroitly turned the conversation in a different direction. Few ever noticed, unless they thought about it later, that he never answered their questions. He left the residents of the city with the impression that he was a friendly and likeable person.

Chapter 5 - The High King's Table

The Great Hall of Tara was a flurry of activity as the evening meal commenced. The usual participants were there: the royal family and the king's closest friends and advisors; but also present were the leaders of the trading ship from Hamburg and the fur-laden canoe from the north that had arrived that day, as well as Trademaster Notaku and Shipwright Finn.

Brigit made sure she sat next to Wulf. She had enjoyed their walk to the Great Hall after his fall into the river. For some reason, she felt a sort of kindred spirit with him. Others in the hall noticed the interest she took in the young man, but no one commented about it.

Mealtime was filled with excellent food and engaging conversation. Official details of trade and diplomacy would be worked out later, but it never hurt to establish friendly relationships with those with whom you intended to negotiate such deals. Skoth was in the process of tying up the dinner conversations and dismissing his advisors, that they might go off and negotiate their trade deals with the visitors, when Brigit spoke up.

"I know you gentlemen will be off to discuss your trade agreements, but before you go I have a request. I'd like to have an archery contest with some of our visitors tomorrow morning. Maybe Wulf could represent the German delegation. Would there be someone from the northern traders who would be willing to join us?"

The northern traders looked at each other, and then one responded, "As enjoyable as that sounds, both of us have other responsibilities. But there was a young man who traveled with us as a passenger. We saw him shoot his bow a few times at our stopovers. He looked quite skilled."

"Perhaps you could ask him to join us."

"We can try to find him. As I mentioned, he was a passenger. He left us when we docked. But he is probably still in the city."

Erik spoke up, "I know where he is. His name is Maengun. I'll send a message to him and invite him."

All eyes turned to Erik.

Brigit looked at him incredulously, and voiced what most of the others were thinking, "And how is it that you know where he is? Or even stranger, how do you know his name?"

This prompted Evlin to laugh out loud. "Darling daughter, by now you should know, for he has demonstrated time and again, that although Erik professes to have no magical powers, he somehow manages to gather all manner of information. So, Erik, would you, indeed, be so kind as to invite young Maengun to our archery range in the morning for a friendly competition?"

Erik, showing just a wee bit of smugness, replied, "Why, yes, your Highness. I'll see that it is done."

Evlin then turned to Brigit, "And Brigit, since the meal is over and the others have work to do, would you please join your father and me in our private quarters? There is something we wish to discuss with you."

Curiosity covered Brigit's face, but she she made no objection. A private conversation with her parents was usually a result of her having gotten into some sort of trouble. But she could think of nothing she had done wrong. She excused herself from the table, saying goodbye to Wulf and letting him know that she looked forward to seeing him in the morning, and then went with her parents to their private reading room.

Young Wulf wasn't involved in the trade discussions so when the others started to gather around tables to discuss particulars of trade agreements, he aimlessly wandered around the large room of the Great Hall. Erik, who also had no specific function with the trading parties, was also left alone in the hall. He had gone to the entrance and talked to one of the guards, no doubt sending a messenger to Maengun at Tante's Table. He then returned and pulled up a heavy wooden chair in front of the hearthfire of the Great Hall. It was the custom of the people for the ruler of the land to always keep a hearthfire burning in the Great Hall as a symbol of welcome to the people of the land and their visitors. So even on this pleasant spring evening, a fire was burning.

Erik beckoned for the kitchen staff to bring him a tankard of ale, and then he called out to Wulf to come and join him by the fire. Wulf settled himself into a chair next to Erik, albeit a little uncomfortably. They sat in silence for a few moments as the fire crackled before them and the murmured voices of the men behind them filled the air. Finally, Erik spoke to him.

"Well, young man, it seems you have made an impression on our young princess. Let me warn you that she is quite accomplished with the bow, so I hope you have a wee bit of skill to challenge her at the competition tomorrow."

Wulf's eyes were downcast. "I'm afraid I'm not very good."

Erik kept his face turned toward the fire, but with a sideward glance he studied the young man.

"So, you can't swim. And now you tell me you can't shoot a bow?"

"Oh, I can. It's just that I'm not very good at it."

"Have you practiced very much?"

"Not really."

"What about sword fighting? Are you at least competent with that?"

Wulf hung his head, "No. Not that either."

Erik bobbed his head slightly, deep in thought, "Now you have me wondering why it is that you have come on this journey to our fair land. You must have quite the story to tell."

Wulf slowly shook his head, but he did reply, "It's not really a very exciting story. It is actually sort of dull."

When Wulf hesitated, Erik prompted him to continue, "Go on. I'm listening."

Wulf took a deep breath and then exhaled. He wasn't at all sure that he wanted to confide his story to a stranger, but there was just something about the old warrior that put his mind at ease. So, drawing another deep breath, he began.

"I'm the fourth son of Deter, Marshall to the Lord of Hamburg. My older brothers are the talented ones. Father likes them, and they are following in his footsteps. But I'm just not interested in swords, bows, and fighting, like they are."

Erik resisted the urge to interrupt him and ask him what it was that the young man was interested in. The young man was opening up on his own, so Erik remained silent and let him go on.

"I like to read, and study, and look at the world around me. I enjoy picking up my staff and spending the day walking in the woods. My father calls me a 'dreamer.' That's why he sent me on the voyage with Uncle Walt. He thought that forcing me to work the life of a seaman might be my calling, and that it wouldn't allow me the time to read and dream."

There he stopped. His eyes had remained on the fire as he spoke, and now it seemed like he had lost himself in the flames as he reflected on his life. After a few moments of quiet, Erik spoke.

"But it hasn't worked out that way, has it?"

Wulf sighed, and went on, "No it hasn't. I'm no good at the sailing skills either. Oh, I can do them, but I don't enjoy them. Except for the navigating part, that is. I enjoy figuring that out. What I have enjoyed most about this journey was the wintering over in Greenland. There was time for me to sit in front of a fire and read."

"There's no shame in being a scholar, young man."

Wulf gave a small snort, "Tell that to my father."

"If he was here I would. But he's not, and you are. And you are the one who needs to hear it."

Wulf took his eyes from the fire and looked directly at Erik. "Why are you telling me this?"

Erik smiled slightly before responding, "You seem a decent enough fellow; and Brigit has taken an interest in you. That, in itself, would be reason enough. But let's just say that you remind me of a young man I knew about twenty years ago."

Wulf gave him a quizzical look, but Erik shifted the conversation.

"Now, what are you going to do about tomorrow? If you can't really compete at the bow, how will you handle the competition?"

"I don't know. Do you have any advice?"

Erik chuckled, "Be yourself. Always be yourself. Don't try to be something you are not. Give it your best effort, but don't give any pretense that you are great at it. And if, or shall I say when, you should be defeated, be gracious in defeat."

When, later that evening, the trading envoys left the Great Hall, they left with a young man who was more self-confident than he was earlier in the day, and who felt that he had at least one friend in this new land.

Chapter 6 - Moonstones

While Brigit was unsure of what was about to happen, Skoth was unsure if what they were about to do was the right course of action. However, he said nothing and let Evlin take the lead.

Skoth, Evlin, and Brigit had entered the family reading room and sat down in their usual comfortable chairs arranged in a semicircle in front of the hearth. Although she was extremely anxious, Brigit contained herself and said nothing. After a few moments, Evlin reached out and pulled a small pouch from the satchel that she often carried with her. She turned it over in her hands several times, looked at Skoth with a long gaze, and then turned her attention to Brigit.

"Daughter dear, apple of my eye, there have been discussions about you . . ."

At that comment, Brigit's brows furrowed in a mixture of displeasure and curiosity. She didn't like people talking about her, but she was curious as to what they were saying!

Evlin went on, "When you were only a few months old, Ayenwatha bestowed upon you the Loon's Necklace. You know that we believe this to be the object of Skoth's quest. As you also know, your father and I were entrusted to guard this relic for you until the time came for you to use it."

Mention of her "using it" displeased Brigit even more, for she felt deeply her failure to make any connection with the necklace. Despite all the coaching and suggestions that her mother and father, and their multitude of advisors, had showered upon her, there had been no connection between herself and the necklace. Still, Bridgit held her tongue as Evlin continued.

"Those of us entrusted with the necklace have come to a decision. It is time for it to be in your care. Totally. Without any reservations or limitations by us. It is your responsibility. We didn't come to this decision lightly, and not all of us are convinced that it is the right thing to do," she glanced at Skoth, "but you are of age. Some of us are of the opinion that it is yours, and yours alone to use, that only with close proximity and time will its power be revealed."

She stopped speaking. Brigit's eyes narrowed as she contemplated the situation. Then she turned to Skoth.

"Father, is this also what you think?"

Slowly Skoth nodded, "I can't say that I'm completely at ease with this. Finding the Loon's Necklace was central to my quest. Yet the acquisition of it does not seem to have completed the quest. I sense that a moment of crisis is drawing near to us. I believe I need the power of the Loon's Necklace to complete my quest, yet I am unable to use it and I am asked to give away control of it. Can one gain success by giving up power?"

"Then why do you agree to this?"

"Because I have learned to trust the ones I love." He paused and looked at Evlin for several moments, and then again looked to Brigit for several moments before he continued. "It is yours. From this day forth. Use it as you will."

Brigit almost wailed, "But I don't know how to use it!"

Evlin took the necklace from its leather pouch and went to stand before Brigit. Motioning for her to rise, she said, "Then simply wear it. It is believed by some of our druids that moonstones help people achieve the fulfillment of their desire. Sometimes there is a difference between that which we want and that which we need. I've wondered at times if that might be part of the symbolism of the black and white pattern of these moonstones. Now, stand up and let me place it around your neck."

Brigit did as she was told and Evlin placed it around her daughter's neck. Then she took a step back and looked at it with admiration.

"I looks beautiful on you, especially when you have your black hair loose and curling around your face like it is tonight."

At this point Skoth had also risen and come to stand beside her. Taking his daughter in his embrace he said, "Ah, the beauty of the moon and land standing here before me," and then he whispered in her ear, "I trust you. Always follow your heart."

After Brigit left them to retire for the night, Skoth and Evlin sat together in front of the fire for a long time. The fire had burned down to but a few glowing embers before they spoke.

Skoth broke the silence, "I hope we made the right decision. I don't doubt her good heart, or Gluskabi's good intention by sending us the necklace. But will she ever have the power to use it? And I worry that perhaps we have made our daughter a target of Malsum. He is still out there, and we know not where he lurks or what schemes he plots."

"Dear Skoth, we don't know what the future will bring. But we can still hope. After all, there is more of you in her than just the color of her hair and eyes."

"Be that as it may, what I'm hoping for is that there is more of you in her than has yet been revealed. Perhaps a bit of the Bear-witch of the North that will always protect her people."

"Time will tell, my love, but I suspect there is more to her than simply fragments of ourselves. She is most definitely her own person. We must trust her."

"O, trust her, I do. But that doesn't mean I won't worry about her or try to protect her."

She went to him and hugged him tightly as she whispered, "As will I."

Chapter 7 - Friendly Competition

The day dawned with crystal clear blue skies and promised to be a pleasant spring day. After a morning meal in the Great Hall with her parents, Brigit, attired in her normal hunter's jerkin and breeches, grabbed her bow and made her way to the archery range. The practice range lay across a small vale to the west of the Great Hall. She hoped to get a few practice shots in before anyone else arrived.

To her surprise, she was not the first one to the open glen which spread across the vale. She could see a young man, bow in hand, striding across the range as he went to retrieve his arrows. She couldn't see his face, since he was walking away from her, but from the look of his hair, his large frame, and easy stride, she guessed him to be Maengun. She looked beyond him to bring the archery target into her focus and could see that his arrows were clustered about the bullseye. She eagerly anticipated the competition that was to come.

The man walking across the vale turned suddenly and glanced back at her. She thought she caught a glimpse of a smile upon his face as he quickly turned away and continued on his way to the target. The thought of him smiling at her both pleased and irritated her. She was just beginning to consider what it was that pleased her and what it was that irritated her, when she heard footsteps behind her. Spinning quickly about, she saw Wulf and Erik walking toward her.

From several yards away, Erik said, "Well, now. It looks to me like you came out a little early to get some extra practice in."

"Aye, you caught me. I was going to get a few shots in to warm up, but it looks like some of my competition," she pointed across the field to Maengun, "has beat me to it. And you're also early. Could it be that you had the same idea?"

Erik laughed, "Not I. I'm not competing in your contest, but Wulf here, thought that he'd need a few shots to regain some skills. I'll bet he's pretty rusty after all those days at sea."

Wulf smiled at her. Some of the smile was purely for her. He thought she was quite attractive in the morning light: fresh faced, with her long wavy black hair braided with the braid falling forward over her left shoulder, and the stunning black and white moonstone necklace about her throat. He was quite taken with her. She was a sight to savor. However, part of his smile was for Erik, for he realized that with that comment, the elder warrior had just helped to lower her expectations for Wulf's demonstration of what he knew to be his limited archery skills.

The bright light of the morning sun highlighted the freckles on Wulf's face and Brigit couldn't help but return his smile.

Erik commented, "I see you're wearing a new piece of jewelry this morning. It looks good on you, and I like the way it lays high around your neck. It won't get in your way when you pull the bow."

"Thank you, Erik. Mother and Father seemed to think it was time for me to have it. They gave it to me last night. Mother thinks I should wear it all the time."

Erik raised one eyebrow at that, "Well, I can't say I disagree with her. I wouldn't let anyone else get their hands on it. It is rightly yours, and I figure it is about time you took responsibility for it."

Wulf wasn't sure what the conversation was about, but he said, "You're beautiful, I mean, it's beautiful," and he blushed.

Brigit also started to blush slightly, but by then the young man who had gone to retrieve the arrows was striding up to them, and they all turned to him.

"Good morning! I'm Maengun," declared the young man as he looked at Brigit, "I received word that I was invited by Princess Brigit of Tara, to participate in an archery contest this morning. You must be her."

"Indeed I am. I had intended to arrive early and to loosen up with some practice shots before anyone else arrived, but I see you have beaten me to that."

Maengun's eyes flickered from her face to her moonstone necklace, and then to her hickory bow, and then to Wulf and Erik, before returning to rest upon her face again.

"Ah, I didn't know that I would be competing against you. Perhaps, it would have been wiser for me to not have warmed up. You look like you like are an accomplished archer. I doubt I can challenge you."

He again glanced, longer this time, at her finely crafted bow, and then to the necklace at her throat. Brigit wasn't sure if he was trying to flatter her in some way, or if, perhaps, there was a bit of arrogance in his voice. Then Maengun turned his gaze to Wulf and Erik, eyeing them over.

Wulf felt a challenge in Maengun's stare. Wulf, taller than average though he was, noticed that Maengun was even taller than he, perhaps more strongly muscled, and certainly more handsome. At least, Wulf supposed, the young Anishanaabe man would be more handsome to the eyes of a young woman.

In response to the stare Wulf introduced himself, "I'm Wulf, from Hamburg. That's far across the sea to the east. I too was invited by the Princess to this contest, though I'm sure she is much better at archery than I."

Erik said, "And I'm Erik, a simple old servant of the Chief."

Maengun responded with a nod of acknowledgement to Wulf, and a brief glance and nod to Erik. Brigit briefly cocked her head to the side and looked at Erik. She had never heard him introduce himself that way before, almost as if Erik was encouraging the young man to be dismissive of him.

"Well then," Brigit said, "Now that we all know each other, I think it is time to get on with the shooting contest. I like to see how folks from other lands handle their bows. Let's get started."

She proceeded to lay out the simple rules for the contest. They would take turns, with each of them shooting three arrows. In each of the rounds they would vary their order. Erik would judge the winner of each round.

Brigit won the draw to lead off the first round. With a steady and sure motion, she nocked her arrow, lifted and sighted the bow, and then released it. They could see it fly into the target, just touching the right side of the bullseye.

Wulf went next. He didn't look at all experienced or accomplished as he lifted the bow Erik had provided for him. When he loosed the arrow, it surprised none of them that he missed the target entirely. He made no excuses, and when Brigit said it was a nice try, he said a polite thank you.

Maengun then stepped forward, and with the self-assurance of a skilled bowman, he loosed an arrow that plunged into the bullseye just inside of Brigit's.

Erik declared, "Our visitor from the north, Maengun, wins this round."

The second round saw Wulf taking the first shot. He missed the entire target for the second time. Then followed Maengun, whose arrow was just outside the bullseye. Brigit hit the bullseye with her shot, and Erik declared her the winner of the second round.

Maengun shot first on the final round and he landed his shot just inside the bullseye. Brigit followed with a shot that hit the dead center of the bullseye. As Wulf stepped forward to loose his final shot, Erik leaned forward and whispered to him, "Just relax, boy. Focus on the target, and just imagine seeing your arrow hitting it. Then release."

Wulf took a deep breath and did as he was told. To the surprise of all of them, his arrow hit the target. It wasn't a bullseye hit, but Wulf let out an exclamation of satisfaction. He could hear Maengun give a little snort of derision, but he didn't care. He had hit the target!

Erik made his declaration, "Well, it appears to me that the centermost hit was by the lady, but I'd say that just hitting the target was a major success for Wulf. So you'll have to forgive me your highness, but I declare him to be the winner of this round. That means all three of you have won a round, but since the most accurate overall shot was made by Brigit, she is the overall winner."

Brigit said, "Thank you, Erik. And thank you, Wulf and Maengun, for so graciously accepting my invitations."

Maengun's response was smooth, "I am honored you asked me to participate. The pleasure of your company, and the challenge to compete against your considerable skill, was an unexpected delight. I hope this will not be the last time we have the opportunity to spend a few moments together."

41

Wulf was going to say some words of appreciation, but he was completely nonplussed by the smoothness of Maengun's response, and he could only manage to stammer out, "Yeah, thanks."

Brigit giggled at their responses, "Well, this won't be the last time we spend time together. You can be sure of that. Let's go get our arrows."

The three young people walked together across the practice range to retrieve their arrows. More archers were now arriving at the practice range, but they would wait until the young folks returned before beginning their practice. A couple of older men, friends of Erik's and instructors for the men-at-arms, walked up to Erik and one asked about the contest.

Erik replied, "That young Maengun from the north has a shot that can rival our best archers. I think we'll have to find out some more about him. Wulf? Well, he's a good lad, but his talents don't lie with the bow. And, Brigit, I'd say she's nearly the best there is, and still improving. I'm not at all worried about her skill." Then in a softer, almost conspiratorial tone he went on, " Her Highness seems to be quite enamored by these two young men, so I'd appreciate it if you spread the word, quietly of course, for your men to keep their eyes open concerning those two. I want to know if anything unusual happens."

Chapter 8 - Plans

Brigit spent the day enjoying the company of her new friends as she escorted them throughout the local shops and environs of Kingstown (now commonly referred to as "Tara" since it was the home of the High King) and over the bridge to Euanglen, which lay on the other side of the Wissawkin River just before that river entered the Mahakentuck. They returned to Tara and parted before the evening meal with plans to meet again on the morn and make a visit eastward, across the Mahakentuck, nearly a mile wide at this point, to visit the apple orchards that had been developed with plants and seeds brought from Ireland fifteen years ago.

The topic of discussion, among family and close advisors, around the evening meal was the impending journey to the south. Although a possible contact with the people to the south had been under consideration for several weeks, High King Skoth had just decided that day to make the diplomatic and trade mission southward to the land of Moran Doyin - the "land of many people" that was inhabited by the people called the Powhatans. Plans needed to be discussed and finalized so that this mission could commence in a couple of days.

It was not intended to be a military expedition, but would still require a sizeable show of strength. High King Skoth would be taking his flagship, the longship *Peacemaker,* and two other fully manned longships. They would be accompanied by the Hamburg trading cog captained by Walt, though young Wulf was to stay at Tara and learn the ways of Eirgalon. In addition, they hoped that King Bjorn of Glesga, and King McLean of Drogheda would see fit to add their envoys to the fleet as it passed their territories on the journey south.

43

To no one's surprise, Evlin was planning on accompanying her husband. They often traveled together on official business, for they made a good team in the way they worked together and presented the goals of Eirgalon to those with whom they dealt. Notaku, as the Master Trader of the Eirgalon League and a close confidant of Skoth, was also a natural choice to be going on the mission.

Brigit would be staying at Tara. Although she was of age, and considered an adult, Skoth did not want her to be burdened with running the day-to-day affairs of the kingdom. He designated Master Unaine of the Academy (the former King of Fada Innis) to be Steward of the Kingdom in his absence. Brigit was welcomed and encouraged to assist Unaine in any way she could. Both Evlin and Skoth felt that she might well learn a few lessons of leadership from the wise elder man.

In private, Skoth talked with Erik about what Erik's responsibilities would be during this time. Officially Erik was to give advice and counsel to the Steward and the Princess, but more importantly he was to watch and protect Brigit. Skoth couldn't shake his concern that because Brigit now possessed the necklace, Malsum would be seeking to attack her.

"Erik, I know you might be tired of running after her, but I need you to keep watch over her."

Erik chuckled, "Thor knows, the girl has enough energy for three people. You can imagine what it must have been like for Unaine so many years ago. There he was, with his three daughters, and then with you on top of it!"

Skoth smiled and nodded as he recalled his childhood days. "But there is a difference. We didn't have the evil of Malsum lurking about. And, though you

44

may be loath to admit it, you are getting older."

Erik nodded back, "Aye, there is that. But I know Brigit and her ways. I'll keep an eye on her. It would be nice to have Anoka with me, but I know he will be going with you and Evlin. Evlin may not need a bodyguard, and Anoka may have slowed down a step, but he stands in the shadows and watches. He'll have her back wherever you take her. And don't you worry, I have plenty of folks here who will be helping me watch Brigit."

"That's good to know."

Erik hesitated and said, "Oh, and by the way, I saw a boatload of those sheep fleeces, from the farms up north. Taking them down the river, they were. Those sheep got me thinking."

Erik paused. Skoth waited. By now Skoth had learned to wait out his older friend. Erik liked to pause for effect. When he figured he had he listener's full attention and had piqued his or her curiosity, then he would gone on.

Erik's mouth curled into a little smile and he went on, "Yep. Those sheep made me think. I recalled something I first heard when I was but a little welp running about the fields of Fada Innis."

Patient, though Skoth was, he knew Erik would keep on like this until he was prompted to get to the point, so Skoth said, "You have my attention, old friend, what is it you recalled?"

"To beware of a wolf in sheep's clothing."

"And do you sense a wolf among us?"

Well, there is that young Wulf, from Hamburg. He's caught your daughter's eye for sure. But I don't think it's him."

Skoth asked, "The other one?"

Erik nodded, "Yep. That young fella from up north. There's nothing specific I know about him, and believe me, I have plenty of folks keeping an eye on him, but I just have an uneasy feeling concerning him. He comes across as so likeable. Downright smooth, he is."

"So let's just tell Brigit to stay away from him."

Erik looked at Skoth askance. "And just how do you think she'd react to that?"

Skoth thought a moment before replying, "I see what you mean. If I did that, why she be running right to him. Well, keep your eyes and ears open. Don't forget, I'm trusting you with what is most precious in my life."

Erik nodded and assured him, "Aye, you can count on me. No wolf in sheep's clothing, or any other such threat, is going to hurt our girl. Not if I have anything to say about it."

Chapter 10 - Message from the North

The delegation to the south had only been gone for a couple of days when a message arrived from Chief Ayenwatha of Tionnontoguen. Master Unaine, now Steward in the King's absence, immediately summoned Brigit, Erik, and Waneek to the Great Hall to discuss what the cryptic message might mean and what the response should be.

Unaine started the conversation off by noting that he wished that Skoth and Evlin were still in Tara, but they had departed, taking Teite with them as she was returning home. She would part with them at Glesga and then return to her home and husband, King Gunnar of New Caledonia.

Unaine then got right to the important message. Holding the piece of parchment before him, he began, "This is from Ayen. Sure enough, it has the flare of Enat's hand about it, but it's got his mark on it."

Brigit burst out, "If you say it is from Ayenwatha then I'm sure it is. You don't have to convince us. What does it say?"

Waneek cleared her throat but said nothing. Erik was about to speak, but when he saw Waneek almost imperceptibly lift a finger in motion toward him he held his tongue.

Unaine looked at Brigit for a moment before continuing his words, "Granddaughter, for you are as that to me, a wise leader should learn and practice the arts of patience and politeness. For it is often in the moments of silence, and in the times between, when one may learn what is crucial to future success. Now, I'm not saying that this is necessarily one of those times, but what if it is?"

Brigit's face reddened as she blushed with embarrassment, and she mumbled an apology.

Unaine went on, "No harm done. Even in times of considering important matters, we can still be learning our manners and be learning that which makes us better. Now let's get on with the communication from Ayen. He writes: The time of crisis is upon us. When in need - remember the necklace."

Brigit waited this time, yet no one else spoke. A scan around the room revealed that the other participants were deep into their individual thoughts. After several moments of silence, Brigit spoke up.

"I, for one, have never forgotten about the necklace. And I know that none of you here have either. And now that I wear it at all times, how could I forget it?"

Erik mused, "It seems to me that we have remembered it. Perhaps he means more."

Waneek said, "That would be like Ayen. I wonder what has prompted him to send this message now. And I wonder why he isn't a bit more specific about what this time of crisis is."

"Perhaps," added Unaine, "we need to refresh our minds as to what we all think we know. It is possible we are missing something. As well as remembering the necklace perhaps we need to recall the legend itself."

Brigit said, "I've heard that story a thousand times. How would remembering the legend help now?"

"I wonder. We've been focusing on the power of the necklace and hoping you could use it. But lately I've wondered if it might be more about the story than the necklace."

Waneek commented, "So, you are thinking that we have to go back to the ancient story from my people and re-examine that?"

"Yes, that's my thought. Let's consider the story. Brigit, since you say you've heard the story a thousand times and know it so well, please tell us the story as you know it."

Brigit hesitated. She knew full well that the others had also heard the story many times, and that Waneek of the Mohak in particular knew it very well, since it was from the history of her people. She wondered if she could tell it as well as they certainly knew, but she accepted the challenge and began to tell the tale.

A long time ago, when the world was young and the people were new in the land, there was a young man of the people. His father died when he was young. His grandfather yet lived, but this old man's eyes had grown dim, and were now blind, and he had trouble providing food for the people. Therefore, the responsibility to feed his family and clan fell to this young man. Sometimes there was but little food to be found, and some of the people would have to do without. Some would sacrifice their food for the good of others, but some would fight and steal from others so that they might have more to eat.

The young man wished for all his people to have enough to eat and to live in peace, so he would take his grandfather's bow and go out hunting. It was a fine, strong bow, for though grandfather was now blind, he had crafted it years before. It was a strong bow; and as the young man grew in stature, he grew to pull it with ease. But his father was not there to teach him the skills of hunting, so often the young man would return from the hunt with empty hands.

One evening, as they sat around the fire, grandfather told him, "My eyes are dim and my strength is spent. I cannot walk the woods with you and teach you the skills of hunting. You must call on Gluskabi to help." He then lifted a fine black and white necklace from around his neck and handed it to the young man. "Take this to Medawisla, Gluskabi's messenger. You know him as the one with the wailing and laughing calls that echo across the lakes and woods. Medawisla often takes the form of the diving bird we call the loon. Take this necklace and tell him your need. Give him the necklace, and ask for his help.

So the next morning, in the growing light before rising of the sun, the young man made his way to a nearby lake in hopes of hearing the echoing laughter of Medawisla. He stepped into a canoe and softly paddled his way to the center of the lake. Soon he spotted the form of the diving bird emerging from the morning mist rising above the waters.

There he made his supplication. With words, true and humble, he told of the need of his people, and of his failure to provide for them. He asked for the help of Gluskabi.

When the loon approached the canoe, the young man lifted the necklace from around his neck and tossed it toward the loon. To his amazement, it fell around its neck and lay upon the back of the loon. Then he heard Medawisla's laughter.

The loon spoke to him, "Jump into the water. Put your hands around my neck and hold on tight as I dive."

The young man did not hesitate. He did as he was told. They were under the water for a long time and when they surfaced they were near the far side of the lake.

"Look to the shore," the loon told him, "Can you see the wild game to hunt upon this shore?"

"Yes, I can." the young man replied.

"Good. Then hunt here and you will have success and your people will eat."

To the four directions of the lake, the loon carried him. Each time it would dive beneath the waters, emerge with him, and repeat the words to him. It then returned him to the canoe and repeated the promise. Then it promised, "There is game enough for all the people. Care for all of them. You have given me the necklace. When your people are in need, remember the necklace."

Then the young man climbed back into his canoe and paddled to shore. When he went hunting with his bow, he found abundant game for his people. He taught them how to work together and to see the abundance that lay around them and to give thanks for it. There was enough for all. And so there is.

Waneek nodded as Brigit ended the tale, and said, "You have told this story of our people true."

Unaine was also nodding his head, but he started his comments with a question, "I wonder if we have it right? For a long time I have been comfortable thinking that the necklace may have no power in and of itself. That the whole story was sort of symbolic for how Skoth ended up uniting the people of this land and helping build a common future. Others have suggested that the necklace has some innate power, perhaps like a druid's staff that is infused with power. But what if neither is right? What if this time of crisis is upon us, and we don't have the foggiest idea of what the necklace is really about?"

Erik added, "Aye. That is a problem. To my mind, the even bigger problem is that we don't even know what the crisis is."

The other three turned and looked at Erik, but said nothing.

Erik sputtered, "Well, I sure don't know! Do any of you?"

All three of the others slowly shook their heads.

Brigit offered, "But maybe Chief Ayenwatha knows. He is the one who just sent us the message."

Waneek nodded, "That is possible, although I suspect he would have informed us if he knew what it is."

Brigit replied, "I say we go ask him."

Unaine sighed, "Young folks always seem to think that the first action to be taken is to go running off. You may be right, but let's think this over for a couple of days before we take any action. Let's try thinking about what Skoth and Evlin would have us do." He looked pointedly at Brigit and added, "And I'm pretty sure that doesn't mean running off without giving some adequate time to think it through."

They agreed to think about the situation overnight and then to gather again at noon on the morrow to discuss it, and then to make some plans. Brigit was the first to leave, and Unaine quietly motioned for Erik to stay as Waneek followed her out.

The two men looked at each other for a few moments, and then Unaine asked, "Do you know what this means?"

Erik responded, "Aye. I'd better go assemble my gear and get ready to go. She'll probably be off as soon as the sun touches the sky, and you want me to tag along and keep an eye on her. Sort of like I did when you sent me with Skoth on his quest."

Unaine smirked as he said, "I can't think of a better man for the job. Take who you need with you. Send any message you need to send and make any arrangements you need to make. But protect her."

"You can count on me, Chief," Erik answered as he turned away and walked to the door. Already his mind was deep in thought as to preparations he needed to make.

"Wait a moment," Unaine called out, "Come back here. I have this walking staff I want you to give to young Wulf."

Erik took several paces back toward him and spoke with admiration as he saw the staff. "Tis' a fine staff. Is it a druid's staff?"

Unaine laughed, "Not yet. But who knows. Perhaps in time it will come to be so. Give it to Wulf and tell him that it was made from a fine young oak sapling. I've been engraving it and polishing it for the past several months. I was rather looking forward to walking the woods with it this summer. But my inner voice tells me that it belongs to Wulf. Please ask him to take good care of it."

Erik hefted the fine staff in his hand. "It does have a good feel to it. Be assured, old friend, the next time I see him, I'll give it to him."

Erik had only taken a few steps outside the door of the Great Hall when Waneek stepped out of the shadows to walk with him.

"Well," she said, "I assume we are to be ready to leave with the morning light. I know that young woman, and I can figure that you two old men are sending you to protect her. I'm going along. What can I do to help?"

Erik shook his head in amazement. Waneek was indeed a Wise Woman of the Mohak, but sometimes she was eerie the way she knew what he was about. He knew better than to try and hide his plans from her or to argue with her about her going along. They discussed and made their plans and then went their separate ways.

They had much to accomplish before the morning light.

Chapter 11 - Heading North

Erik and Waneek sat on a bench near the waterfront, enjoying a light breakfast, as they watched the sun rise over the Mahakentuck River. Somewhere, and in some way, there was a gathering storm approaching the land of Eirgalon, but at this moment, in the glory of a serene spring morning, the river was a scene of beauty and calm. Erik wondered if this was the real world, or was it perhaps just a veneer that covered the chaos and destruction that might soon devour them.

His reverie was broken by the voice of Brigit coming up behind him.

"Erik? And Waneek? What are the two of you doing here at this time of day?"

He turned slowly to face her. He had been expecting her. But he had not entirely expected to see Maengun standing next to her.

"Why, greeting the morning sun, we are! And may I inquire as to your presence here at this early hour? Out and about so early, and with young Maengun of the North?"

"Well," she hesitated, "I might as well tell you. I decided after our meeting last night that I should go north to Ayen. I have the necklace. It is my responsibility. When I told Maengun I was going, he insisted on coming along to help me. After all, he is from the north lands. He can be of help to me. We came down here to see if there was a boat heading north. If so, I was hoping to catch a ride on."

Erik gave a little smirk, "Well, sure enough, there is. I happen to have a boat waiting."

He pointed to a small skute (a trading vessel with one sail and several sets of oars that could navigate small, shallow rivers better than the larger seagoing karves and longships) that lay tied to the wharf in front of them.

Brigit stammered, "What? Why? How did you arrange this?"

"Oh, I know we were supposed to talk about this a bit more, but I just reckoned we'd be heading that way soon, so I wanted to be ready. Would you like to join Waneek and me on the boat?"

Brigit reddened a little in embarrassment. Erik and Waneek were obviously planning on going north with her, but she had intentionally avoided telling them she was leaving. Well, she thought, there is nothing to be done about it now, so I might as well make the best of it.

She politely accepted Erik's invitation, and the four of them began making their way to where the skute was moored. She was already mentally readjusting her plan and accepting the fact that Erik and Waneek would be traveling with them, at least until she had a chance to visit directly with Chief Ayenwatha. Then, as they stepped up to the skute, she was startled when one of the laborers in the skute straightened up from securing a bundle in the hold of the ship and turned toward her. It was Wulf. Erik could see her face brighten with a smile, but he also noticed a scowl flash across Maengun's visage.

"What?!" she exclaimed. Then she turned to Erik. "What is he doing here?"

Erik, non-plussed and even slightly amused, replied, "Wulf? Well, we all know Wulf isn't much of a seaman, and we sure don't want him falling off our boat when we don't have our eye on him, but since his uncle left him here to learn about Eirgalon, I thought it might be good for him to take a trip up north. You don't mind if he goes along, do you?"

"Of course not! I didn't think to ask because I thought he had to stay at Tara until his uncle returned, and I didn't know that he would want to go on such an adventure."

"Ha," retorted Erik, "he right jumped at the chance when I asked him. Of course, I don't know if it was because of the adventure, or because I let slip that it would be the Princess Brigit he would be traveling with." He winked at her and turned away.

Wulf jumped out of the boat onto the dock and came over to them. He wore a smile that spread across his face from ear to ear. It lessened slightly when he noticed Maengun, but returned fully when he looked back to Brigit.

"Good morning, Brigit!"

"Good morning, Wulf. So you are going up the river with us. I'm pleased," then with a wink to him she added, "Be sure to warn us if you decide to go for a swim."

Wulf laughed, "Oh, don't worry about that. I plan on staying out of the water."

Maengun interjected, "Don't worry about it, Wulf. We're heading toward my homeland. I'll take care of you."

Wulf thanked him, but was slightly taken aback by the manner in which that phrase was said, and the way in which Maengun smirked as he said it. But there was nothing to say about it now, and no need to spoil the positive mood of the moment. However, it would bear remembering, and it wouldn't hurt to keep an eye on his rival.

Soon the travelers were in the river boat, and with Erik's small crew of ten men at the oars, it had slipped away from the shore and they were headed upstream. Their first destination was the city of New Alba.

New Alba was the place where, as a infant only a couple of months old, Brigit had confronted the evil limikkin shapeshifter, Senadondo. At the sacred grove of maple trees surrounding a small lake, just outside the city, Evlin had laid Brigit in on the ground before a small shrine at the water's edge. Her attention, and that of her companions, had been distracted from her child by the attack of Senadondo's henchmen. This had allowed Senadondo, in the form of a rattlesnake to approach Brigit. As he rose in attack, he suddenly was frozen in action, enabling Evlin and her attendants to seize and kill him.

While Brigit could remember none of this, she had been told the story many times. The tellers all assumed that there was some power in Brigit that had stopped Senadondo in mid-strike. But Brigit wasn't so sure. She felt no such special power inside her, despite all her attempts to find such; and despite all attempts by her mentors to help her reach, or learn, those powers.

Brigit had been to New Alba with her parents several times since that event, and every time she felt a strange uneasiness overcome her. This would be her first visit to New Alba wearing the black and white moonstone necklace, and she set out on this trip she wondered if she would feel any different.

Chapter 12 - New Alba

New Alba had prospered and grown in the years since the peace accord with the Haudenoshonee League. Located near the confluence of the Mahakentuck and Mohak rivers, it was a prime location for commerce and communication. The previous leader of New Alba had been a man by the name of MacGregor. He had eschewed the title of King, preferring to be called Chief, but at heart he had been a simple trader. He had been one of the first of the local leaders to give his loyalty to Skoth as High King, when Skoth became the ruler of the Mahakentuck valley.

Upon his death five years ago, his place as the chief trader of New Alba was passed on to his eldest son, also called MacGregor. During the infamous spring of conflict that had brought the days of peace, the younger MacGregor was absent on a trading and exploring mission to the north. He had wintered with men of Eirgalon at the Celtic and Anishinaabe settlements that lay on the Big Waters River, beyond the Lake Between. On the very day that Skoth and Ayenwatha were celebrating the peace treaty, Young MacGregor and his men were making their way overland from the Lake Between to the headwaters of the Mahakentuck River. In the years that had followed, MacGregor and his son had established a thriving trade route between the New Alba and the Celts on the Big Waters River to the north.

The elder MacGregor's only daughter, Lil, had married the former king of Glesga, Duncan. When King Duncan was killed in the skirmishes that preceded the days of peace-forging, Lil had mourned his passing. But when courted by the new king of Glesga (Captain Bjorn), she found new life and became the wife of the new king. They had been blessed by three children. Lil felt that the curse of the unfortunate circumstances of her first marriage and the liaison with Malsum had been lifted by her service to the leaders of Eirgalon.

The crew of the river skute made good time up the river. They had a pilot who knew well the currents of the river and the winds of the river valley. The men who manned the oars appreciated his skill, for most of the work was done by the single-masted sail amidships. When they made port at the docks of New Alba, Erik insisted that they all go to MacGregor's Hall and make a formal presentation of themselves.

MacGregor's Hall had never been so much a "Great Hall" of one of the Eirgalon kings as it had been a trading center. Young MacGregor hadn't changed that, for he was at heart the same kind of trader as his father had been.

MacGregor was not at the hall when they arrived, but was busy at work in one of the storage barns near the docks. He did, however, send word asking them to wait at the hall and to join him at the evening meal when he returned.

MacGregor had not yet returned to the hall when it was time to begin the evening meal. Apparently, this was not an usual event, for the kitchen matron matter-of-factly announced it was time to serve the meal. She instructed them to sit at MacGregor's table and to begin. A hearty meal of bread, chicken stew, and sauteed vegetables, was served.

Several minutes into the meal, an energetic and muscular brown haired and bearded man barged into the hall acting like he owned it. In a manner of speaking, he did. It was MacGregor. He started talking with his guests as though he needed no introduction, which was true except for Maengun and Wulf.

"Ho, there my friends. Erik, so good to see you again! And the Princess Brigit! It is my honor. Waneek, looking as wise as ever," he winked and went on, "and these two young men. Now here's a couple of fellows I've never met before. I'd say one was a son of the Anishanaabe and the other a son of the eastern lands."

Erik laughed in response, "Tis a good eye you have, my friend. Maengun here, is indeed a son of the Anishanaabe. The other lad is Wulf, and he is a young man who has traveled to us from the German lands of Europe."

MacGregor's eyes widened and he laughed. "Two young wolves on my doorstep! What gifts you bring me, Erik!"

Erik and the others appeared puzzled. Erik was thinking about what MacGregor had said, when Brigit, who knew MacGregor well from her many visits to New Alba, gave voice to her question.

"What do you mean by 'two young wolves on your doorstep'?"

MacGregor responded, looking first at Wulf, "Well, I reckon that 'Wulf' in his tongue probably means wolf." Wulf nodded in assent. Then MacGregor looked at the young Anishanaabe man, "And I've traveled among your folk enough to know the tongue of your people well. Your name means 'wolf,' doesn't it, Maengun?"

All eyes turned to Maengun, who licked his lips and responded politely, "Why, yes, good sir. It does."

Waneek and Erik made eye contact with each other but said nothing.

Brigit directed her next question to Maengun, "But why didn't you tell us what it means? It's sort of funny, and strange, that the two of you have the same name, so

61

to speak."

"It's not the sort of item that one just throws out into a general conversation. After all, have you told me what 'Brigit' means?"

"Why it means: power or strength. Although Erik, here, has said that what it really means is 'strong-willed one' because he thinks I'm stubborn. Although I don't know that it was actually given to me because of those qualities as much as it was given to me because I was born on Brigit's Day."

Then she stopped, and looked around the table. She realized she had been going on for a bit, and then she said, "Oh. I see what you mean. We don't usually explain our names unless asked."

Maengun gave her a reassuring smile.

Then Maegun smoothly said, "It's not names, or their supposed meaning that really matters, is it? Isn't it what a person does that really counts?"

MacGregor snorted, "Aye, laddie. Tis what a person does that shows them true, but tis often the telling of such in a name that proclaims it to the world."

The conversation at the table fell silent, then MacGregor spoke again, this time with a lightness in his voice, "There are those say that my name means watchful and alert. I'm thinking that my trading partners and customers would probably agree with that. I doubt many of them have ever witnessed me get the bad side of a deal."

From there the conversation transitioned into more mundane matters. Typical table talk of weather and news predominated, but through it all Erik kept one eye and both ears tuned to Maengun. The interaction with MacGregor had done nothing to alleviate Erik's uneasiness concerning Maengun.

Chapter 13 - Gone

The plan was to spend one day in New Alba and then to head west up the Mohak River. They would stop and visit the trading post at Nealsfort, and then continue up river to the Mohak castles of Skenektedy and Tionnontoguen. Tionnontoguen was Ayenwatha's city, and it was there that they would meet with him to discuss what he meant with the message he had sent. They stayed the night at accommodations MacGregor had provided for them near his hall. They would meet there to break their fast in the morning and then depart.

But plans do not always come to fruition. For early on the morning of their intended departure, when it was light but before the sun had touched the sky, Waneek came to waken Erik.

"Get up, old man. I fear the child has run off."

Groggily, Erik replied, "What? What are you talking about?"

"The Princess! I can't find her anywhere. She's gone."

Erik jumped up and hastily clothed himself. As he did so, he tried to reassure Waneek that there was probably a simple answer. Maybe Brigit had gone out early to practice with her bow. Maybe she was making a special trip to the shrine at the sacred grove.

Waneek was having none of it. "She visited the shrine yesterday. I was with her. We meditated and made supplication there. She is gone I tell you. I can feel it."

They spent the next couple of hours searching for her, but couldn't track her down. They found Wulf, as he was coming to get some breakfast, but he knew nothing about her absence. Compounding their concern was the fact that they could not find Maengun either. After a frustrating day-long search for clues, they met with MacGregor to hear his report from the search parties he had sent out.

The only possible clues were that someone had spotted several miles north, on the Mahakentuck River, a two-person canoe paddling north; and that there was a report of a missing canoe on the northern outskirts of the city.

Erik shook his head when he heard this news, as he said to MacGregor, "That's not like Brigit. She's not one to steal a person's canoe."

Waneek said, "But don't forget about Maengun. We don't know that he wouldn't steal it. Why he may have even told her he'd brought it from up north, or that he'd bought it the day before. It might be she'd think it was his."

"Well, if he did, and if indeed she has run off with him, I'm still wondering, why? Why wouldn't she tell us?"

Wulf spoke up, "She didn't tell us when she was going to leave Tara with him."

"That's true enough, boy," replied Erik, "What can she be up to?"

Waneek offered a possibility, "Perhaps Maengun has some control over her will . . ."

Erik shook his head, "I don't think so. She's a strong-willed lass, if ever I've seen one. No, if she's with him, then she's with him of her own free will. At least at this point she is."

"Is is possible that she decided to do this, and that she is just taking Maengun along as a guide? Isn't he from the land to which she is headed?" asked Wulf.

Erik sighed deeply, "Yes, all too possible. She has a

mind of her own, and though she has always listened to us, she still makes up her own mind. She was about to leave Tara of her own accord with Maengun, so it is possible she left here, with the same thought in mind. Maybe we just helped her on her journey."

Wulf said, "So then let's go after her. If we know she's going north, let's go that way."

Erik and Waneek looked at each other, and then Waneek spoke, "We are pulled in different directions. She went north up the Mahakentuck, but Ayenwatha lives to the west on the Mohak. I deem it is of vital importance for me to go west and meet with Ayenwatha and his wife, Enat. They have knowledge and skill that helped usher in this time of peace and cooperation in Eirgalon. Their words of wisdom might well help us survive the crisis upon us."

Erik nodded in agreement. Wulf was going to say words in protest, for his desire to pursue Brigit was obvious, but Erik raised his hand to forestall him.

"Young man, I appreciate your desire to pursue her, but we must be wise in our action. I agree with Waneek. She must head west to Ayen."

He paused as he looked at Waneek and they both nodded as unspoken words passed between them. Then he continued.

"I will send her onward with our skute. Tis early in the year and the river is high. The pilot will make all speed to get her to Tionnontoguen. They will leave the skute if they must and take smaller canoes, but they will get her there as quickly as possible. There she will confer with Ayen and Enat. They will do what they deem best. I will pursue Brigit and Maengun. I may be old, but I can still follow a scent."

"What about me?" queried Wulf.

"What about you?" the elder warrior replied, "What would you do?"

"Why, I'll go with you to follow Brigit. I may not be the greatest fighter, but I'll not let her run off with Maengun. I'll tell you true - I don't trust him. And I don't trust her to be alone with him."

"Ahhhh, Wulf. What will I do with you? You can't swim. You're not much with a bow. You've confided to me that you aren't very adept with a sword. You could tag along, but you may even slow me down."

"Listen, Lord Erik, I agree I may not be the greatest warrior around or even a decent warrior. But I do know my way through the woods. I told you how I would spend my days walking the woods near my home. Give me a stout staff, and I'll keep up with you!"

"Well, first of all, young man, don't ever call me 'lord' - I'll have no man bend a knee to me. Second, I do believe having you with me might come in handy. I have this feeling in my gut that there is more to you than meets the eye."

Wulf nodded somewhat smugly and replied, "Okay. When do we leave?"

"We'll leave at first light. I'll hire the fastest river canoe and crew in port to speed us up the river to the North Falls. From there the river, what's left of it, turns west. From that point, the trade route goes by land to the Lake Between, then another portage to the North Gate Lake, and then on to the Many Waters Rivers. You better get some rest. I have the feeling you are going to need it."

Chapter 14 - Teachings of the Fires

Brigit and Maengun traveled nearly twenty miles up the Mahakentuck River that first day. The Mahakentuck ceased to be a tidal estuary near the vicinity of New Alba and paddling against its current was more difficult than what Brigit was accustomed to in the waters near Tara. They made camp that evening on a small island in the middle of the river. They could have easily found lodging in one of the settlements that dotted the course of the river, but while Brigit was not intent on concealing herself, she had no desire to broadcast her presence to the locals residents.

They made camp and then made a small fire to sit near, sharing some of the food they had brought with them. The effort of the paddling had been substantial and Brigit was tired enough to have gone directly to sleep, but she also wanted to enjoy the company of Maengun, so they sat near the fire and talked.

They sat gazing into the fire, and in response to Brigit's request for Maengun to tell her some of the history of his people, he told her the tale of the Teachings of the Fires.

A long, long time ago, prophets came to the people. This was when our people were living along the eastern shores of this great land. They left fires burning in our hearts and minds. Our people would move and grow as we moved to these fires.

The first fire was for the people to rise up and move to the turtle-shaped island. It is the place we now call Hochelaga. We were told that if we did not leave our homes on the eastern shores, we would be destroyed as a people. So we left our lodges and traveled to the place of purification. We settled and made our hearth fires at

68

Hochelaga.

The second fire was when the people grew to be many. There would be some who would move to live by the great waters. They spread from the first fire to the second fire and then going beyond to the furthest of those great waters. Our people would scatter about the shores of those great waters. But there would be so many clans, so many villages, so far apart. The people would struggle to be united as one.

Then would be time for the third fire. The third fire would be a calling together of the people who had scattered from Hochelaga to those scattered about the waters. The clans and villages would unite as one by sending leaders to meet. Our people do this now, and although we are many, and although we live scattered about the great waters, we are as one. But there are dangers for us.

The fourth fire foretold the coming of the pale ones from the lands beyond the sunrise. It is the time we live in. It speaks of danger for us. We are warned that the pale ones may wear the face of death for us and our ways. We are told that if they come with weapons and promises of peaceful brotherhood, but with greed for our land, we should not trust them, for if we do, then we shall perish."

Maengun concluded his story and looked into Brigit's eyes. He held her gaze for several moments and then his eyes darted a glance at her necklace. She noticed it and involuntarily she lifted a hand to it.

Then Maengun asked, "What would you say if I told you that wise and powerful men among my people believe that your people's promise of peace with the Haudenoshonee was but a sly way to weaken them, so that they would lose their ways and their lands?"

69

"But that's not the way it is," protested Brigit.

"No? Have not the Haudenoshonee joined the kingdoms of Eirgalon? Have not the ways of the pale ones spread throughout the Haudenoshonee lands? Where now is the vigor of their warriors?"

"They are still strong. They are feared by their enemies."

"Who are their enemies? The Wabanaki - who but imitate the pale ones? The Lenape - who are lap dogs to the traders of the pale ones? No, the only ones who still stand as true people of this land are the Anishinaabe. And even many of our people have come under the spell of the pale ones."

Brigit sat in silent thought for a few moments, and then asked, "If you believe this, then why did you come to Tara? And why are you guiding me north?"

"You came to me. You asked me to accompany you on this journey. You did not explain to me why you wanted to go north. You are the reason I am guiding you. Perhaps it is you who should answer my question: why are you making this journey?"

Brigit's forehead furrowed in thought. She had only known Maengun for a few days. While he was her companion on this journey, she felt she didn't she trust him fully, and a tinge of doubt teased her mind as she wondered if it had been the best action to make this journey alone with him.

Maengun sat silently, watching her, and watching the flickering flames of the campfire reflecting off the polished black and white moonstones that lay strung around her throat.

Brigit's head gave an almost imperceptible shake and then she explained, "This trip is just something I have to do. I thought you would be a good guide, since you come from the lands of the north. If you don't want to go with me, then just say so."

"No. I didn't say that. I do want to go with you. If you don't want to tell me your purpose, you don't have to. I'll help you as I can. After all, I do enjoy the pleasure of your company."

Brigit gave a little smile, "Thank you. I think we had better lay down and get some sleep. I'm not used to the paddling and and we have more of it to look forward to tomorrow."

They laid down on their separate pallets on opposite sides of the fire. Brigit turned her face from the fire and though she was tired, her eyes remained open for sometime before the lapping of the river waters on the beach lulled her to sleep.

On the other side of the fire and for a much longer time, Maengun lay with his eyes open and focused on Brigit. The flames flickered out. Only the coals and Maengun's eyes glowed in the night.

Chapter 15 - Pig's Eye Landing

Brigit and Maengun arrived at Pig's Eye Landing tired from their exertion of paddling. They eagerly anticipated the change to walking.

Pig's Eye Landing was the name of the southern end of the Grand Portage that ran from near the southern end of Lake Between to the Mahakentuck River. The landing was below the North Falls of the Mahakentuck. Above the falls, the river turned to the west and diminished in size. Pig's Eye Landing had acquired its rather strange sounding name as a result of the trading post that a Celtic trader had established there when the the Celts had first entered the region. This early trader had one "lazy" eye that did not track with the other. His friends jokingly referred to him as "Pig's Eye" and the name came to be applied to his trading post as well. Generations later, it was still called that.

A storm front was rolling in and the cloud cover had been building for hours. The rain had started falling only minutes before Brigit and Maengun paddled the canoe into the landing. They pulled their canoe up on shore and grabbed their gear out of it. They quickly flipped the canoe over and then ran to the main hall of the trading post.

One side of the hall was dedicated to the process of buying and selling trade goods, and the other side was used as a tavern where travelers could find food and refreshment from their journeys.

Brigit and Maengun inquired about a place where they might find lodging for the night and then sat down to order a meal of bread, stew, and ale.

They were deep in enjoyment of this fare when Erik and Wulf came through the main door of the hall shaking the rain off of their cloaks. Brigit jumped up and ran to them. She was surprised, but obviously pleased to see them.

"Erik! And, Wulf! What are you doing here? I thought you were going to see Ayen in Tionnontoguen."

Erik hugged her and replied, "Indeed, that's where I thought we were all going. Then, you up and disappear."

As Erik was making his greetings with Brigit, Wulf looked beyond her to where Maengun was sitting at the table eating his food. To Wulf, it appeared that Maengun was sneering at him. As Maengun wiped his mouth after taking a drink of the ale, he made an expression that Wulf likened to that of a cat licking itself after enjoying a mouse.

Wulf was shaken out of this thought by Brigit moving from her embrace with Erik to giving him a hug. Brigit pulled the two of them over to her table, and Erik beckoned to the kitchen maid asking her to bring out two more meals.

Maengun greeted them politely, but said no more.

When they were comfortably seated, Brigit again asked Erik about why Erik and Wulf had come to Pig's Eye Landing rather than going to Tionnontoguen.

"Well, well. Tis a good question to be sure. I'd be wanting to know the same of you. But my answer is that while Waneek is on her way there to talk with Ayenwatha, I thought it would be wise to see if I could find my way to you. I know you can take care of yourself well enough, but I didn't think that Evlin or Skoth would look kindly on the fact that I let you run off on your own. You can understand that, I'm sure."

A little bit embarrassed, she replied, "Oh, Erik. I'm fine. Other than being a little sore from all the paddling, I'm doing fine." She saw Erik's glance toward

Maengun, and continued, "And Maengun has been a perfect gentleman. Though I'd wager he is just as tired of the paddling as I am. I am puzzled though."

"About what?"

"How did the two of you get here so soon after we did? You certainly couldn't have left any time close to when we did."

Erik smiled. "No, we left the day after you did. But I thought this would be the direction you were heading, so I hired a river canoe of traders heading back north to take us on as passengers. Then I paid them extra to put their backs into the effort. When this storm front approached, we caught the winds from the southeast which fairly blew our boat, with its small sail, up the river. Those river men know what they are doing, to be sure!"

Wulf had been holding his tongue, but finally he blurted out, "What did you think you were doing? Running off like that without telling us what you are doing. We are your friends. We can help you just as much as he can!" Wulf motioned toward Maengun.

Maengun, with a smirk on his face and sarcasm in his voice, said, "Oh, you can? Do you know the ways of the north? Can you navigate the rivers, lakes, and woods? Can you protect her from the evils that walk these lands? What does a pale man from the weak lands across the sea know of this land?"

Erik placed his hand on Wulf's arm to forestall him from answering.

Brigit turned her attention to Maengun, "What do you mean? What are the 'evils that walk this land'? You have told me none of this!"

"They are nothing. I can protect you from any harm from them. My people call them Windigos."

"Windigos? I've never heard of such before."

A weathered man, a traveling trader by the look of him, who was seated nearby and obviously listening in to their conversation, spoke out, "Trolls. Trolls be what he is talking about. The mountains to the northwest of here are cursed by them. The Anishanaabe call 'em windigos, but trolls is what they be. You best stay away from 'em."

Erik asked the man, "Have you had dealings with them?"

The man shook his head, "Not I, but I have friends who have. Man-eating brutes they are! I warn you again. Stay clear of them."

Each of their private thoughts went to considering this new information, but their common conversation shifted to more mundane matters such as the food, the weather, and physical readiness to move on. They ended the evening meal by agreeing that they would meet in the morning to break their fast. Erik made Brigit promise that she would not run off, and that she would consult him about any decision concerning her future course of action. The trading post's workers directed them to go to the next door hostel, where they might get sleeping accommodations for the night. Women travelers were not uncommon, and Brigit was pleased to learn that the hostel had separate sections for men and women.

There was but little conversation between the men at the hostel. It was time for rest, not conversation. There was a tension in the air between Maengun and the other two men, and none of them seemed inclined to take any steps to lessen it. They simply laid down and rested.

The women's side of the hostel was another matter. While Pig's Eye Landing was at what might be considered the northern fringe of the local Kingdom of

Tara, it was still well within the High Kingdom of Eirgalon. The name of Brigit was well known throughout the land, and there was a young woman who had recognized her as Princess Brigit of Tara. The lass was close in age to Brigit and looked to be of Celtic stock for she had the fiery red hair that marked some of those whose ancestors came from the land of Eire.

"Well, glory be, if it isn't the Princess Brigit, herself!" she exclaimed.

Brigit acknowledged her and politely added, "And to whom do I have the pleasure of talking?"

"Why, I'm Shivon. My father brought some furs down the route from Hochelaga. He's planning on taking them to New Alba, then heading back north."

"How is it that you know me?"

"Pardon me, Princess, but you are pretty well known, though I confess that I didn't expect to see you here in Pig's Eye Landing. Last year, I was with my father when he took his goods all the way to Tara. I saw you there, though I doubt you noticed me, with me being only the tag-a-long daughter of a trader from the north."

Brigit gave her a reassuring smile, "I'm sorry to say I don't remember you, but I'm pleased to meet you now."

They conversed for several minutes, and that led into hours, as they rested that night. They had a surprising natural affinity and rapport with each other. The end result of the conversation was that Brigit asked if Shivon would be willing to travel with Brigit and her three companions as she headed north. Shivon agreed, though she did say she would have to get her father's approval.

When the conversation ended and Shivon had drifted off to sleep, Brigit lay awake for a few more minutes contemplating her journey. Her last conscious thoughts were questioning if she knew what she was doing; she wasn't clear on her exact purpose, much less the how of it. She had some doubts percolating about Maengun, and now she had just asked a person she had known for only a few hours to accompany her. Life was becoming more interesting by the day!

Chapter 16 - Decision Made

When morning broke, Brigit awoke with renewed determination to continue with her original plan. She had not previously shared her plan with any others, but now she deemed it wise to speak of it to them and to solicit their advice and support.

Brigit had the trading post manager arrange a private meeting room for the five of them: herself, Erik, Wulf, Maengun, and Shivon. Brigit introduced Shivon to the men and then they ate their breakfast of morning spruce tea, bread, and porridge. Following their meal, Brigit laid out her general plan and asked for their advice. Both Wulf and Shivon knew but little of the history of Skoth's Quest, so she took it upon herself to retell that story and then to finish it by offering them the chance to opt out.

"I wasn't sure what I was going to do when I began this journey, but now I intend to complete what my father began two decades ago. When he undertook his quest, he did not fully understand all of it. I have to admit that I don't either. He did acquire the Loon's Necklace, but had no clear understanding of how to use it in completion of the quest. Before the great crisis with the Haudenoshonee broke out, he intended to follow the waters of the Mahakentuck to their beginnings. That is where I intend to go. We will go to where its waters begin on the slopes of Cloudsplitter Mountain."

She let the impact of that settle in. All present, with the exception of Wulf, would know that meant traveling into the harsh territory of the granite mountains of the Rondax. It was a land that was filled with steep slopes, heavy forests, and numerous lakes. Such wilderness terrain made travel difficult, if not impossible, in places.

Then she continued, "From what that trader said last night, this means we will be going into territory where there are trolls, and perhaps other dangers. I can't, and won't, force any of you to come with me. So if any of you want to leave me, I understand."

Maengun didn't hesitate, and even seemed eager and pleased to go. When Wulf heard Maengun's response, he also quickly affirmed his desire to proceed. Shivon thought about it while the others spoke and then she too added her desire to go with Brigit. In addition, she cautioned them that her father would not be pleased with her choice.

Erik sat thoughtful and silent. Brigit had expected that he would quickly protest her intended course of action.

Brigit eyed him over and waited. She could see him clench his jaw before he responded.

"I'm not sure that it's the wisest course of action, but as you say - you are the one wearing the necklace. Sometimes a gut feeling is the best judge. You have a gut feeling to go this route. I'll trust that. And I have a gut feeling that I should go with you. Mind you, I'm not all that anxious to tangle with any of those nasty trolls that infest the Rondax hills. They're right difficult beasties to kill."

Maengun's eyes widened slightly at Erik's comments, and he asked, "You've encountered the windigos? And you claim to have defeated them?"

"Aye, that I have. And that's the reason I'd avoid them if I could. But if the Princess wants to go where she might have to deal with them, then I reckon I'd better tag along."

Maengun looked at Erik with a calculating eye and asked, "What magic do you possess? When I first met

79

you, you introduced yourself to me 'a simple servant of the chief' yet you were able to quickly follow us here, and now you claim to have the power to defeat the windigo. Are you a shaman of the pale ones?"

Erik could see that Maengun was recalculating his estimation of him, and he responded, "Ach, no! I'm just a simple fellow with a wee bit of luck. It never hurts to have fortune smile on ye."

Then to change the direction of Maengun's questioning thoughts, Erik turned his attention to Brigit and asked her about her traveling plans.

She responded, "I thought that rather than follow the river on its winding course up the valleys and hills of the Rondax Mountains, we would follow the trade route to Lake Between and then travel north on the lake toward the mountain called Cloudsplitter. We will land at Ticonderoga, the settlement at the junction that connects Lake Between and the North Gate Lake, where the waters run north. From there we will go west by land and up the slopes of Cloudsplitter until we come to the ultimate source of the Mahakentuck."

Erik asked, "And how will you know when you have come to the waters of the Mahakentuck, and not to one of the other streams that run off of Cloudsplitter?"

Brigit hesitated. A thoughtful look crossed her face before she replied.

"If I am right about the source of the river being tied to the necklace, then I think that I will feel some sign when we get close to it. If I am wrong, and don't feel any sign, then I can rely on Maengun. He has assured me that he can locate the source of the river."

Erik looked for a moment at Brigit, then shifted his gaze to Maengun, who was nodding in affirmation.

"Young Maengun, what makes you so confident

that you can lead her to the source? Have you been there?" He paused for effect and then continued, "Or perhaps, have you some magic about you?"

Maengun was startled by the question and stammered as he formulated a response.

"Ah, well, I know the north lands. And I assure you that I can guide her to where she needs to go."

Erik noted to himself that Maengun didn't actually answer the question, but let that slide. The fact that Maengun avoided answering with any substance revealed more to Erik than Maengun realized it did. When Erik let the issue drop without responding, Maengun felt reassured that the old man was satisfied. In reality, while Erik put on a public face of being reassured, inwardly he resolved to keep an even more watchful eye on the young man from the north. There was definitely more to that young wolf than met the eye.

Chapter 17 - Portage to Lake Between

On the following morning, after a day of preparations for the trip north, the cool spring morning saw the five travellers fall in with a contingent of traders that had brought beaver furs from the south to trade, and who were now heading back north. Shivon's father was among these men.

Shivon's father had been less than pleased when informed by his daughter about her decision to go with Brigit's party into the Rondax. Their private discussion the previous day had been intense, but in the end he acquiesced to her plans. He had left the meeting with his daughter with a look of concern on his face; and though he walked away alone he occasionally shook his head as if he was still trying to persuade his willful daughter to stay with him.

On this morning, he conversed with Erik as they walked beside a team of horses pulling a wagonload of goods up the portage to Lake Between (which was the name of the village at the southern end of the lake, as well as the name for the lake). Erik was keeping his eyes on the young foursome who walked several paces ahead of them on the path, but he was listening carefully to everything that Shivon's father was telling him about his daughter and about recent developments in the northern city of Hochelaga and beyond. It had been several years since Erik had been on this route, and as far north as Hochelaga, so he paid careful attention, after all, one never knew when a seemingly unimportant bit of information might come in handy.

From his trader's perspective, Shivon's father described the current conditions in the north. For generations Celtic traders and immigrants had come westward up the Big Waters River. As in the rest of Eirgalon, for that is how people now referred to the western continent, the descendents of the European people had intermixed with the native inhabitants of the land. Hochelaga, the turtle-shaped island in the Big Waters River, was the largest of the cities along the river and had the largest population of those with Celtic blood in their veins. People of Celt, Wabanaki, Mohak, and Anishanaabe lived and worked in relative harmony along the course of the river. However, there had recently been an increasing number of altercations between the Anishinaabe and the other inhabitants of the area.

Unlike the Celtic political system of local kingdoms that were each ruled by a chief or king, Hochelaga was governed by a council of Elders that represented the various groups that comprised its population. The Elders had been struggling to keep peace among the factions, but rumours were rife that behind the unrest were machinations of the mysterious shaman sometimes called Megissogwon, and sometimes called Malsum. Shivon's father repeatedly asserted to Erik that while he was a simple man with no power or authority to influence events, it was obvious to him that there was trouble brewing and something needed to be done.

Mostly, Erik just listened to him. Occasionally he asked him a clarifying question, but as he listened, his thoughts grew darker with the realization that undoubtedly the threat that Ayenwatha had been referring to was the the re-emergence of Malsum.

Erik also probed his walking companion with questions to learn about Shivon. A father's pride was evident in the responses to these inquiries. Erik was pleasantly surprised by the numerous talents and abilities of Shivon that were revealed to him.

While looking forward upon the young women and men walking several paces ahead of him, he started to reflect on the group that Brigit had chosen as companions for herself. While he trusted Brigit, and she had shown good common sense as she had grown up, Erik wondered if the way she had so quickly become infatuated by the others was a normal process of her maturation, or if it might be the result of some nefarious work of Malsum. Was that possible?

Erik walked through the relationships in his thoughts. He had no doubts about Wulf. Their time and conversations reinforced Erik's conviction about the essential goodness of Wulf's nature. Maengun was another matter. His presence had troubled Erik from the moment he had seen him, and he merited special attention. Shivon was still an enigma to Erik. She seemed like a nice girl, was talented (at least according to her father), and her father was likeable enough. But was she as she appeared? Erik wondered at the way Brigit was attracted to her and so quickly. She certainly had fine features. And without a doubt, that flaming red hair did have certain appeal.

Then Erik chuckled to himself as he thought, "Ach, even now, a pretty lass turns my eye. I'm old enough to be her grandfather. But if she delights my eye, I'm thinking she has such an affect on others. She bears watching as well."

The distance from Pig's Eye Landing to the landing at the south end of Lake Between was about ten miles as the crow flies, but slightly longer by foot as the portage road wound around swamps, through woods, and between hills. As they walked, Erik noted to himself that there would be several fine spots to ambush travelers, if someone would choose to do so. Fortunately, nothing of the sort happened; and after their hours of walking they came to the landing on the shores of the lake.

When the group turned the final corner and the vista of a valley with sparkling lake waters flanked by verdant slopes of forests lay exposed before their eyes, Wulf stopped as if stunned.

"Ahhh," he said, "so beautiful. I've never seen anything like this."

Shivon, who stood next to him responded first, "Welcome to the northlands, Wulf. If you think this is grand, you should see it in the fall when the leaves are turning color. You'd never forget it."

"I'll never forget this," he stammered, and then as he heard Maengun give a little snort of derision, he blushed in embarrassment for letting his emotions show.

Erik who had come up from behind them spoke up, "I'm with you, boy. This is a right beautiful sight. It never ceases to amaze me with its beauty. I've been to quite a few places in my life, and I must say I rank the views of this lake and valley right up there at the top," and then spinning the conversation to Shivon he said, "As for you, Shivon, your father has been telling me how much you enjoy these trading trips with him. Perhaps these sights are the reason, but beside the view, what is it that makes you want to travel, and even to go on this adventure with Brigit?"

Shivon glanced at Brigit, who was listening intently, and responded, "Da knows I've always liked to get away from home. It's a big world and I want to see it. As for Brigit's quest, well, who could pass up a chance to travel with Brigit, and to maybe do something that matters!"

She then turned her gaze back to Brigit and locked

eyes with her. The connection between the two was obvious to the others. None could identify what the connection actually was, but the fact that there was a spark of some sort between them was obvious.

Maengun spoke up and drew Brigit's attention, "The lake looks calm, and we have a couple of hours of daylight left. Perhaps we can arrange passage on a craft and get a few miles up the lake yet today."

They could see Brigit thinking about the options, and then Wulf asked, "What's the hurry? We just got here. Maybe we should look about for a bit. We can't get that far in only a couple of hours."

Maengun impatiently chided, "Listen. This lake may not look huge to you. It is only a mile or so wide at this end, but it is thirty miles long. It will take us some time to traverse it. You may want to see the sights, but that's not what we are doing here. I say we get started today."

Brigit cocked her head to the side as she looked at Maengun, "YOU say we get started? I didn't realize you were in charge?"

Maengun immediately backed down, "Oh, no. I don't mean it to sound like I'm in charge. You're the leader here. I'm only suggesting what I think is the wisest action. It only makes sense to get under way. The weather is good today. A spring storm could blow in tonight and delay us. There is no reason to delay."

"It's okay," said Wulf, "We can go on today. Whatever you want, Brigit."

Erik said nothing, but listened to the byplay as Shivon said to Brigit, "Can I offer my advice?"

Brigit replied, "Of course. I'd like to hear what you think."

"If we stay we can get a good meal and a good

night's rest. I don't mind going on, but unless there are some strong reasons to move on, I think it would be better to lay in here overnight."

Brigit nodded in acceptance of what Shivon said, and then turned to Erik, "You haven't said anything. Do you have any thoughts you'd like to share with me?"

"Well, I wouldn't mind staying the night here if you had a mind to do so. There's a wise woman of the Women's Circle here that I know. My back has been giving me some pain, and if it would be alright with you, I'd like to visit her, and see if she could do anything for me. "

At this point, Shivon's father who had walked up with Erik, but said nothing to this point, added, "If you wait until the morning, you can travel on the barge my trading company has hired to take us up the lake. You'll have to come on as paying customers of course, and maybe even lend your arms to the oars. It may not be the fastest boat on the lake, but we'll likely travel its course in three days."

"That sounds good to me. We will stay the night and then be off with you in the morning," replied Brigit, who then directed a comment to Erik, "Go look up your friend. I'll be anxious to hear what she has to say about your back."

Erik smirked and replied, "That I will. Now promise me that you won't try to run off again without me."

Brigit laughed, "I promise. Now let's go find some food, some lodging for the night, and some 'back relief' for our elderly escort."

Chapter 18 - Lake Between

The wise woman of Lake Between was not surprised to see Erik walk through the door of her small cottage. She was a matronly woman, who looked to be in her early sixties. She was in the midst of preparing the evening meal for her husband, a blacksmith who had a shop out back of the cottage, but she immediately went to Erik and gave him a warm embrace.

"Erik! What a pleasure to see you."

"Ah, the pleasure is mine, dear Orla. You are looking as lovely as ever."

"Ahh, go on with you, now. You always were the charmer. We're both old enough now to know better."

They bantered back and forth like the old friends they were for several exchanges before Orla invited him to sit while she resumed working to prepare the meal. Erik sat at her sturdy wood kitchen table and explained the mission he was on. He described Brigit's mission and asked about the current state of affairs in the area, including any information she might have concerning Malsum and his minions.

During the course of the conversation, Orla's husband, Knut, entered the cottage from the back door. It was apparent that he was also an old friend of Erik's, and he joined the conversation. Oft times people come to blacksmiths in time of need, and that often results in the sharing of information.

Shortly after Knut entered the conversation, he asked, "Has Olra mentioned to you about the rumors of the baykaak?"

"No. What is a baykaak? I've been all over this land, but I've never heard of that."

"It was new to me, too. You know how I get some

of my ore from the Rondax mountains to the northwest of here, well, my suppliers tell me they have been hearing reports of these creatures attacking our people."

"I've encountered the trolls of the Rondax Mountains before. You're sure these aren't trolls, or as others call them - windigos?"

"No, no. Trolls are nasty, brutish beasts, but they are beasts. And they are of the land.These baykaak sound to be more ghostlike. And they are creatures of the air. They are said to look like skeletons you can see through. They have eyes that blaze like fire, and they shoot invisible arrows. Then they come and rip you open, tear out your heart, and eat it."

Orla said, "It sounds to me like they are demon-spawned creatures. I don't know for sure, but I wouldn't be surprised if Malsum was behind this. There are creatures like this in the legend and lore of the Anishanaabe."

Erik sat for several moments in silence as he thought about this information, then he turned to Knut and said, "Knut, if that forge of yours is still hot and you have a supply of nails handy, there are a couple of small iron items I'd like you to fashion for me."

"Anything for you, my old friend. Let's go see what I can do for you."

With that being said, the two men went out the back door to the blacksmith's shop. They re-entered just as Orla was coming to the door to call them for supper. In his hand Erik carried a small leather pouch. He slipped it into the inside pocket of his tunic and then they sat down and enjoyed their meal together.

When Erik left that night to go and join the other member's of Brigit's traveling party, he cautioned Orla to tell others who might ask about him only that he had come to visit her for some healing remedy to his back pain. No one, other than Brigit, needed to know that the real purpose of his visit was to gather information, or that he had Knut forge six small amulets in the shape of Thor's hammer.

The next morning the group gathered at the lakeshore, and while the boatmen were making final preparations, Erik pulled the four younger members of Brigit's group to the side.

He explained to them, "When High King Skoth was a young man, just starting on his quest, he had a blacksmith forge a small amulet of protection that he wore on his quest."

Brigit interrupted, "I've seen it. He still wears it."

"Has he told you why he wears it?"

Brigit shook her head.

Erik continued, "He wore it, and still wears it, because the old Master Druid, Theofinn, had taught him that an amulet of iron could help fend off attacks by evil spiritual forces."

Wulf blurted out, "Does it really work?"

Almost at the same time Maengun asked, "Why are you telling us this?"

"Easy, my young wolves," responded Erik, "yes, I believe there is something to it. And I'm telling you this because I have something to give you that might help protect you from forces of evil in the days to come. The choice is yours, but as for me, I will wear this newly forged amulet. I will use every advantage I can as we walk into danger."

He pulled out a small leather pouch from his tunic and then pulled a Thor's hammer amulet from the small pouch. A leather cord was strung from it so that it could be worn as a necklace.

"This amulet was fashioned from nails that were forged with iron mined in the Rondax Mountains. If there be evil of a spiritual ilk that seeks to harm me, perhaps this will guard me, as Skoth was so protected."

He placed the corded amulet around his neck so that it lay upon his chest. Pulling out another amulet he handed it to Brigit.

As she lifted it over her head and lowered it round her neck to lay next to the loon's necklace, she said, "Perhaps later you'll tell me more of Skoth's iron amulet. As for now, I trust you and your judgement. I'll gladly wear this amulet of protection."

Shivon also graciously accepted the gift and immediately put it on.

Wulf appeared anxious to receive his; and when Erik placed it in his hands, he turned it over and over as he inspected it.

Erik asked him, "Is there some problem?"

"Oh, no. No problem at all. I just wanted to see it close up. I notice there are a couple of imprints on each side. Would those be the maker's mark?"

"How astute of you to notice. One of them is indeed a maker's mark. Knut the blacksmith is a talented man, and his mark on metal is a sign of quality. The other side is marked with the rune of Algiz - it is the rune of protection. A wise woman of the north has blessed these amulets with all the power she possesses. You asked if really works - I do believe so."

Wulf smiled as he put the cord over his neck and lay the amulet upon his chest. Shyly, he mumbled genuine words of appreciation.

Then Erik pulled an amulet from the pouch and turned to Maengun. He could see a wave of emotion flash across the young man's face. It was a mixture of distaste and possibly even fear. However, when Erik extended his hand with the amulet, Maengun smiled and graciously accepted it. He glanced at it and then placed it into his tunic pocket.

Erik asked, "Aren't you going to wear it?"

"No. I'll keep it in my pocket. If it actually works, it will work as well there as if I wore it. Besides, I don't want it getting in my way if there is any physical action."

Erik said nothing, but raised a single eyebrow. Then he reached into the pouch and pulled out one more amulet. It was slightly smaller than the others and the cord was not yet attached to it.

"Brigit, please hand me your bow. With your permission, I'll fasten this small amulet to it. One never knows exactly what might transpire, but it doesn't hurt to take precautions."

He took a few moments to fasten the amulet securely to the bow in a way the would not interfere with the heft, or the release of an arrow, and then handed it back to her.

"Now we are ready to move on. It looks as though they are ready for us to board the boat. Let's get on the lake and get moving."

Chapter 19 - Bolton's Spring

The barge was heavily laden with trade goods heading north, and even with the help of a slight westerly breeze that the small ship's single sail tacked against, the rowing of the bargemen didn't bring them to their day's destination until late afternoon. It was named Bolton's Spring in honor of the Saxon immigrant trader from West Angland, who had established the waystation there.

As they neared the settlement, Shivon, who had traveled this lake on several trips with her father, pointed out that the main settlement was on the western shore of the lake where there was a freshwater spring. There was also a small settlement on the island that lay less than one hundred feet offshore, but most of the traveling barges docked overnight on the main shore. They would be tying up on the mainland side of the channel and resting there for the night before moving on in the morning.

There was a common hall for travelers that had been constructed near the spring, and it was to this establishment that Shivon directed the group after the boat was securely tied to one of the several docks jutting out into the lake. Erik told the others to go to the hall without him and that he would join them later.

Several other boats, some from the north and some from the south, had also made their way to these docks for an overnight stay. The manner in which the boatmen from the various crafts greeted each other made it apparent that many of the boatmen knew each other, for as their barges plied the waters of Lake Between, they often crossed paths.

Men from those boats also made their way to the

hall, and soon the hall was filled with tired and hungry men waiting for the evening meal to be served. Some of the men recognized Shivon, for she had made this trip with her father a couple of times, and that red hair of hers was hard to miss.

After Brigit and the others left the barge, Erik went among the bargemen who were securing their craft. Some would leave and go to the common hall to eat and bunk there overnight, but others would stay with the barge and watch over their craft and goods during the night. There was an unwritten code of brotherhood among the men who plied the waters of Lake Between and North Gate Lake as they moved trade goods along the north south corridor through the mountain range of northern Eirgalon. They trusted each other and often helped each other out, for they knew that there were very real dangers on the waters and along the shores of these northern lakes. Constant vigilance was needed to guarantee their safety.

Erik asked the men of his barge to spread the word among the men of the other boats that they should act as if they didn't know him. This would be a major challenge, for Erik, advisor to High King Skoth, was certainly well-known. His decades of traveling the lands of Eirgalon as a warrior and advisor to kings had left him oft-recognized, but at this moment he wanted to show a low profile.

Some time later, when Erik walked into the common hall of Bolton's Landing to rejoin Brigit's group, men would glance up at him, give him a wink or a nod to acknowledge him, but then turn away. To all appearances, Erik was an ordinary traveler, perhaps looking a little weathered through the years, but nothing out of the ordinary.

Brigit saw him and motioned him over to join them at their table near the rear of the room. They had already begun eating and Erik joined in. The fare was a hearty fish stew and bread meal, accompanied by an ample ale. The men and women, for there were a few other women travelers like Brigit and Shivon, enjoyed the friendly atmosphere and camaraderie around a satisfying meal. But as the evening wore on and the day slid into the darkness of a spring evening, conversations turned to local events, and then to dark rumours of strange occurrences.

The common room was a place where hard-working people ate and drank; and while it could get boisterous in the way that a town tavern might, the folk knew full well of the work that lay before them on the morrow. It wasn't long before they made their ways to their accommodations to get their rest, for the sun would rise soon enough.

Shivon had helped Brigit's party secure bunks at the hostel attached to the common hall, so when the meal ended and the conversation began to wind down, they headed to their bunks. Erik told the others that he was going to step outside for a short while and then he asked Wulf if he would walk with him.

They ambled together toward the lakeshore, where the boats were tethered.

Once away from the others, Wulf asked Erik, "Erik, do you think those stories are true?"

"Which stories?"

"The ones those men at the table beside ours were telling. The ones about banshees, and trolls, and baykaak, and the like."

"I don't know about the accuracy of all the details, but behind the tales lie elements of truth. There is evil in this world. Sometimes the evil is in the hearts of people, and sometimes there is evil from the spiritual realm that grasps out at us."

"Erik, can I tell you something?"

In the darkness, unseen, Erik raised an eyebrow.

"Of course. What is it?"

"I think there is some evil about Maengun. I mean, I don't know for sure. I thought maybe it was the way he treats me and speaks to me, or maybe that I was jealous of the way Brigit looks to him, but . . ."

He paused.

Erik encouraged him to go on, "But what?"

"But I get this feeling about him. You know that feeling one gets when you see the hackles on a dog's neck rise up. He just doesn't feel right to me. I don't trust him."

"Neither do I, my young friend. But I caution you not reveal the depth of our suspicions. If he senses that we are overly suspicious of him, he will be more guarded around us."

"Is that why you act like you are just a simple king's servant around him?"

"What do you mean?"

"I know you are one of the king's most trusted men. I know you have traveled far and wide, and that you have had grand adventures. I have heard of your exploits. Yet, around Maengun, you reveal none of that."

If Erik had turned his head, and if there had been enough light, Wulf would have seen the old man smile.

"Ah, yes, there is that. You are indeed observant, young Wulf. I think it is best that he knows as little about me as possible. He's already suspicious enough, either by nature or by intent. Tis best if he knows the least amount possible. I'd just as soon he underestimate me."

The men arrived at the barge and checked in with the crew. Watchmen from the boats were posted along the shore, and all seemed in order. Erik invited Wulf to sit with him for a spell. They found a sizable boulder on the shore past the final campfire and watchman and sat down. From their seat they could see the small campfires on the island beyond the narrow channel.

Erik asked Wulf for his impression of Shivon, and was not surprised by the reply. It was too dark to see Wulf blush, but Erik could sense it in his words.

"She's quite impressive. There are her looks, of course, but she has a fine wit and she seems to have a genuine heart. I feel I can trust her."

Erik agreed, "She certainly is impressive, and I think you might well be right about her. I've talked with her father and what you say goes along with what he says. Yet, we would be wise to be cautious about her as well. Even good people may get twisted by the evil designs of others."

"So, I should avoid her?"

"Oh, not at all. Let your friendship grow. Yet stay alert. Don't let the charm of a young lady dull your senses."

Suddenly a wailing scream pierced the darkness. Erik and Wulf leapt to their feet. Erik drew his sword and Wulf seized his walking staff. They heard sounds of a struggle coming over the water from the direction of the island. The guards on the barges strained to see into the darkness, and the men who had been resting soon scurried to alertness. But there was little they could do at that moment but peer anxiously into the gathering gloom. The skies were clear, but the last vestige of sunlight had disappeared several minutes ago and the moon had not yet risen to give its light to the night.

Immediately after hearing the scream, the light from the campfires on the island disappeared. It was as if they had been covered by blankets. Desperate shouts of "help" echoed through the night.

The men guarding the barges could be heard uttering "banshees" and "bloody baykaaks" as they held their weapons tight. There were canoes on the shore, but none of the men volunteered to get in the canoes and venture across the channel of water to the island. They weren't cowards, but their job was to protect their trade goods. Besides, who knew what evil might now be lurking on that island, or in the waters near it, just waiting to pounce upon any would-be rescuers.

Wulf whispered to Erik, "Shouldn't someone be going over there to help?"

"Aye," Erik whispered in return, "but none of these men have that responsibility. Their job is to protect what is here."

"Then what about us?"

"You would go? You can't swim. What if our canoe was attacked and capsized in the dark?"

"It doesn't matter. Someone needs to help them!"

Resolutely Erik nodded his head, "Aye, you have the right of it. Let's go."

While they were getting into one of the canoes, a bargeman holding a torch in one arm and a sword in the other came up to them and said, "I'll go with you." He motioned for Erik to take the front, Wulf to the center. He handed Wulf his torch, laid his sword into the canoe, and then pushed them off. He jumped into the stern of the canoe, where he deftly lifted his paddle and steered them to the far shore.

Within moments they had traversed the channel and

run the canoe up on the shore. They quickly disembarked. The sputtering torch cast its dancing light upon the towering trees around them. The bargeman motioned that they should make their way to the right, where the largest fire had been, and where there were a couple of small cottages.

As they moved in that direction, a group of people emerged from the shadows. They held weapons at the ready, but seeing the friendly face of someone they knew in the bargeman, they didn't attack.

One of the men told of how they were sitting near their fire when the fire when out, as if buckets of water had been dumped upon it, and then they had heard the scream. They insisted it didn't come from their fire, but from somewhere north of them on the small island. As they lit more torches from the one Wulf was holding, they explained that they lived on the island but that there had been another fire north on the island, where a group of travelers had set up camp for the night.

Together, they made their way up the path along the shoreline to where the other fire had been. Upon reaching the campsite they discovered a grisly scene. Three men lay dead on the ground before them. They had obviously struggled with their attackers, for their weapons were out and the camp was in disarray.

The investigating men kept a watchful eye out for the attackers as they examined the scene. Whoever had committed this attack was still out there and could return.

The unpleasant smell of death filled the air about them and Wulf became nauseated. He stepped several paces to the side, knelt and retched, and then stood up and wiped his mouth with his sleeve. The others, men who had experience with the harsh realities of life and death, said little to him. They gave him slight nods of recognition, and here and there a muttering of "it's alright" or "nothing to be ashamed of."

Erik led the men in summarizing a survey of the scene. It revealed that the fire was stone cold, not even warm embers to relight a fire. There were the two old men and one youth lying dead before them. All three had been shot by arrows. It appeared as though the arrows didn't kill them but that knife wounds did. The youth had the most gruesome wound, for it appeared that his chest had been brutally ripped open and his internal organs torn out.

The bargeman muttered, "That is work of a baykaak, for sure. Spawn of the demon world and pure evil they are."

The bargeman suggested to Erik and Wulf that they should return to the far shore, share the news, and give warnings to the people at Bolton's Spring. Though fearful, the local folk of the island made assurances that they would keep watchful for a return attack. They thanked Erik, Wulf, and the bargeman for their help and promised that they would provide a proper burial for the deceased men in the morning.

Before leaving, Erik took one of the deadly arrows from the scene. He took it to the water's edge and rinsed it off, then carefully wrapped it in a leather cloth. While he secured it to the sheath of his sword, he noticed Wulf watching him.

He said to Wulf, "This will bear some careful examination in the light of day. Let's get going."

Chapter 20 - Questions

Brigit and Shivon had not yet fallen asleep in their bunks when that piercing wail split the night. They immediately roused themselves and grabbed their weapons. For Brigit this consisted of her bow and a long dagger, as well as the smaller knife she always wore at her side. Shivon's normal gear was a short bow and long knife. After conversations with others in the traveler's hostel, they all left the building together and went toward where the boats were secured on the lakeshore.

By the time they arrived, the small watch fires had been stoked into raging bonfires. The shoreline was ablaze with light and people milling about. No one knew what had happened, though the air was filled with speculation that there was an attack by banshees, or baykaaks, or perhaps a war party send by the mysterious shaman, Megissogwon.

Brigit and Shivon looked for Erik, Wulf, and Maengun among the crowd, but could see none of them. They did learn that Erik and Wulf had gone with one of the bargemen by canoe to the nearby island where the shrills sound and the cries for help had come from. Brigit was questioning one of the watchmen about what he had seen, when out of the corner of her eye she saw Maengun come alongside her. She turned to him with a puzzled look and a stream of questions.

"Where have you been? You weren't at the hostel. We looked for you when we heard the wailing. What have you seen? Did you see Wulf and Erik leave? Why didn't you go with them?"

Maengun held up his hands as if to forestall her rapid fire questioning.

"Whoa, there. Give me a chance to answer. Which

question first?"

"Wulf and Erik, do you know anything about them?"

"I don't see them anywhere."

"But have you seen them? I mean, folks here say they took a canoe over to the island. Did you see them leave?"

"That was before I got here. I had gone out for a walk, but I followed a path that went inland. By the time I got here, they were already gone."

"Why didn't you follow them?"

"I thought it would be best to wait here for you."

Shivon had a puzzled expression on her face, "How did you know we would come here? You knew we were at the traveler's hostel. If you went up the path into the woods, then you had to go right past the hostel on the way to get here. Why didn't you stop there first?"

Maengun gave her a hard glance but replied calmly, "I knew you wouldn't stay there. I just knew you would come here."

Shivon shook her head, as if she didn't believe him. She thoughtfully looked him up and down, and then her gazed focused for a moment on his hands. But she said nothing.

Maengun turned his attention back to Brigit, "Let's get closer to the shoreline. There are lights again over on the island. Perhaps we can make out what is going on."

They could, indeed, make out the re-ignited main fire where the small cottages were, and they could see figures holding torches further to the north. They also observed a group carrying a torch and walking from the north back toward the main fire.

Minutes later, the people standing on the shoreline of Bolton's Spring saw a canoe returning from the island. All eyes were on that torchlit canoe as it made its return trip across the channel. The waning half-moon had risen and now cast its light on waters of the lake. Erik, Wulf, and the bargeman were returning. As they neared the shore, the grim set of their faces could be seen.

Men helped pull the canoe onto the beach and the passengers jumped out. Wulf and Erik said nothing, but let the bargeman take the lead in describing the events that had transpired.

"A bloody, gruesome sight it was. The main camp wasn't attacked, although their fire went out. But, alas, the three travelers who had set up their camp on the north end of the island were all slain. We saw none of the attackers. Whoever, or whatever, they are, they are still out there somewhere. All of you, be on your guard!"

Voices asked for more, "Where did the screams come from? Were there banshees? Or Baykaaks? How did their fires go out? Tell us more!"

"We don't know more. The deed was done before we arrived. But this I tell you. I think there was some magic involved - for their fires were snuffed out completely. There were not even warm embers to light a new fire. They re-lit their fires and torches from the torch we carried with us."

One of the men on the shore said, "That doesn't sound like banshees to me. I think you're right. Some sort of evil magic is at work, as sure as my mother raised no fool."

The bargeman went on, "Aye, evil magic is about, yet those men were killed by human weapons: arrows and blades! We need to be on our guard. Keep the fires burning. Keep guards posted. No one goes out alone."

By this time, Erik and Wulf had worked their way

over to where Brigit, Shivon, and Maengun were standing. Brigit leaned forward and gave Wulf a hug and told him she was glad he was safe.

When she put her arms around Erik, he whispered in her ear, "I need to talk to you. Soon. Alone."

She released him, looked up into his eyes, and gave him a nod that was imperceptible to the others.

There were still hours of darkness before the dawn, but at least the half-moon washed the small village in its light. The men and women would be vigilant throughout the night. No one would be left alone. While some slept, the others would be on guard.

When Brigit's party returned to the hostel, they went to their bunks to get a couple of hours of sleep before the sun would rise and they would continue their journey on the lake. Erik whispered a few private comments to Brigit before they separated. It was a conversation that left a worried expression on her face. Then, before they settled into their bunks, Shivon whispered she needed to tell Brigit something. They sat close together on Shivon's bunk while they talked in hushed voices.

Shivon whispered, "Did you notice his hands?"

"Whose hands?"

"Maengun's, didn't you notice the blood?

"Blood? What blood?"

"He looked like he had washed his hands, but I swear there were traces of blood on his hands and sleeves of his jacket."

"Are you sure?"

"Well, as sure as one can be when seeing something by the light of a torch."

"Maybe, he was hunting in the woods, and had just shot something and was field dressing it."

"In the dark?"

Brigit was silent for a long time. Then she whispered back, "He might have an answer for it."

"Sure, he might. But I thought it was information you'd want to know. He might talk his way out of it, but I warn you, there is something strange about him."

They stopped their conversation and lay down to rest, but neither of them slept long, or well, throughout what remained of the night.

Chapter 21 - Odin's Point

The trip through the narrows of Lake Between was filled with tension, but it was uneventful. The narrows were approximately in the middle of the long lake. It was here that the lake shores approached each other to less than a mile in width. There were also numerous small islands which were scattered throughout the waters of the narrows. The bargemen put their backs into rowing the barge northward, but they also kept a watchful eye on the shorelines of the mainland and the many islands. There was only a slight westerly breeze, so there was little help from the wind.

Quarters on the boat were too close on the crowded barge for there to be private conversations, and Wulf and Maegun had joined the bargemen at the oars to speed their journey, so any probing discussion of the previous night's events was avoided. It was obvious to Erik that Brigit was deep in thought.

They made landfall at their planned stop for the night, Odin's Point, a foreland that jutted into the lake from its western shore. Other boats traveling north had already landed at Odin's Point and shared the news of the attack at Bolton's Spring, so the town was already buzzing with conversations about it.

The bargemen dutifully and securely fastened their boat for the night and made arrangements to set a guard on it similar to the previous night. The passengers made their way to the common hall for a meal and secured lodging there for the night. There was time after the meal to visit with the locals and other travelers who plied the waters of the lake, so the group left the common hall and returned to the area along the shore. Some men, and a few women, were gathering around bonfires that were beginning to flare as dusk was settling in. After what had happened at Bolton's Spring last night, no one wanted to take chances on this night. There would be no individuals left alone or in small groups.

Brigit indicated that she wanted to talk to Maengun privately. The two of them walked a short distance away, still within sight of the others, and sat down on a log by the water's edge. Soon they were deep in conversation.

Meanwhile, Erik beckoned Shivon and Wulf to step aside with him. He led them several paces away from the fire, where they would not be overheard by the others. He carefully pulled a leather-wrapped arrow out of his quiver. Wulf immediately recognized it as the arrow from the attack, but Shivon looked at it with a questioning look upon her face.

Erik began, "This arrow was embedded in one of the victims last night. It looks ordinary enough to me, but is there more to it? Could it be the arrow of a creature, like the baykaak, which the local folks speak of?"

Wulf said, "It seems ordinary enough to me. I don't see it being any different than the arrows normal folks use, although it is a little different from those we use back in Hamburg. Even if it is an ordinary arrow, couldn't monsters like the baykaak use it?"

Erik nodded, but Shivon spoke, "I suppose so. Look, see the way the fletching is tied and marked. While anyone could use this, this is a design of our native friends. And I'm not sure, but if I had to guess, I'd say it was most likely of Anishanaabe manufacture."

Their eyes all flickered to where Maengun and Brigit sat deep in conversation.

"Hmmm," was Erik's comment, followed by a long

pause, and then, "The two of you don't like him very much do you?"

Wulf snorted, "You know I don't."

Shivon curled her lip a little as she spoke, "You have the right of it. I don't like the way he looks at her. It makes my skin itch. And I don't understand why she is so taken by him. I keep thinking there must be something in him that she sees, that I don't."

Erik paused thoughtfully and then asked, "Would either of you trust him in a fight?"

Wulf quickly responded, "Do you mean trust him to fight for you, or to stick a knife in your back? No, I don't trust him at all."

Shivon was a little more circumspect in her reply, "Well, if it was a fight where he was fighting to save his life, then perhaps."

"Perhaps?"

"Aye. I think he might help, but I think he'd put his own survival before mine."

They continued their conversation about the arrow and Maengun for several minutes, and Shivon shared the information about seeing the blood on Maengun. They discussed this until they saw Brigit and Maengun stand in preparation of returning to them. Erik quickly placed the arrow back into his quiver, and they made their way toward the fire.

Brigit smiled when she stood. She felt reassured by her discussion with Maengun. The longer she listened to his voice, the more confident she became that he could be trusted. When asked about the blood Shivon thought she had seen, he reassured her there was nothing to it.

"I'm sure Shivon was mistaken in the light of the flickering fires. There was no fresh blood. I know the sleeves to my jacket are slightly spotted. It is indeed blood that it is spotted with. You can see that now." He held out his arms so she could see his sleeves, and then went on, "But you know I am a hunter, and occasionally I will get blood on my clothes when I am field dressing an animal. This dried blood is nothing more than that."

He put on his most disarming smile and continued, "I know that there are those who have prejudice against the Anishanaabe from the west and north. But I have never seen that from you. You are open and accepting of all people. That's a credit to the way you were raised. I assure you that I will do my best to help you. Why, I even have some friends in Ticonderoga who can help us on your quest. If you think that we might need extra help, then I'm sure I could persuade them to come along and strengthen our party as we go into the rugged hills of the Rondax that your friends seem to fear."

That smile that had spread across her face after hearing these words, melted away when she turned and saw the dire expressions on her friends faces as they walked toward the fire. Suddenly she felt unsure of herself again. She gave a little shake of her head, as if to clear her mind.

As they walked toward the others, Maengun whispered to her, "Don't worry. They'll follow your lead. They need a strong leader. That's what you are."

They made small talk with the people around the fires for a time; but since all seemed secure for the night, they soon made their way to their sleeping accommodations next to the common hall.

The night passed without event, and the sun rose to clear skies. Without fanfare the crew and passengers of the Ticonderoga-bound barge ate their morning repast and resumed their journey northward on Lake Between.

Chapter 22 - Ticonderoga

The barge made its way into the docks that lined the shore at the northern end of Lake Between. There its goods would be unloaded and put onto wagons to be portaged to North Gate Lake where they would be loaded onto a boat that was bound for Big Waters River and Hochelaga. The water that spilled down the waterway from Lake Between to North Gate Lake was too shallow and filled with rapids to carry boatloads of goods, though for the challenge and sport of it brave men often descended it in small canoes.

The sizable trade town of Ticonderoga had developed at this intersection. For centuries it had existed as a hub of trade for the natives who had lived in the region, and when the Europeans arrived they added to what already existed. The population seemed to be close to evenly split between the Celtic "new-comers" and the various native groups of the region: Wabanaki, Mohak, and Anishanaabe.

Brigit's party said their good-byes to the men they had traveled with and quietly waited for Shivon to say her farewell to her father. He would be moving on north with his trade goods, while she would be going westward into the Rondax Mountains with Brigit. He gave her a huge bear-hug and as he did so, he whispered into her ear.

"Trust Erik. In a pinch, trust him like you would me."

She looked up into his eyes as they parted and she nodded. Then she quickly stepped away and went to Brigit. They turned and walked to to find a place to eat and to spend the night before beginning their journey into the west and up the slopes of Cloudsplitter

Mountain. There they intended to find the headwaters of the Mahakentuck River.

Erik subtly directed their path to a tavern and inn that he knew catered to travelers such as themselves.

At the door, before they entered, Brigit stopped them and said, "We'll make our accommodations for the night here. However, I'm going to send Maengun to find some of his friends that live here and ask if they would accompany us on our journey."

Maengun said nothing, but gave a slight bow and then turned and left them.

Shivon said to Brigit, "Why do you want him to bring his friends along? I thought you felt that we could do this ourselves. Do you really trust him? And them?"

Brigit held up her hand to forestall more questions.

"It's alright, Shivon. He and his friends know this area. When they join us in the morning, we'll have a much stronger group to deal with any of the dangers that might confront us in the mountains. Please, don't worry, Shivon. He explained the blood on his clothes. Everything is fine. We can trust him."

Wulf said nothing, but Shivon standing next to him could hear him emit a slight growl under his breath.

Erik kept a stone face and simply nodded. Then he raised his hand to his beard and rubbed it as if in thought.

"If you don't mind, Brigit, I'd like to go look-up an old acquaintance that lives here. I don't imagine I'll be gone too long. I promise not to desert you. I'll be back for the evening meal. You know I wouldn't miss that."

Brigit chuckled as she responded, "Oh, I know you wouldn't miss a meal. Go on, then. Visit your friend, if you can find him or her. Don't worry about me. Shivon and Wulf will keep me safe."

Erik hurried off down the street while Brigit and the others went into the inn. After securing accommodations for the night, they sat down at a table in the common room of the tavern and waited for the evening meal to be served. They sat sipping on their mugs of ale for several minutes and enjoying light conversation. Then Wulf turned the conversation to a more serious matter.

"Brigit, I know you like Maengun, and trust him, but I wonder about the friends you say he is getting to help us. We know nothing at all about them."

Brigit reached out and placed her hand on Wulf's arm, "I know you mean well, Wulf, but please don't worry. Maengun is from the north. He knows these lands and these people. I'm sure the men he brings us will be of great help to us."

Wulf slowly shook his head, "Brigit, I just have this feeling about him. He bears no good intention to me, and I wonder if he really has good intentions for you."

"What do you mean? He has been a perfect gentleman with me. He is considerate and helpful. Perhaps you are a wee bit jealous?"

"Achh, I'll not deny I am. But that doesn't change the gut feeling that I have about him. And Shivon feels the same way. Don't you Shivon?"

Shivon nodded, "It's true. You know I do."

A flicker of doubt flashed across Brigit's face, but she said, "I know both of you mean well. But I trust him. Please give him a chance to prove himself."

Wulf sighed. He knew there was no use trying to convince her to feel the same threat he felt from Maengun, but he also knew that he would keep a watchful eye on him. When he looked at Shivon, he could see in her eyes that she would also.

Their conversation shifted back to more routine

matters and, and a short time later Erik entered the tavern. Seeing them drinking their ale at a table, he motioned for the serving girl to bring him a mug of ale and then he went to sit with them.

Brigit smiled up at him and teasingly asked, "Were you able to find your friend?"

"Oh, yes, indeed I did. He was occupied with other matters, but we had a few moments to share news and information."

"Is there anything of interest or importance you want to share with us?"

"Aye, I did find out that the beastie trolls, or windigos as some folks call them, have been harassing some of the mining operations in the mountains. We'd best be on our guard."

"We will, and having some of Maengun's people with us will help."

Erik's jaw hardened a bit, "Well, we'll see about that. Ahh, it looks like they have the meal ready. I say, let's eat."

Chapter 23 - Towards Cloudsplitter

Morning came, but the sun was not to be seen. The skies were heavy with clouds and there was a feeling of imminent rain in the air.

Maengun and his men met them outside the inn. The three men all looked to be Anishanaabe, for they wore the traditional puckered buckskin footwear of such people, but they shared their greetings in the Celtic language of Eirgalon (which was actually a polyglot mixture of Celtic and Norse, with a generous smattering of the Wabanaki, Haudenoshonee, Lenape, and Anishanaabe words.) Even if they were not fluent in the language, they would certainly know words of greeting. They were young men, perhaps a little older than Maengun, but only in their twenties.

Brigit stepped forward to greet them, and as she did so, Erik leaned over to Shivon and whispered to her, "Don't let them know you understand their native tongue."

She said nothing, but nodded in understanding.

Maengun introduced them as Asin, Mikom, and Noodin. They were friendly and seemed anxious to embark.

After the introductions, Maengun said, "It looks like it might rain soon. I think we should be on our way. I suggest we start by taking the valley road to the west. It is the easiest path westward to the valleys which run to Cloudsplitter."

Brigit replied, "That makes sense. Has there been any troll activity reported that way?"

"None that we have heard of. My friends told me that there has been reports of windigos further north, near the mining villages, but none where we are going

114

today. May I suggest that my friends take the lead? They are familiar with the area, and they would quickly notice if something were amiss."

She acquiesced and soon they were on their way. It was a well-worn path, for indeed it was the easiest route to the western valleys, but it was narrow, and they walked single file. The three men led the way, followed in single file by Maengun, Brigit, Shivon, and Wulf. Erik brought up the rear.

After a short while on the trail, Wulf turned back to Erik and asked, "I enjoy having my feet on a trail in the woods again and walking, but haven't you folks ever heard of horses? It would make this part of our trip a lot easier."

"Aye, that it would. But there are some treacherous and dangerous ways ahead of us. Horses may help here, but they would be an encumbrance in the miles to come. Besides, they get right skittish when they are in bear country. And on top of that, the beastie trolls seem to have almost as much of a taste for horse meat as they do for human flesh."

Wulf muttered as he turned his head back forward, "You sure do have a way of brightening the day and bringing joy to one's heart."

In spite of the weather, the situation, and the dangers which lay before them, a grin spread across Erik's face.

The morning hours of the hike were over terrain that was relatively easy. The path wound through trees and gradually upward through a valley whose sides were bursting with the verdant growth of a mild spring.

For the first time since leaving in home in Hamburg, across the sea, Wulf had a of feeling of being at home. The hills were higher than the hills south of

Hamburg, but the sights, smells, and very feeling of the forest stirred memories. With the oak walking staff of Unaine in his hand and the numerous sounds of birds around him, his mind wandered away from the others on the trail. He followed in their footsteps, but his mind walked elsewhere.

There had been times in the woods of Hamburg that he was sure he heard the voice of what was called by the people of his land "der Grune Mann." Now, as he heard the songbirds of the Rondax singing, he felt he was hearing such a voice. Then suddenly it struck him. He was being told something. Then, in a flash of understanding, he knew what the birds were saying.

He stopped in his tracks and turned to Erik who walked behind him. "They're speaking to me. It's Brigit. The blood of the Green Man flows in her veins."

Erik looked surprised. "What? Keep your voice down. What are you saying? Who is talking to you?"

"The birds are speaking to me. They are telling me that the blood of the Green Man flows in her veins. How can this be?"

Erik replied in a hushed voice, "I don't know how you heard this, but it is true. She is the granddaughter of the Green Man of the Woods. Now be quiet. Keep walking. Don't let our 'friends' hear you say that. I'll explain that to you later."

They resumed their walk, and soon caught up to the rest of them. Shivon had noticed that the men behind her had stopped and had a brief conversation. When she glanced backwards at them she raised a questioning eyebrow, but said nothing. Those who walked in front of Brigit appeared not to have noticed the brief event.

Twice they encountered groups traveling the opposite direction. The first was a group of three men with backpacks of beaver pelts piled high upon their backs. The men didn't stop, but muttered greetings as they passed by.

The second group was a mule train of six mules and their handlers. The mules were loaded with sacks of iron ore from the mines near Cloudsplitter. The road was narrow at this point and Brigit's group stood to the side to let the others pass.

From the snippets of conversation that were shared as they passed by, they learned that there had been increasing troll attacks near the mines and that hair-raising screeching wails had been heard during the night for several weeks.

By late morning, they were making their way along the southern shore of a long lake. The rain that had been threatening them finally began to fall as a light drizzle upon them. There was no thought from any of them that they might stop and take cover. They intended to make it to the small village that lay where this valley joined another. It lay beyond this lake, and then yet another lake of similar size. They weren't even halfway yet and they had to keep moving.

They kept moving without stopping for a noon meal. As they walked, they nibbled on venison jerky and hardtack biscuits.

They were mid-way along the southern side of the second long lake, and following the path single file through a narrow defile, when a couple of boulders came crashing down the steep slope. Quick reflexes and swift movements meant no one was hurt, but it had been a close call. One boulder had tumbled down right behind Brigit and another had almost hit Wulf.

When they had exited the defile and come to where the path widened and the slopes to their sides lessened, they gathered in a group. Shivon and Wulf wanted to go up the slope and work their way back along the ridgeline.

Shivon said, "Those boulders didn't come down by themselves. Someone wanted to do us harm. I say we go get them."

Maengun replied, "We would be wasting our time. There was no one there. I'm sure those rocks were loosened by the spring thaw. Then these rains allowed them to slip free."

Wulf argued, "The longer we talk about it, the harder it will be for us to catch them." He raised his staff and pointed it toward the ridgeline. "Or maybe they are circling around to ambush us at this moment."

"Fool. Don't you realize that if there really was someone there, you would be dead by now. A hidden archer could easily have put an arrow through your heart."

Wulf began to protest, but Shivon cut in, "So why don't you want us to check it out?"

Maengun answered her, "I don't want us to waste time. Brigit wants to get to the source of the river. I'm trying to help her. What are you doing? Chasing after ghosts?"

During this time, Erik had been scanning the landscape around them. Now he spoke up.

"I think we might as well do as Maengun says. We're wasting daylight and we want to get to the village before darkness sets in. We still have hours to go."

Brigit, who had surprisingly remained silent to this point, said simply, "We'll go on."

As they reassembled their walking order, they heard Maengun's men speaking to him in their native tongue. He responded to them and they chuckled. Then they took the lead again as they proceeded down the path.

When they had gone and Maengun was several steps away from them, with Brigit right behind him, Wulf asked Shivon, "What did they say? What were they laughing about?"

"They asked what we had said and then they laughed when Maengun said to ignore us because we are just a silly girl and a boy with a stick."

Chapter 24 - Little Falls

At the western end of the second lake, the valley widened as it joined a second valley that ran on a north-south axis. The rain had stopped by the time they reached a fork in the road. They took the path that headed northward up the new valley. After two more miles of walking, they came to a small village which was located on the banks of a small river. The village was called Little Falls, as this location had a modest waterfall of only a few feet in the river.

It wasn't much of a village. Several small cottages and shops comprised the entirety of the valley village. The one small tavern was filled when the eight travelers joined the local inhabitants. When queried about lodging, the proprietor laughed at them and said, "I've got ale to wet your throats, but no rooms. You folks will have to camp out like everyone else does who spends the night at Little Falls. There's a couple of empty lean-tos near the woods that traveling folk use. You're welcome to them. Mayhap, one of the crofters will let you ladies stay in their cottage. I could ask if you'd like."

Brigit replied for her group, "Why, thank you. We'll take you up on the drink, and we'll check out those lean-tos. But as for lodging, Shivon and I will stay with the rest of our group."

"Do as you like. But you folks stay on your guard. Strange things have been happening at night around here. I wouldn't want you getting hurt."

They enjoyed their drinks and then left the tavern to go set up camp near the lean-tos. The leans-tos were small and offered little shelter, though it would be a place to keep their gear dry if the rain resumed. They made two small fires. One was for the Anishanaabe men who indicated that they wanted to stay apart. They gave every indication that the only Eirgalon words they understood were the few words of greeting they had shared at the beginning of the day. The other fire was for the original travelers, although Maengun did go back and forth between the two fires that were only twenty yards apart.

About an hour after they had set up their camp, just as the sun was setting, a group of four men came up the same path to the village that they had come. The men waved hands to signify general greetings, but kept to themselves and made their camp about fifty yards south of them, near the bank of the river.

Shivon, who was seated next to Wulf by the fire, nudged him and speculated, "Maybe those are the ones who rolled the boulders down at us."

Wulf considered what she said, and looked them over carefully. "I don't think so. I can't say for sure, but I get a good feeling watching them."

"Why? What do you see?"

Wulf hesitated, glanced around and saw the Maengun was with his three friends at the other fire, and then went on. "They are quite a distance away, and the light is growing dim, but it looks to me like they are a father and his three sons. The one is obviously older, probably about the age of your father, and the younger ones bear a noticeable resemblance to him. Even some of their attire seems to be cut from the same cloth. And look at the way they give deference to him."

Brigit, who was seated on the other side of Shivon said, "I don't know that you're right about them not being a threat, but you have good observations. Regardless, they came up the same path we did. I'm going to greet them, and ask them if they saw anyone else on the trail. Any of you want to go with me?"

Both Wulf and Shivon stood up to go with her, but Erik stayed seated. "You young ones go on. Check them out. That was a long hike today. I'm going to rest my weary bones here."

Brigit gave him an odd look, and then turned and started walking with her friends toward the new arrivals. As soon as Maengun saw this, he jumped up and moved swiftly to join them. Erik watched them go with an amused look on his face. As he watched them, he noticed that Maengun's three friends had stopped their activities and also had their eyes turned to the new arrivals.

Brigit greeted the men politely and introduced herself and the other members of her group.

The elder man replied, "Nice to meet you. Folks call me, Rolf." He pointed at the others. "These young whippersnappers are my boys." He motioned toward the boys. "There are the twins: Olaf and Lars; and over there is their younger brother, Finn."

Warm smiles and handshakes were shared around the circle.

Rolf went on, "We didn't mean to seem antisocial, by not setting up camp right next to you folks, but sometimes folks like to be off a wee bit by themselves. Hope you're not offended. I'd say you don't appear to be, since you came right over to welcome us."

Brigit smiled. "Not at all. We understand. But the tavern keeper did say to keep our guard up. He said there have been strange goings-on hereabout."

"Oh, we will, lassie. Don't worry about us. We'll keep a watch out."

Wulf noticed that Rolf glanced at Maengun when he made that comment.

Shivon had waited patiently through the introductions, but now she asked, "Did you men notice anything strange on the trail, today?"

Rolf replied, "Well, lassie, can you be more specific? There lots of strange things out there, if you have a mind to look for them. What sort of things do you have in mind?"

Wulf thought to himself that the way Rolf responded reminded him of the way Erik talked to him at times.

Shivon replied, "Well, I was thinking about those boulders on the trail."

"Yep. We noticed them. Lars, there, even commented on them. We've been on this trail before. Sure as not, those boulders were never there before."

"Did you see anyone else on the trail?"

"Aye. We crossed paths with some fur traders and a iron ore mule train."

Maengun spoke, with a hint of sarcasm in his voice, "You mean there wasn't anyone lurking about hoping to ambush you on the trail."

Rolf looked him over with a long stare before he answered. "Nope. We didn't encounter any lurkers, bandits, or other such scum. Did you folks have some problems?"

Brigit replied, "Oh, no. Those boulders you mentioned, did tumble down the slope into our midst. But that was just happenstance. A natural result of the spring thaw." She turn to Maengun. "Right, Maengun?"

Maengun thoughtfully answered, "I can't imagine what else it could have been. The winter freezing and spring thaw pushed the rocks apart and then maybe some small creature sensed our presence, and in scrambling to get away from us, put enough pressure on them to send them tumbling down the hill."

Rolf nodded, "Perhaps your friend is right, missy. Some dumb critter trying to get out of the way. Sure, that could be the way of it."

Wulf caught the cynicism in Rolf's voice and wondered if the others had. They didn't seem to have noticed.

Rolf then added, "If you folks don't mind, we've been jawing here a bit, but my boys and I have a camp to set up before it gets too dark."

Brigit was slightly embarrassed. "Oh, I'm sorry. Of course. Thank you for the information, and please, if we can be of any help, let us know."

"Thank you, lassie. But we can manage on our own. You be careful now. As the tavern man said, you'd best be keeping your guard up in this country."

Shivon and Wulf were quiet and full of thoughts as they walked back to their campfire. Both of them were hesitant to say a word with Maengun walking next to Brigit. Maengun excused himself and left them for few minutes so that he could go and to talk to his men at their fire.

When he was several paces away, Shivon whispered to Brigit, "So? What did you think about them?"

Brigit replied, "What do you mean? What did I think about them? They seemed like nice enough men."

"I mean do you believe them?"

"Yes. They didn't see anything. And they don't seem a threat."

"Aye. But they seemed to be in a hurry to get rid of us."

"Relax, Shivon. There is no threat in them."

By this time they had returned to their fire and they quickly relayed to Erik what Rolf had said. Erik nodded and said, "I see Maengun is returning to us from his friends." He raised his voice so Maengun could hear him as he approached the fire. "Say there, Maengun, I have a mind to take my young Wulf here to the tavern and get him a drink. I want to show him what life in the backwoods of Eirgalon is really like. Would you mind being a good lad and staying here with the young ladies? I know they can take care of themselves, but it is getting dark, and I'm not sure how soon we will be back."

Maengun readily agreed and soon Erik and Wulf were gone, leaving Shivon to feel out of place as Maengun focused his attention and conversation on Brigit.

Chapter 25 - Tavern Talk

Erik and Wulf entered the small tavern, which was already empty of the local inhabitants. They got their mugs of ale from the owner of the tavern and sat down at a table by the wall. When the owner handed them their mugs, he warned them that he wouldn't be open much longer. He said that since the beginning of the strange wailing sounds at night and the rumour of unnatural beasts in the wild, the men of the village had been going home early and securing their doors.

Erik assured him that they wouldn't stay long - just long enough to finish their ale and have a short conversation.

After the owner left them alone and went about beginning the process of straightening up the place for the night, Wulf spoke first and in a soft tone so that, even though the tavern was small, the proprietor wouldn't be able to hear him.

"You know those men, don't you?"

"Why do you think that?"

"Well, first of all, the old one, Rolf, sounds a lot like you."

"Lots of men sound like me."

"Not really. There's a fine way about the manner in which you use your words and your facial expressions. I haven't encountered such similarity before. And then there is the fact that you didn't seem at all surprised to see these men show up right behind us. And that you didn't feel the need to go talk to them where we might see you interact with each other."

A long sigh of satisfaction came from Erik. Whether it was from the ale, or from what Wulf had said, was unclear to Wulf at first.

Then Erik said, "You have the right of it, my laddie. The older gentleman of that quartet, Rolf, was one of my men-at-arms a couple of decades ago."

"So how did he get here."

"Why he walked, of course."

Slightly exasperated, Wulf said, "Erik, I know that. I meant how and why did you arrange for them to get here?"

Erik smirked. "Oh, then why didn't you ask that?"

Wulf rolled his eyes. "Right. I should have been more precise. Now, are you going to explain it to me?"

"We went through some real adventures together. One of which was trekking around and over hills like this as we chased the men who had abducted Evlin, Brigit's mother." He hesitated as if remembering those events. "We lost a good friend on that chase, but we helped rescue Evlin. I knew Rolf was in Ticonderoga. Yesterday, I tracked him down and asked him and his boys to follow us. I thought we might need some back-up, now that Maengun's added those three lackeys of his to our traveling group. That's why I brought you to the tavern. I wanted to explain the situation to you out of earshot of the others. I'm impressed that you figured some of it out."

"Does Brigit know? I mean does Brigit know who he is and what you have done?"

"Those are some good questions. The answer is that I'm not sure. Rolf and his boys never lived at Tara, but he did pass through several times in the past years. I wouldn't be surprised if she did recognize him. She is usually rather perceptive. Perhaps she did recognize him. But her brain has been so addled with Maengun, and with this quest to the source of the river, that I don't know. You were with her when she met him. Do you

127

think she recognized him?"

Wulf reflected silently for a couple of moments as he tried to recall her words and reactions.

"I'm not sure. She seemed really friendly, but then, she usually is. And she didn't ask a lot of probing questions. My hunch is that she did recognize him and just went over there to verify who he was. If that was the case, she was careful not to let on to Maengun about who Rolf is."

Erik nodded thoughtfully and stroked his beard with his hand. The conversation lulled for a moment with both men deep in thought.

Then Wulf said, "Erik, I want to ask you about my walking staff. It is a real beauty. It feels like it was made for my hand, and all the detailed engravings are done with such skill and artistic flair. This can't be just a normal walking stick. I know you said Master Unaine wanted me to have it, but why?"

"I asked him that very question. His response was that he felt you should have it. He said something to the effect that while it wasn't yet a druid's staff, perhaps one day it would be. Wulf, were you trained in the druid ways back in old Hamburg?"

Wulf's eyes went upward as if he was trying to remember. "Well, not specifically, that I know of. I read everything that I could, and Meister Gerhardt sometimes walked the woods with me, teaching me what he called 'skills of the earth and sky' and directing my thoughts in certain ways. But we didn't call him a druid."

"Hhmmph. Sounds like a druid to me. I'd say that Unaine sees in you the makings of a druid. He said he was crafting the staff for himself. I've known that old man for a lifetime, for him to give it to you is no small gift. You may not be the soldier your father wanted, but others see in you the potential to be a druid."

"But, if that is true, how will I learn? Who will teach me?"

"Well don't look to me. I'm only an old soldier. Actually, it seems to me that you already have some of the marks of a druid. You are unusually perceptive when you want to be. You have a connection to the natural world few others do - you did hear the birds speaking today. Plus, you do have the staff."

"Sure, I have the staff. And those men of Maengun's make fun of me by calling me 'a boy with a stick.' They have no respect for me."

Erik chuckled. "That's a good thing. They don't recognize the power within you. They underestimate you. If, in the long run, our fears become reality and we come into conflict with them, then their underestimation of you will become your advantage."

"Is that why you let Maengun think you are nothing more than an old servant tagging after the princess?"

Erik chuckled again. "See, you are perceptive. Let him think less of me and that strengthens me in the future."

At that moment they hear a loud wailing scream. They slammed down their mugs and raced to the door.

Chapter 26 - Attack

Shivon was sitting by the fire and wondering how much longer this torture was going to continue. Brigit sat between her and Maegun and the two of them had been deep in conversation, and ignoring her, for what felt to be an eternity. She thought that surely Erik and Wulf must be finished with their drinks by now. What was taking them so long?

Then the wailing scream pierced the air. At each of the three fires the people sprang to their feet in readiness to fend off an attack.

No attack came. Erik and Wulf came barrelling out of the tavern and rushed to join their comrades. The wailing stopped and nothing else happened. The people around the fires looked across the open clearing at each other and each could see that all stood ready, but that there was no action. After several minutes, they relaxed and guardedly resumed their places by the fire. Eventually, although guards were posted, the others lay down and tried to get some sleep.

Few of them got any rest. Several times during the night, that same wailing scream pierced the darkness. Each time the travelers leapt up to fend off an attack, but none ever came. The weary folk welcomed the sight of the first light of the dawning day touching the eastern horizon.

As they gathered that morning, Maengun told them, "We will follow the waters of this stream up the valley for several miles, then turn west up a different valley. We will have to go several more miles before we go over a pass and then down to touch the waters of the Mahakentuck. When we do, then we can follow that stream up the slopes of Cloudsplitter."

Brigit responded with, "So be it. Let's get on the move. I doubt any of us want to stay in this valley of the wailing screams."

"I certainly don't," said Shivon, "those screams make my hair stand on end."

Maengun quietly said, "I was a little concerned when Brigit said you were coming. You are an innocent young woman. I wonder if you have the mettle to confront the dangers before us. Perhaps it would be better for you if you didn't go any further. Maybe Erik would be willing to go back with you. I think the rigors of what is to come may be too hard on his old body." He looked at Erik. "I mean, no offense to you, old man, but there is some extremely rough going ahead of us."

Shivon's eyes blazed and she took a deep breath in preparation to respond, but before she could begin Erik spoke.

"Why, thank ye for being so considerate of me. As much as these old bones appreciate the offer, I rather think young Shivon is determined to go on. And for that matter, I'd like to see how this all turns out. So unless you have more to say, I'd suggest we get going. We're burning daylight."

Brigit declared, "By all means. Let's hear no more talk of this and let's get moving."

Without any more fanfare, Brigit and her people struck camp and resumed their journey toward Cloudsplitter. They followed the path that wound northward along the edge of the winding stream that came down the valley.

They spaced themselves on the path in the same order they had on the previous day, with Maengun's men leading the way.

As they fell into line Wulf gave Erik a pat on the

back and chuckled, "Hang in there, old man."

Wulf couldn't see it, but Erik grinned as he fell into step behind the young man. He also couldn't see that Erik looked over to where Rolf's group was still packing up their camp. Erik raised his hand in a wave. Rolf stopped what he was doing and waved in response. Across the distance they smiled at each other.

They trekked for several miles that morning. There were higher hills and bluffs on their left as they followed the path north. Wulf was thinking that this was certainly more rugged terrain than he had ever experienced before, and he suspected it would get even more so as they continued. As noon approached, they came to a place where there was another small gathering of cottages. Here the path split again, with one path heading up into a cross valley to the west. This is the path they took.

They continued to gain elevation as they followed the general course of a small stream as it rushed down the valley. Often their path veered away from the stream because of its steep banks, but they could still hear the water tumbling over rocks and boulders. Some of them tensed because this would be a good place for an ambush. But nothing happened.

By mid-afternoon they came to where the valley widened and they could see openings to several other valleys.

Maengun pointed to a gap in the western hills, and said, "We go between those peaks. We'll cross a pass that will enable us to turn north again toward Cloudsplitter."

Brigit asked, "How much longer will we be on this path?"

"Only for the rest of the day. After the pass, we'll

come to a lake that we can camp near. This path goes west from there, but we must turn north at that point. We will be bushwhacking from there onward."

They went on. During the course of the next couple of hours, Wulf's mind drifted through many thoughts. If not for the fact that Wulf didn't enjoy the presence of Maengun, and the fact that they were in territory that Wulf thought of in his mind as "a land of screaming demons," he would have been thoroughly relishing this adventure. With his staff in his hand, and with the wilderness about him, he felt a sense of belonging.

That feeling of near serenity was shattered by the high pitched squeal of pain from the front of the column. They had traversed the pass and were descending into the wide valley. Trees lined the path, but there were gaps in them through which one could see their surrounding area. When Wulf heard the squeal, he looked forward and could see that the three Anishanaabe men and Maengun had their bows drawn and were shooting arrows to the right side of the column. He couldn't see what they were shooting at but he could see Brigit running forward and yelling at them to stop.

The men stopped and turned to look at Brigit. Then they heard a loud snorting sound and the sound of something crashing through the undergrowth to their left. Before they knew what was happening a large bear had charged out of the brush and was charging Asin, the furthermost of the Anishanaabe warriors.

Within moments the bear was upon him and knocked him to the ground. Mikom, Noodin, and Maengun, ignoring Brigit's yelling to stop, raised their bows and fired upon the bear. Then, dropping their bows, they pulled out their long knives and rushed the bear. Blades slashed and the bear tried to retreat. But it didn't get far, for one of the knives had plunged into its throat and severed a major artery. It fell bleeding to the ground.

The men stood still and the air was filled with the moans of the dying bear and the crying of its dying cub several paces away.

Then Brigit spoke in anger, "Why did you do that? They weren't harming you."

The men looked at her with stunned looks on their faces.

Maengun responded, "We've done nothing wrong. My friends saw the young bear, knew we were nearing the time to set up a camp for the night, and decided to get some fresh meat."

"But it is a bear," she shouted, "we don't eat bears."

"Perhaps you don't, but we do. They are creatures of great power. When we eat their meat, we gain their power. See how ferocious it was when it attacked us. We had to defend ourselves."

Shivon stepped forward and demanded, "But you shot the cub first. Of course it attacked you. What mother wouldn't defend its child?"

The mother bear was still bleeding and moaning while the cub's cries of pain were getting weaker.

Erik interrupted them and said, "What's done is done. Don't stand here arguing. Go and put those dying beasts out of their misery."

That silenced them and they did as Erik ordered. Meanwhile, Asin, the warrior who had been knocked to the ground lifted himself off the ground and brushed the dirt off his clothes. Some of his garments were torn, and they could see that he was bleeding from the arm he had raised in his defense.

Brigit's anger hadn't subsided, but she held it in

check. She went to him and examined his wound. She wrapped a cloth over and and tightly tied it, telling him that it would need to be cleaned and bandaged better when they stopped for the night.

From where they stood, they could see a lake shimmering in the distance. This is where they intended to camp, so Erik suggested that Brigit, Shivon, and Wulf go on ahead to set up camp, while he would stay and help the Anishanaabe men. When Wulf gave a questioning look to Erik, the older man flickered his eyes to glance back to the pass from whence they had come, and Wulf saw the forms of Rolf and his boys cresting the summit of the pass.

Brigit and Shivon were easily persuaded to move on and away from the slaughtered bears. As they walked toward the lake with Wulf, they discussed what had happened. Both of them were completely outraged that the men had attacked the cub. After listening to them vent their anger for several minutes, Wulf through it might be good to change the conversation.

He asked Brigit, "I am told that you are the granddaughter of the Green Man. How did this come to be?"

She looked in his direction as they walked, but kept on walking. "So no one has told you? I guess I assumed you probably knew. It seems most people do. But since you are from Hamburg across the sea, I suppose you never heard the story."

"No, I haven't. But I would like to hear it."

So as they walked she told him a short version of the story.

"Fearglas, the Green Man of the land of Eirgalon, had walked this land and loved it for many years. One day he spotted a Wabanaki maiden running through the fields. They fell in love and he took her for his wife. They had a daughter, Evlin. When evil Malsum attacked the child, Sheela sacrificed her own life to save her child. Fearglas raised his daughter and taught her the ways of the woods and the ways of humankind. This child, now a young maiden, encountered Skoth as he was beginning his quest. They fell in love. After Skoth was proclaimed High King of Eirgalon, uniting the various kingdoms and chiefdoms, he was called upon to protect his people and land from the threat of the Haudenoshonee League to the west. Evlin went with him to help him. She was taken captive by limikkins, shapeshifter minions of Malsum. She was dying in captivity so to free her and save her life, Fearglas sacrificed his own life. As he did so, he learned that he was also saving the life of his granddaughter, for Evlin was pregnant with Skoth's child. I am that child."

Wulf seemed puzzled, "How can it be that the Green Man is dead?"

Brigit replied, "What do you mean? He breathed his last and was buried under a fallen oak tree."

"I mean, I have walked the woods where I grew up, and I know I heard the voice of what we called the 'Grune Mann', or in your tongue, 'the Green Man.'" He paused, considering what he was about to share. "Brigit, I have heard this voice speaking to me as we walk these paths."

Brigit shook her head. "I can't explain that. I only know that I was told that my grandfather died."

Shivon broke into the conversation, "Sorry, to interrupt, but we are here by the lake, and this looks to be a good place to camp. I say we get a fire started and set up camp as we can."

Chapter 27 - Wolf Lake Camp

The fire was burning and the surrounding area cleared, when they heard the voice of Rolf come booming into the clearing. They quickly turned to seeing Rolf and his sons as they strode into view.

"Ho, there, my friends. 'Tis only us folks from Ticonderoga. That old fellow, Erik, he said his name was, sent us on ahead. He thought it might be good if we camped with you folks tonight if that is alright with you, Lady Brigit. Then he said to tell you that he, and the others, would be along shortly."

"Of course, you are welcome to camp with us. Though we may have to start another fire so everyone can get close if they want."

"Yes," Rolf agreed, "that way there will be more light, when night falls. I'm also thinking those men will be wanting to roast some of that bear meat over a fire, and I'm not sure you'd be wanting that at your fire."

"Right you are about that." She hesitated as she scanned the surrounding area. "By the looks of it, there is another spot it appears that previous travelers have had a fire at, just thirty yards along the lake shore. That is close enough for safety, though not as far away as I would truly like, if they are going to be cooking the meat."

"I'm certain they intend to, my lady. But at least you won't have to be sitting next to them while they do it."

Rolf's boys dropped their packs and took their bows to go hunting. As they went off with their bows, they said that they hoped they could get a grouse or two before dusk fell, perhaps even a whitetail deer if they were lucky enough. Rolf smiled for he knew that their intention was to scout out the area more than to find game. They had enough food for the day. He had taught them well.

Rolf looked at Wulf and said, "It looks like you have a nice fire going. How about if you grab some of those burning branches and help me get a fire started over yonder.?"

Wulf jumped right to it, and in short order the two of them had a fire started at the other location. While working together on the fire, Rolf quietly mentioned to Wulf that Erik had confided in him that Wulf was aware of who Rolf and the boys were and what they had been asked to do.

Both fires were blazing nicely after several minutes. Maengun and his men came trudging down the path with their normal packs and each of them carried an additional bundle. The men had both bear pelts with them, and well as meat to roast over the fire. Brigit pointed them in the direction of the far fire, and then called for Asin to come over to her fire so that she could take care of his injured arm.

The sun was setting behind the clouds, but she could still see clearly enough to clean and bind the wound. She took him over to the lakeshore and had him remove his tunic and shirt so that she could wash the wound with the clear mountain lake water. She noticed him glancing several times at the moonstone necklace she wore, but he said nothing about it. After washing the wound carefully with clean water, she took some ointment from her pack. Asin's eyes went wide with a glint of apprehension, and he muttered some words in his native tongue. Brigit gently smeared some ointment into the wound and then she re-bandaged the arm.

After he went back to his friends at the other fire,

Shivon whispered to Brigit. "When you took out the ointment, Asin commented that he hoped your 'magic' would heal him and not hurt him."

Brigit chuckled at the thought. "If I wanted to hurt him, I'd have just left his wound alone. I may not be able to 'touch my magic' as others say, but my mother and aunties have taught me a few of the healing arts."

Rolf's boys returned to the camp a few minutes later. Finn was carrying two grouse they had shot.

Olaf jokingly said, "Here are two fine grouse to roast over the fire. We would be eating some nice venison tonight, but Finn missed a clear shot at it."

Finn protested, "It wasn't a clear shot, and you know it. I'd say you caused me to miss, because the way you stumble about in the woods. You startled it and it took off."

Lars laughed at the two of them and pointed to the grouse that Finn had slung over his shoulder. "At least I was able to take down these two fine birds.

They bantered back and for for a few minutes as they prepared the birds to roast on spits over the fire. Their attitude helped lift the heaviness that Brigit felt as the other men brought the remains of the mother bear and its cub into the camp, and then prepared portions of the meat to be roasted over their fire.

Erik and Rolf weren't saying much as they prepared their sleeping pallets for the night and rested from the exercise of the day. They were content to watch the younger folk scurrying about making preparations before nightfall. Both men had found protected places near large boulders From their places on opposing sides of their campfire they could see what lay between them, and each could see what lay behind the other man who was positioned on the opposite side of the fire. And both could clearly see the other campfire where Maengun and his men were roasting their bear meat.

As darkness descended, they felt a chill fall over them. The air was still and damp, and the temperature on this spring evening was cool. The crackling fires drew them closer and the shadows that the fires threw on the surrounding boulders and trees gave an eerie atmosphere to the wilderness about them. After finishing their meal for the evening, Olaf and Shivon moved away from the fire and took up positions where they could look away from the fire as they kept watch.

Wulf told the rest of them that he needed some time to sit and think, so he went near the water's edge and sat against the trunk of an old and gnarled oak tree that loomed above them. They could see him sitting there, fiddling with his staff, making scratch marks in the soil beneath the tree. Occasionally he would pick up a pebble and toss it into the lake.

From the distant fire came chortles of laughter. Those who could understand the Anishanaabe tongue heard the men making fun of the boy with a stick who was scratching the ground. Brigit was about to get up and go to Wulf when Erik made a small motion and caught her eye. A gentle shake of his head was enough to tell her that Erik wanted her to leave Wulf alone.

Brigit remained at her fire and made pleasant conversation with Lars and Finn. Erik and Rolf were both away from the fire, leaning against their respective boulders and seeming to doze off.

The men at the distant fire had finished their meal and were settling in for the night. One of them stepped away from the fire as he went to assume a guard position. Maengun stood up and took a couple of steps toward Brigit's fire.

It was at that point that Brigit heard Wulf call her. "Brigit, would you please come here?"

She immediately stood and started moving toward Wulf. Maengun saw her going to Wulf and turned back toward his fire. He walked beyond it and went as if to go talk to the man on guard duty and then disappeared into the darkness.

When Brigit reached Wulf he moved slightly to one side and patted the ground next to him indicating for Brigit to sit next to him. She sat down and was shoulder to shoulder with him leaning against the tree. They didn't look at each other, but looked out over the lake. There were no heavenly lights on this cloudy night, and in this wilderness there were no lights of civilization on the opposite shore of the lake. The only light was from their cook fires, and the reflections they cast.

Wulf began the conversation, "Brigit, I have words I must share with you."

"Go on then."

"First of all, I must confess to you I'm not sure what has been happening to me. Ever since Erik placed Unaine's staff in my hand, my world has been changing."

Brigit was intrigued. "How?"

"I see and hear that which others do not. I can't explain it, and I certainly don't understand it; but when I hold this staff, my senses seem expanded."

"Go on."

"I'll try. I told you that I felt I have been hearing the voice of the Green Man. The birds and animals around me sometimes speak to me. The woods and trees as well. This old oak here," he patted a gnarled root that ran out from the tree, "it gave me a message. A message that it said is intended for you."

"For me?"

"I assume it is for you. As best as I can make out it is for 'she who is of the blood of forest and the spirit of the bear.' That fits you. Doesn't it?"

Brigit nodded thoughtfully. "It would seem so. As the granddaughter of the Green Man and the daughter of the Bear-Witch of Eirgalon, it seems to mean me. What is the message?"

Wulf paused, took a deep breath, and then went on. "You may not like hearing this, but the message is about the moonstone necklace you wear."

"Is it about how to use it?"

"I don't think so."

"What do you mean?"

"It didn't sound like using it. The voice said to be ready to give the necklace away. At the right time and the right place - give it away."

They sat in silence for several moments.

Then Brigit asked, "Is there anything else?"

Wulf sighed. "There is more."

"What is it?"

"You won't like this either."

"How do you know that?"

"It runs counter to what you are doing."

"Well then, out with it. I might as well know."

Wulf sighed again and then cautiously said, "What you seek is not on the slopes of Cloudsplitter."

Brigit didn't have time to respond to that statement, for at that very moment the spine-chilling howls of wolves sliced through the air.

All members of the traveling party sprang into action, seizing weapons in readiness to defend themselves. The howling continued and the travelers cast furtive glances about them. Lars and Olaf tossed a couple of more sticks of timber on their fire.

Erik calmed them by saying, "Tis good to be alert, my friends, but relax a wee bit. Those howls are coming from across the lake. They're not from behind the nearest tree. Wolves howl this particular way when they sense a threat and they are sending a message that they will protect their territory." Then he paused before going on, "That is, of course, if they be normal wolves."

Brigit asked, "And what other kind of wolves would they be?"

Wulf whispered, "Werewolf."

Erik responded, "That's what you may call them in your land, laddie, but in this land, we'd call 'em shapeshifters, or limikkins."

They kept their eyes roving along the dark edges of the camp for several minutes. Those on guard duty, Shivon and Olaf returned to the group about the fire. Slowly the howling from across the lake ceased and was replaced by the normal night sounds of the forest in springtime.

While the others had been scanning the dark shadows of the woods and avoiding looking at either their fire, or the fire of the Anishanaabe men, Wulf had been looking at what those men were doing. He could make out the shapes of Asin, Mikom, and Noodin as they also looked out into the woods. But he didn't see any sign of Maengun while the howling was echoing through the night. Shortly after the howling had died out, he could make out the form of Maengun slowly emerging from the forest on the far side of the Anishanaabe fire.

Maengun's absence and his reappearance were proof of nothing, but Wulf's eyes narrowed in suspicion and he could feel the hair rise on the nape of his neck.

Something smelled wrong. And then he chuckled as he thought of the worst rotten fish smell he had ever inhaled. Wulf thought to himself that it may not literally smell as bad as that god-awful lutefisk that the Norske people were fond of, but this was fishy enough!

Chapter 28 - Leadership

In the middle of the night, a gentle wind from the west began to blow and by morning the clouds were gone from the sky. Twice more during the night the wolves had howled, but from much further away. Erik pointed out to the others that the howls were different from the first ones, and suggested that it was if the wolves were trying to locate each other. Wulf said nothing out loud, but thought to himself that what he heard in their voices was a call for distant members of the pack to come together.

After they packed up their gear Maengun told the gathered group, "We don't have much farther to go. One more day, up this valley and over one more small pass, and we will be able to touch the waters of the Mahakentuck."

Brigit asked, "Are you sure this is the way?"

"Don't you trust me? I have led you safely so far."

Shivon muttered under her breath, "Or so you say."

Brigit sighed slightly and said to Maengun, "Yes, you have led us as I have asked of you. And no harm has come to us. No trolls, windigos, baykaaks, or wolves have attacked us. It is just that I am wondering if this is the right course of action. What if that which I seek is not at the headwaters of the Mahakentuck?"

Maengun looked deep into her eyes and said, "Tell me. What is it you seek?"

"That's the problem. I don't know. I thought it would become clearer to me, as we came closer to the river's source, but I'm as unsure as I was before."

Maengun glanced down at the necklace Brigit wore, smiled, and then said, "You are a wise woman, I am confident that you will find the answer." Then he leaned forward and whispered to her so that only she could hear, "The necklace is beautiful, but with that piece of iron also hanging around your throat its beauty is marred. Why don't you just take it off and put it in your pocket." Then leaning back and speaking louder so that others could hear he said, "Shall we proceed?"

They shouldered their packs and began their journey for the day. With the addition of Rolf and his boys, the order of the marching changed slightly. Maengun and his men still led the way, but they were now followed by Rolf and Erik. Brigit and Shivon followed close behind them, with Wulf and Rolf's boys bringing up the rear.

The file of travelers wound their way around the lake they had camped near and went through the area from whence the howls of the wolves had come. They could see no sight of the wolves, but they stayed on the alert for them.

By mid-afternoon they had reached the summit of the pass Maengun had spoken of and began descending into another valley.

Erik sidled up to Brigit's side to give her a warning.

"This is troll country. As sure as I can be. The beasties are about."

Brigit eyes seemed slightly fogged over, and she replied, "Don't worry so much Erik. Maengun will alert us if they are near." She sighed went on, "I feel so tired."

Erik looked her over with a searching eye.

"Where is the iron amulet of protection I gave you?"

"I took it off. I thought it detracted from the beauty of my necklace. The harsh iron next to the moonstones didn't look right."

Erik shook his head. He knew how headstrong she

was; and that if he insisted that she wore it, then she might well rebel even more strongly against his wishes. So he tried a different tack.

"Aye, you may be right about that. But I think there is something to its power. Could you humor this old man and either braid it into your hair, or perhaps fasten it to your skin by tying it about your arm?"

Brigit smiled at her old friend, "Just for you, my old friend and protector, I will do so."

Brigit called on the party to halt for a brief rest and she asked Shivon to braid the amulet securely into her hair. Maengun's eyes flared for a moment when he saw what Shivon was doing but said nothing.

When Shivon was finished Brigit stood up. Her eyes looked brighter and she said, "That little rest stop did me good. I'm ready to go on."

They went on and soon they came to a small brook that wound its way down the valley. They followed it westward. About an hour before sunset, they came to the place where it joined a larger stream which was coming from the north.

Maengun announced to them, "We have come to the Mahakentuck. If we follow this water to its source then we will go up the slopes of the high mountain called Cloudsplitter. We will get our reward."

Shivon noticed the Anishanaabe men smile when he said that. It made her uneasy and she glanced around to see if anyone else had noticed the smiles. If they did, no one said anything.

The river was high, for it was spring and the snowmelt was still heavily feeding it. Where the river had receded from its spring high water mark there were a few open places, but the river bed was filled with rocks and boulders and there was no place to set up in those open spots. They would need to set up camp in the heavily wooded areas on the river's edge. They walked up the shoreline of the river several dozen paces and found an area where there was a high canopy of chestnut trees and little underbrush. The ground was rocky and strewn with boulders but they deemed it adequate for the night and they quickly set up camp and made a fire.

Even though the sun was near to setting, some of the men were about to take their bows and go hunting for game to roast on the fire when Rolf gave them a warning.

"You go on and scout the area if you like, but don't bother getting game. We'll not be roasting meat tonight. This is troll country. And sure as not, if there be trolls about, the smell of roasting meat would draw them to us as certain as bees to a flower."

Noodin, of the Anishanaabe muttered to his friends in his native tongue, "Weak men, afraid of wind and windigoes."

They chuckled to each other, but when Maengun gave them a glare they quickly stopped. Noodin and Mikom took their bows with them and went into the woods with Maengun. Asin, his arm still healing from the wound the bear had given him, stayed in camp. When Brigit beckoned him to come to the river with him so she might examine the wound and re-bandage it, he meekly went with her.

Rolf motioned to Erik that he wanted to talk, so they went walking northward along the riverbank, saying they were scouting to make sure the area was safe.

When they were out of range of the others hearing them, Rolf said, "This is rock-cracking troll country, to be sure. I'm worried about tonight. This is not the place

I'd have chosen to camp. If I'm right, our mining camp of Ironhill is only a few miles down river from here. We'd have been better off, using what was left of the light to make our way there. There we'd stand stronger against any trolls."

"Aye, true enough. But here we are, and we'll make the best of it. Let's have the boys gather plenty of wood so we can keep a hearty fire burning all night. Those beasties may like to eat roast meat, but flames can hurt them. Let get some torches prepared too."

They continued to make their plans as they walked back to the campsite. There they found that Shivon, Wulf, and Rolf's boys were already gathering wood for a fire. The elder men told them to continue and to gather as much as they could. They directed Wulf and Shivon to grab some branches and begin wrapping them with cord and cloth to make torches. When Brigit returned from the river with Asin, they set him to work with Shivon and Wulf, and they took Brigit aside to speak with her.

Erik began, "Lady Brigit, you are the leader of this party. The decisions you make lead us into and out of danger. Like it or not, you now have the responsibility for a dozen people riding on you and your decisions. Rolf and I will use whatever fighting skills we have to protect you and the others if it comes to that, but we are only men - and aging ones at that. You have chosen to follow Maengun's advice in coming this way, and we haven't been harmed yet, but I'm worried about tonight. There are trolls out and about in this land, as well as wolves, baykaaks, and Thor knows what else! To top it off, I'm not so confident of Maengun and his friends. What if they should turn on us in the moment of an attack?"

"What would you have me do?"

Erik put an edge to his voice, "What would I have you do?"

"Yes. What should I do? Maengun is no threat. He has been helpful, and so too his men."

"Achh, my lassie. Don't let your heart be charmed by some sweet-talking, dashing young man."

Rolf interrupted them, "Excuse me. I think Erik knows you best and this is a conversation the two of you should have in private. I'll go check on how the preparations for the night are coming along." Without another word, he turned and walked off.

Brigit seemed more contrite than Erik expected. "Do you really think I've been charmed by him?"

"Lassie, you'll have to be the judge of that. But what I need you to think about is leadership. You've seen your mother and father in action. Now is the time for you to step up and assume such a leadership role."

"What do you mean?"

"You have lives depending on your decisions. In matters of heart, yes, always follow your heart, but matters of leadership are often more than that. Trust those who have earned your trust - if it be truly earned. But beware of those who may be deceiving you. Make your decisions based on what is best for your people, not on what pleases you."

"Can't they be the same?"

"Yes, they can. But they aren't necessarily so. Sometimes you must set aside your personal desires to protect those who depend upon you."

Brigit paused in thought before saying, "I suppose this is what father means when he says that being the king means to serve the people."

"Aye, lassie. That it is. To be a true leader is to be

more a servant than a master."

Brigit nodded her head slightly and said with determination, "I hear what you are saying. I'll try to keep my head clear, and I'll do my best. Now let's go back to the others and help them get ready."

Erik smiled and said, "Proud of you, I am. But there is one more thing."

She looked at him with questioning eyes.

"It's about the trolls. Remember - fire hurts 'em. You're one of the best in the land with a bow. A flaming arrow to the heart is one of these best ways to kill those beasties. If you get a shot, don't hesitate. Take it!"

She smiled and said, "I'll do my best."

"That's all anyone can ask of you."

Erik smiled in return as they made their way back to the others.

Chapter 29 - Fire in the Night

The sun had set and the moon would not be rising until well into the night. All members of Brigit's ensemble had returned to the fire. As directed, none had brought in any game to roast. They sat about the roaring fire nibbling on venison jerky and hard crackers from their packs, and sipping cool water from the mountain river.

They had spaced themselves out around the fire, and at all times they had at least a couple of people seated with their backs to trees and looking outward from the fire. Whenever they were replaced by another person coming onto guard duty, they allowed several minutes for that person's eyes to adjust and restore their night vision, before leaving them and returning to the fire.

There was noticeable tension in the air. What little joviality there had been on previous evenings was absent this night. When anyone did speak, it was in hushed tones. They would fiddle with their weapons, glance furtively around themselves, and try to calm their nerves.

For a long time Wulf sat by the fire, fidgeting with his staff and mumbling to himself as he touched the runes and symbols carved into it. The Anishanaabe men smirked at him, but said nothing.

As the minutes and hours ticked by, each one became settled into their own reverie. As the moon started to lift its head above the eastern horizon, Maengun suggested they might as well take turns trying to get some sleep.

"Listen, there is no reason some of us shouldn't get is a few hours of sleep. We fear an attack, but one may not come. We have a hard day ahead of us as we go upward through the steep and narrow defile of this river. We will need our strength and wits about us. It won't be easy going. We can take turns sleeping."

"Aye," Rolf responded, "we do need to get some sleep. But we must stay on our guard as well. Only half at a time should sleep. The rest should be awake and alert."

His suggestion was agreed upon and soon half of their number at a time was attempting to sleep. It was fitful sleep - but at least it was some rest for their weary bodies. The fires were kept brightly burning at all times. Those on guard watched and waited.

It was hours after midnight and the moon had risen high in the sky when the windigos attacked. Mayhem ensued as the ravenous brutes rushed the camp. Wielding huge clubs and throwing large rocks, they roared as they startled the those on guard duty. The long hours of watchfulness had dulled their minds momentarily, but they quickly sprang into action. Those at rest also came to full alertness.

The putrid smell of the gaunt beasts with inhuman strength was nauseous and caused even the strongest of the group to blanch in disgust even as they attempted to repel the attackers. Arrows and sword strokes appeared to have little effect on the beast, other than to briefly slow them down. Defenders were being knocked to the ground.

Brigit grabbed one of the fire arrows she had prepared and set by the fire. She plunged its point into the fire to ignite it and lifting it to her bow she turned to fire it at one of the beasts. As she turned, she saw Asin leap in front of her and take a blow from a windigos club that was intended for her. He fell in a heap to the ground. She fired the arrow at the windigo and it plunged into his heart. In a scream of agony it fell to the rocky earth.

She grabbed another arrow, ignited it, and fired it at a windigo that had was forcing some of her party to hide behind a couple of large boulders near the river. It also went down in a scream of agony. She looked to her side and saw Erik and Rolf brandishing torches as they attacked one of the beasts.

Then Shivon was at her side handing her another flaming arrow. She shot it between the moving bodies of Erik and Rolf, missing them and hitting the windigo.

Her people were falling back closer to her and closer to the fire, as more and more windigos appeared out of the darkness of the woods. Through the sounds of the screaming and roaring beasts, and the din of battle, the yelps and snarls of attacking wolves could be heard in the forest.

Brigit glanced to her left and saw Wulf, like a madman, leap to the top of a large boulder. He had a crazed look in his eye as he lifted his staff high over his head and swung it in a large circle. He shouted one word, "VERBRENNT"!

Bright flame went searing out from the end of the staff. The men and women went temporarily blind, and the windigos and surrounding trees, green though they were from their spring growth, went up in flames. Wulf fell from the boulder and the flames from the staff stopped.

As they struggled to recover their vision, they grabbed their fallen comrades and what supplies they could and retreated to the river's edge, to avoid the consuming fire.

As they cowered behind the boulders along the

river's edge, Brigit took stock of their casualties. Asin lay dead from the wound he had suffered while protecting her. Mikom and Noodin were also dead from injuries. The twins had twin injuries; Olaf had a broken right arm and Lars had a broken left arm. Wulf was sitting beside the river in a daze, saying nothing. The rest had minor scrapes and bruises, but nothing debilitating. And Maengun was missing.

Erik, kneeling beside Wulf, looked up at Brigit, "I think he'll be alright. Seems a bit stunned by what he just did. I'll admit, so am I."

Brigit raised her eyebrows as she thought of what she had just witnessed in Wulf's display of power, "So are we all," and she repeated softly, "so are we all."

Erik said, "And I've got to add, that was a fine bit of shooting on your part. You didn't hesitate, and you didn't miss."

"Thank you. Your words of advice helped me," she touched the iron totem attached to the bow, "and perhaps this did too. But it wouldn't have been enough. There were too many of them. They would have overrun us." She nodded in Wulf's direction, "He saved us."

"That he did. I'd say that if he didn't already have your trust, he sure earned it tonight. As did your arrow maiden." He nodded toward Shivon.

"True. On both accounts. Do you know what it was that Wulf shouted?"

"I'm not really sure. I reckon it must be something from his native tongue. It sort of sound like 'burn' in old Norske, but I couldn't say for sure."

From where he was sitting, Wulf muttered, "Burn. Yes. Burn is how you could translate it."

From where they stood, they turned and looked directly at him. His head had been bowed, but now he

155

lifted it and looked at them. His eyes had lost that glazed far-away look they possessed after he fell from the rock. They were back to having their normal spark, but his face looked drawn and tired.

"Are they all gone?" he asked.

"The trolls who were upon us are burning as brightly as newly lit torches by the look of it. I don't know if there were more in the woods beyond where your fire reached. We'll have to wait until morning to find out. It looks like the fire you kindled in those trees will burn til at least then. None of the beasties will be coming through that. And I doubt they would try to cross the river to attack us, seeing what happened to their friends. We may think of them as dumb brutes, but they're smart enough to steer clear of what just scorched them. However, we'll keep a watch until the dawn."

So in the light of the still burning trees, they settled amongst the boulders on the river's edge. Brigit tended to their wounds, as she had been taught some of the healing arts by the women who raised her, and they waited for the dawn.

Chapter 30 - Morning Decision

When the skies brightened with the dawn of the new day and the sun broke the horizon, Erik and Rolf cautiously ventured through the still smoldering sentinels of the trees to scout the surrounding area.

Shivon talked with Brigit about what should be done with the fallen Anishanaabe warriors, "If we just leave them lay here, carrion and the wolves will come and savage their remains. We can't allow that. But do we have the time to do anything else?"

Brigit answered, "You're right. They died fighting for us. And I know Asin gave his life for mine. He stepped in front of a troll that was about to crush me. We may have doubted their loyalty to our cause, but in the height of battle they fought on our side. We will not leave their bodies to be torn apart by carrion."

Shivon gestured toward Olaf and Lars. "Well, those two won't be much help. With those broken arms they can't dig a grave. Why, they probably won't even be able to carry their own packs."

"No, they can't do much digging, but the ground here is really too rocky to dig anyway. I think we'll have to scrape a shallow grave and cover them with rocks."

Wulf, who had been sitting several feet away, apparently overheard them, for he said, "Finn and I will find a proper spot and get started preparing it."

By the time Erik and Rolf returned, the two young men had found a slight depression and scrapped what little topsoil there was out of it. They carried the bodies of the dead men to the site and placed them in it. They began collecting rocks and covering the bodies. Olaf and Lars had also begun to help. Even though each one only had one useful arm, they carried the rocks they could lift. They paused briefly when the elder men returned to camp and Erik explained what they had found.

"There were more trolls beyond where the fire reached, but it appears the wolves attacked and scattered them. Or at least chased them back to their dens in the rocky slopes. I'm not sure why the wolves would do that, but they seem to have done us a good turn."

The corners of Wulf's lips gave a slight curve upward when he heard that. Erik noticed and wondered if Wulf knew something about the wolves.

Brigit asked, "Did you find Maengun?"

"Not hide nor hair of him, my lady. He has right disappeared without a trace."

"Maybe the trolls captured him and took him with them."

"Not likely. Those beasties who were closest to us went up in flames. Those beyond the flames the wolves dealt with. If the wolves were attacking them, they'd be running for their lives, they wouldn't stop to take a captive."

"Then where can he be?"

"Your guess is as good as mine. We can spend more time searching for him if you'd like. But I don't think we'll find him."

"We have to look, but I don't want to spend another night in this place."

Rolf interjected, "I know your plan is to head upstream, but I'm pretty sure that the mining village of Ironhill is only a couple of miles down stream. We could search for a bit and head there."

Erik added, "I know you want to search for the headwaters of the river, but our numbers have diminished and a couple of us are injured. We could regroup there."

Brigit sighed as she thought and then responded, "And I have been told that what I seek is not upstream." She glanced at Wulf. "We stay long enough for Wulf and his crew to finish burying the men. Meanwhile you and Rolf, and Shivon and I, will search again for Maengun. Then we head to Ironhill."

They went quickly to their tasks. Despite a careful search of the surrounding area, no trace of Maengun or his gear was to be found. It was as though he had vanished into thin air. The activity of the trolls and wolves, as well as Wulf's fire, had obscured any trail he may have left. If the two expert trackers, Erik and Rolf, couldn't pick up a trail, then there wasn't a trail to be found.

Once the deceased warriors were interred in the cairn of rocks, the remaining members of the traveling party shouldered their gear and followed the general course of the stream as it flowed down the valley. Rolf led the way, followed by his sons. Then Brigit and Shivon, followed by Erik and Wulf.

As they walked, Erik talked to Wulf. "Do you feel like you have recovered from last night?"

Wulf nodded, "Surprisingly, I do. I was feeling sort of drained, but the physical activity seems to have reinvigorated me."

"Aye, sometimes the best course of action, when mentally drained, is to be physically active. Now, iffen you don't mind me asking, how did you learn to do what you did with that flame?"

Wulf sighed. "I don't rightly know. I had been sitting there and focusing on the staff, and the glyphs that are carved into it. When the attack came, I guess it just sort of took over. I knew I wanted those critters to burn. So we, the staff and I, ordered it."

"So, who is in control? You or the staff?"

"I believe I am. The staff could have done nothing without me."

"But what could you have done without the staff?"

"Good point, Erik. I'm not sure what I could have done, but I am sure that I could use someone to teach me."

"Well, don't look at me. I can't teach you a mule's kick worth of that druid stuff. I'm just a simple soldier, using my wits the best I can to do my duty."

That made Wulf chuckle as he responded, "You once told me that High King Skoth learned the druid ways when he was already grown. How did he learn?"

"Aye, tis true enough. He was no longer a youth, but he had the Green Man and Evlin to teach him. Unfortunately, the Green Man is dead and gone."

Wulf looked thoughtful and was quiet for several moments, then he said, "Brigit told me about the death of her grandfather, Fearglas, the Green Man. But there is still Evlin. Do you think she could teach me? Or maybe Unaine, at the Academy?"

"A sure as a dog wags its tail, they could teach you. I don't know that it would be what you need to learn, but they are knowledgable and wise."

"Yet," said Wulf, "I can't leave Brigit. I have this feeling I must stay with her. As much as I would like to find someone to help me understand what is happening to me, I can't just leave her."

"Responsibility and desire often come into conflict with each other," mused Erik.

Wulf snorted, "An observation which is of no real help to me in figuring out what to do."

"Would you have me tell you what to do?"

"Yes," said Wulf in exasperation, and then he

added, "well, no. Not really. I have to make my own decisions."

Erik grinned at the young man. "Then you've learned an important lesson already. People can tell you what they know, and they can make recommendations. But when it comes down to it, you are the one who has to live with whatever course of action you choose to take. Make the best decision you can, and then make the best of what happens."

At that point they came up to the rest of the group. They had stopped at the bank of the river near a cairn of rocks. They could see the sides of the river were soon to become steeper as they were entering a small gorge. Rolf was pointing to a cairn on the far side.

Rolf said, "I reckon these cairns mark where we must ford the river. Then we go around that hill, and there we will find Ironhill."

They forded the river with some difficulty, since the water was high with the spring melt. In addition, the two young men with broken arms had some difficulty balancing and needed to take extra care. But soon all members of the party had crossed the river and were trudging down a path that wound around the hill. In short order they emerged from the wooded path and saw the village and mineworks of Ironhill.

Chapter 31 - Ironhill

Ironhill was a small village dedicated solely to the purpose of extracting iron ore from the surrounding hills. There were several small cottages where some of the long-term residents lived with their families, but the site was dominated by two large structures: the larger common hall and dormitory on the shore of a small lake, and the mineworks further up the hill.

Rolf directed them to the hall near the lake. This large ramshackle building had obviously been added onto several times as the mining operation had grown over the years. Rolf was the first one in the door; and as soon as he entered, the others heard a booming voice.

"Rolf Strongarm, you old has-been berserker! What are you doing here?"

Rolf responded with an equalling boisterous voice, "Angus Mulerider, you son of a goat. It looks like you're still swilling ale in the most disreputable of places!"

A hearty belly laugh from the red-bearded and barrel-chested Angus reverberated through the common hall as he took in the sight of the men and women who followed Rolf into the hall. When he saw the last member of the group enter, he yelled out, "And if it isn't the old wanderer, himself, Erik - King's Shadow and Protector. Your hair has whitened a bit since I saw you last, but there is no mistaking that ugly mug of yours! What brings you to my fine establishment?"

Erik was not one to let such a greeting go unanswered.

"Angus! Larger than life you are! And I don't think it's taller that you are, it must be that you're getting wider! By the look of it, you may have to make a bigger door to this place."

162

Again a hearty laugh echoed through the hall as the two men stepped toward each other and then embraced each other in a genuine bearhug.

Wulf turned to Brigit and whispered, "Does he know someone everywhere we go?"

Brigit grinned as she replied, "It appears so. I knew it seemed he knew everyone that came through Tara as I was growing up, but sometimes he still surprises me."

Erik quickly made introductions, though it was already apparent that Angus knew Rolf and his boys. Accommodations were secured and plans were made to spend the night. Angus insisted that after supper they share with the assembled miners and workers the story of the previous night's troll attack.

When all had come in from their daily labors and filled their plates and then their bellies, Angus silenced the crowd with a bellow. He then introduced the travelers to the assembly. Brigit had not hidden her identity from Angus, but she was surprised when Angus openly told the crowd that she was the Princess Brigit and that she was on a quest.

As the workers came in that evening, it quickly became apparent that many of them knew Erik, and they looked to him to begin the telling of the tale.

Erik stood up and cleared his throat. One could see in their eyes a greedy hunger for the story of the events of the quest. Eric told the story with a few embellishments as to the actions of the others and minimized his own deeds. Again Brigit was surprised, for he told the tale without sharing the doubts he had shared with her about Maegun and the Anishanaabe men. Perhaps he did so because several of the workers present were Anishanaabe. When he elaborated about the fire Wulf had ignited as he torched the trolls, the crowd looked at Wulf with wonder and amazement. Wulf blushed and hung his head a little in embarrassment.

Erik had just finished telling about Maengun's strange disappearance and asking them to keep their eyes open for any trace of him, when the outer door of the hall swung open and Maengun stepped inside.

Brigit gasped when she saw him and the hall fell silent. She jumped up and ran to him.

"Maengun! You're safe! What happened to you? Are you hurt?"

She gave him a hug before he could respond. All eyes were on them. Erik, standing near the hearthfire of the hall, stroked his beard in thoughtfulness. He looked about the room trying to read the faces of the crowd to see if any of the local folks showed signs of recognizing the newcomer. He noticed none, but he did notice Shivon's eyes narrow in suspicion and a look of puzzlement flicker of Wulf's face.

When Brigit stepped back from Maengun he began his explanation. He spoke to her, but spoke loud enough so others in the hall could hear him.

"What an ordeal I've been through. Have you told the others about the attack of the windigos?"

He called the creatures by their Anishanaabe name, and the Anishanaabe men in the crowd nodded respectfully.

Brigit responded, "Yes, Erik was just finishing the story and had just told them about how you were missing. We looked all over for you. What happened?"

"I was to the side, dodging blows from one of the windigos and trying to strike at it, when there was this huge fireball. I was thrown to the side and must have hit my head on a rock. When I awoke, one of the beasts had

164

me slung over its back and was no doubt carrying me back to their lair. I gave it no notice that I was awake and alert. After several minutes, the windigo stopped when it met up with others of its ilk. It tossed me to the side thinking I was still unconscious or dead. The windigos started arguing with each other, and as they did so, I crept away from them and then fled. I knew of this mining village since some of my people work here. I thought that if any of you survived the attack, you would make your way here. I see you did."

Shivon, who was sitting next to Wulf, lean over to him and whispered, "I don't believe him. Why hasn't he asked about his men?"

Wulf nodded his head slightly in agreement, but said nothing.

Brigit said, "What a relief it is to see you. We searched and searched for you. Are you sure you are alright? Let me take a look at that bump on your head."

She reached her arm forward to touch his head, but he stepped back.

"No, no. Don't worry about me. I'm fine now."

She withdrew her hand and a puzzled expression formed on her face.

Then she asked, "You just said you knew this village was here, so you came here to find survivors. Why didn't you lead us here and have us spend the night here? Why camp out and risk an attack, when this village was so close?"

"I have only been trying to help you. You wanted to press on toward your goal. We would have had to backtrack had we come here. Your journey would have been delayed. You didn't want that."

Shivon leaned over to Wulf to whisper again.

"He trying to blame her for this. And he still hasn't

asked about his men - or about any of the rest of us!"

This time Wulf responded with a whisper back to her, "I agree. He's lying, but we can't prove it."

A clouded and confused expression came over Brigit's face.

The voice of Angus boomed through the room, "Well, come on over here young man. Have a mug of ale. An encounter and escape from the trolls is no small matter. This drink is on the house."

While Shivon and Wulf may have doubted Maengun's story, there were obviously many in the hall who believed him. Shouts of approval and the sound of mugs being knocked against the tables echoed through the room.

Maengun made his way toward Angus, and several of the Anishanaabe men rose to join him. The survivors of the traveling party remained seated and exchanged glances with each other. Brigit remained near the door for several moments with that confused expression on her face and then went to rejoin her friends.

Before she got to them, Shivon once more said to Wulf, "And never once did he ask about his friends."

Chapter 32 - A New Direction

Shivon and Brigit talked long into the night as they lay near each other in the room that Angus had arranged for them. At first, Brigit defended Maengun against everything that Shivon said, but as they talked, slowly her mind cleared and she came to question Maengun's truthfulness. They had no proof that he was lying, and he had offered no proof that his tale was true, so the questions Shivon raised remained unanswered.

For quite some time Brigit remained awake after Shivon had drifted off to sleep. She knew that she was the one who would decide what course of action to take. She suspected that no matter which direction she choose to go, there would be some who disagreed with her. There was no clear path open to her. She only knew that she strongly felt in her soul that the culmination of Skoth's initial quest and the crisis that Ayen declared to be upon them, was ultimately her responsibility.

Early the next morning Brigit assembled the crew that had been traveling with her. She started out by first saying some words of thanks to her companions. Then she explained the course of action she would undertake.

She would be descending the river by raft. It was often the way that ore was transported out of the mountains. Each member of the traveling group was welcome to join her or to go their own way. She would not force anyone to accompany her.

A moment of initial silence greeted her announcement. A slight smile creased Erik's face and he was about to ask her why the change of plans, when Maengun spoke.

"Why are you doing this? I thought you wanted to go to the headwaters of the Mahakentuck. We are so close. I'm sure we can safely get by the trolls. If what you need is there, we should go on. I can help you."

Brigit shook her head. "I have decided. What I seek is not there." She glanced at Wulf, but said nothing more.

Maengun protested, "But you were never sure about what it is you seek, only that you felt it necessary to go to the source of the river. How do you know it isn't there?"

Erik could see the muscles in Brigit's jaw tightening. He knew that look. He knew from watching her as a child, and then as she had matured into a young woman, that when she got that look she was setting her mind and there was little that would change it. He chuckled to himself as he recalled giving advice to Skoth and Evlin about how to deal with their headstrong child. He often reminded them that Brigit was like a rope - you could give her some direction by pulling, but you wouldn't accomplish much by pushing.

Erik mused inwardly, "Just keep pushing, Maengun, just keep pushing."

The exchange between Brigit and Maengun continued for a couple of more rounds, but after it became obvious to Maengun that nothing he said would change her mind, he gave up trying. He then changed his approach.

Maengun's voice took a softer tone, "Brigit, I apologize for disagreeing with you. You know I only want to help you. I will go with you wherever you go, and I will give you whatever assistance I can."

Shivon said, "I'll go with you. And might I add, I much prefer the idea of floating downriver, rather than tangling with those trolls again."

Wulf grimaced slightly as he said, "I don't relish the

thought of being on water again, but I'm with you."

Brigit smiled, "I knew the two of you would want to go with me. I know I can depend on you." She turned and looked at Erik, who had been whispering with Rolf. "What about you? I can't imagine you would leave me go off by myself."

"Right you are, lassie," he replied, "I was just talking matters over with Rolf here. He's figuring to stay here for a spell and let his boys' wounds heal up. Then they'll be going down river. If you want to wait, they'd go with us. But if you want to leave sooner - well, then I guess you're stuck with just me."

"I feel the urge to move quickly. So I guess that means we'll be without them." Turning to look at each of them in the eye, she said to Rolf and his sons, "Thank you for your help in getting this far. We haven't been travelling together very long, but I appreciate what you have done for me, and I won't forget it."

Rolf looked at his boys and then spoke as he turned his attention back to Brigit, "You are welcome, Princess. Perhaps our paths will cross again. If so, you can count on us."

Brigit said, "Well, then, that is settled. I'll go make arrangements with Angus to get us passage on one of his iron ore caravans rafting downriver."

After she left, Erik sidled up to Maengun. He pointed to Maengun's bow and and said, "Iffen you don't mind me asking you something?"

Maengun replied, "What?"

"You know how I have admired that fine northern bow of yours, how is it you still possess it? I mean, with you being knocked out, the trolls dragging you off, and you sneaking away from them. How is it you managed to keep your bow through all that?"

Maengun looked momentarily stunned, and then squinted his eyes in thought.

"I must have had it slung over my shoulder when they attacked. I guess they didn't notice I still had it. I'm just lucky, I guess."

Erik let out a thoughtful hum as he stroked his beard. Then he said, "Some say the gods shower good fortune and misfortune upon us. Others say we make our own luck. Whichever it may be, you certainly came through that scrape in good shape. Guess you are lucky."

When Brigit returned she informed them that Angus had a caravan of rafts heading downriver on the morrow. She laughed as she told them that he had welcomed them to travel with it, though he did say they'd have to pay their way - after all, he was running a business.

She finished by saying, "So spend the day resting and recovering. We leave bright and early in the morning."

Chapter 33 - Mahakentuck Gorge

Riding the ore-rafts down the mountain river was an exhilarating experience. At least it was for most of the travelers. It seemed as though there was whitewater and serious rapids around every corner. Wulf suffered through it. Although he wasn't afraid of the water, he dreaded the thought of falling overboard into the tumbling waters.

They made it safely through the first day's series of rapids and then the ore crews pulled to the shore and tied up. They spent a couple of hours readjusting and retying their rafts. The ore crew chief told the travelers that even though they had hours of daylight left, this was a necessary precaution, for the next day would see them descend through the Great Gorge of the Mahakentuck. He described it as deep trench cut through the mountains with nary a good place to beach and make any repairs. The cliffs sometime rose a couple of hundred feet above the river, and the waters rushed with furious speed beneath them. They needed to be rested and ready to deal with it.

During that evening of preparation, Erik pulled Brigit aside for a conversation.

"I've been wondering what is was that changed your mind. You were so set on going to Cloudsplitter. Now we head away from it. Can you explain?"

"Erik, you have always been one to tell me to trust my instincts. I know that sometimes I am rash and impulsive. I know that sometimes I have let my desires get the best of me. Some of that may have been driving me into the mountains. I want so much to find the key."

"Lassie, I know how much you want to prove yourself. Finding the ultimate key to Skoth's quest would certainly do that. But ..." his voice drifted off to silence.

"But what?"

"What if we are looking at this all wrong?"

"What do you mean?"

"What if the key is not a thing? What if it is something you must do?"

Brigit nodded. "That's what I am starting to think, too. And when Wulf told me that what I seek is not on the mountain . . ."

"He did?"

Brigit chuckled, "Oh, I know he can be kind of clumsy and he is outright strange at times, especially these last few days, but there is a genuineness in him. I know I can trust him, and if the man who can talk to birds and ignite fires like he did when the trolls attacked, says that what I search for is not on the mountain, then I should take that seriously."

Erik nodded and gave her a penetrating look. He then decided to venture into dangerous territory. "You have been very trusting of Maengun. Do you still trust him after the troll attack?"

Brigit furrowed her brow and narrowed her eyes in thought, then released the tension in her face and said, "Yes, I do. Well, sort of. I mean, he has always been helpful, and he did know his way into the mountains. I think he means well. At least I hope he does."

Erik could tell by her comments that though she still thought well of Maengun, she had some doubts about him. That was enough for now. Any more questioning on this issue might push her back to defending him.

"Since we are talking about your companions, I've been wondering about Shivon."

"And what is it that you have been wondering."

"Ach, I don't really know how to say this, but I've noticed that that two of you have been getting really close to each other, and ..." Again he took a long pause. Then he went on, "I really don't know how to say it, but, how close are you?"

Brigit gave a light-hearted laugh. "My dear old protector, you don't need to worry about me. I can take care of myself. I'll not deny there is an attraction between the two of us. I enjoy her wit and appreciate her insights, but there is nothing for you to worry about."

It was Eric's turn to laugh as he glanced toward where Shivon was regaling the men of the ore rafts with one of her stories of adventure.

"Maybe you need to worry. I see she is using her charms on the men."

Again Brigit laughed, and she smiled as she said, "She is free to charm whomever she wants. Now, if you're done worrying about me, I'd like to go have a talk with Wulf. He seems a little withdrawn this evening."

She got up and and went to sit with Wulf who was perched on a large boulder next to the river. His eyes were focused on the swirling waters but his thoughts roamed far away.

When Brigit sat down next to him, she said, "You look so deep in thought. Is there anything you want to talk about?"

"I was thinking about what one of my instructors, Master Gerhardt once said."

He stopped and she had to prompt him. "Go on."

"He said that sometimes you choose your own fate and sometimes fate chooses you."

"That's a deep thought. It sounds like something Master Unaine might say. And here I thought you were

173

just looking at the river and worrying about falling in it tomorrow as we pass through the gorge."

"Oh, I am plenty worried about that. But there doesn't seem to be much I can do about it."

"If you'd like, I could ride the same raft as you, and jump in to save you, if you need it. I did that once before you will recall."

That comment made a slight smile appear on Wulf's face.

"Yes, you did. You rescued me and I will always be grateful for that. Riding with you tomorrow would be reassuring. According to the raft men, we have miles and miles of almost continuous white water tomorrow. Today, I asked one of the men about tying me into the raft, but he said it wasn't a good idea, because if the raft capsized I was just as likely to be held under the water as I was to be saved by the rope."

"Then that's settled, we ride together tomorrow."

"Brigit, can I ask you a question?"

"Fair enough. I asked you one."

"Are you choosing to go on this search, or are you being forced to?"

Without hesitation she answered, "No one is forcing me to undertake it. I go of my own free will."

"Yet, would you being doing this if you were not the daughter of Skoth and Evlin, and if the Loon's Necklace had not been bestowed upon you?"

She was quiet in thought for a few moments and then her face brightened as if seeing a light.

"Ahh, so you are suggesting that fate is choosing me as well as I am choosing my own fate."

Wulf sighed. "So you see my point. I, like you, have been placed into a situation that is not entirely of my own choosing." He gently laid his hand upon his staff that lay on the boulder between them. "Yet I have choices to make, and those choices determine what will happen. So is it fate, or is it my action?"

She looked at him and, holding his gaze, she reached out to place her hand upon his that held the staff. Neither spoke for several moments.

Then Brigit spoke, "You are a good and wise man, Wulf. May your choices, and mine, bear good fruit."

From a distance, Maengun watched. His face remained expressionless but his eyes glowed. Perhaps it was only the reflection of the campfire.

Chapter 34 - Past the Gorge

The previous day of exhilarating travel down the rapids of the upper Mahakentuck River paled in comparison to the day of plunging through the whitewater of its Great Gorge. After rounding the final bend of the gorge and emerging from the high slopes into a wider valley with more gentle slopes, the waters took on a gentle flow and the crews of the ore rafts maneuvered them to the western shore. There was a steep cliff to the east, but there were nearly level shores to the west.

They took stock of their cargo and crews. To their satisfaction they had safely traversed the gorge with only minor incidents. The raft that Maengun was on had nearly capsized, and Mangun and one crew man had been thrown overboard into the tumbling waters, but the raft had been righted and the men had eventually been recovered. Both were wet and exhausted, but they were alive.

Once on shore Brigit quickly went to Maengun. She carefully looked him over to make sure he had no serious injuries, and then she examined the other man who had fallen overboard. Both of them only had minor scrapes and bruises from their ordeal.

While Brigit was checking the men over, Shivon and Erik checked on Wulf. Wulf was never so happy to get off a water vessel as he was to jump off the raft once it reached shore.

When Shivon reached him she said, "Whew, now that will be a tale to tell the grandchildren! Wild and wonderful that was!"

Wulf looked askance at her. "Wild and wonderful? Are you crazy?"

Shivon laughed and shook her mass of red hair which was still covered with the spray of the rapids. The water flew from her hair and splattered Wulf and Erik.

"Aye, a wee bit crazy I may be! But isn't it glorious to be alive!"

Wulf looked at her with wonder in his eyes and Erik boomed a hearty belly laugh.

"That's the attitude," declared Erik. "We may be wet, but we are alive. I must say, that was quite a ride. I've never had the thrill of shooting down that gorge before. I'm not sure I want to do it again, but I certainly will never forget it."

Wulf expelled a long breath. "Nor will I! And I am sure that I don't want to have to repeat the experience."

As Wulf slowly took in the fact that he was indeed still living and breathing and standing on solid ground, he continued to look at Shivon reveling in the aftermath of the ride. His gaze softened and he looked at her with admiration. She did look radiant in her excitement. In fact, at that moment she looked rather appealing.

Erik nudged him in the side and said, "Ach, boy, quit your ogling. Put your eyes back in their sockets, and let's go do a quick scout of the area. And you be sure to tell me if you hear any birds talking to you. This sure enough is still troll country."

They turned and walked away, Erik with his bow in hand, and Wulf with his staff. Shivon watched them leave, at first with a bit a quizzical look in her eye, and then with a dawning realization of what that look of Wulf's meant. Then she smiled and turned to go to where Brigit was tending to the men's injuries.

Several minutes later Wulf and Erik came crashing through the underbrush, yelling to get on the rafts and push off. The the air was split by harsh roars and by the

177

sound of boulders careening down the cliff on the opposite side of the river and splashing into the waters.

The men scrambled to get on the rafts and get them untied from where they were tethered on the shore. The final raft, the one with Shivon on it, had just been released and was beginning to catch the current when it was struck by a huge boulder. The raft shattered. People and the ore containers went flying into the waters. The current pulled people and the splintered logs of the raft downstream. Within moments they were beyond the cliff and catching up to where the crews on the other rafts were trying to slow their drift down the river. It was a difficult task, for the rafts had entered an area of light rapids and the rafts were being pulled quickly downstream.

As chance would have it, Shivon drifted near to where the raft that carried Maengun. She tried to reach for the raft, and Maengun reached out to grab her arm, but then there was a jolt as the raft hit a boulder. Shivon was swept away and she went under the water.

For moments that seemed an eternity to those watching she was under the water, then her body bobbed to the surface with her face down. The current pushed her toward the raft Wulf had jumped upon when he had run out of the woods. He reached out and somehow snared her with his staff and pulled her closer. Then with one hand hanging on to the raft, he set his staff aside and reached out to grab her with his other hand and pull her on board.

As Shivon lay on the logs of the raft, he could see she wasn't breathing. Wulf wasn't sure what to do, but he recalled that on his sea passage on the Hamburg trading cog the sailors had joked about the fact that he couldn't swim and that someday they'd "no doubt have to push the waters from his chest and breath the air back into him."

So he took her in his arms and holding her chest above her head, he tried to shake and gently squeeze the water out of her. Then he lay her back on the logs, inhaled deeply, put his mouth to hers, and exhaled forcefully. To his amazement, she coughed and then inhaled deeply.

She opened her eyes and blinked several times as the face of Wulf kneeling over her came into focus. Despite the ordeal she had just been through, she smiled. She held that smile for several long moments, even when she coughed again.

Then the smile became a frown.

Shivon sputtered, "That demon spawned pile of goat scat! He knocked my hand away from the raft. May the crow's curse be upon him!"

Wulf sat back from her in shock. "What? What are you talking about?"

"When I got thrown into the water and was being tossed about, I saw a raft and tried to make my way to it. Maengun was on it. When I reached for the raft, I thought he was reaching for me, but he knocked my arm away. Then I must have hit my head or something. The next thing I remember is seeing your face."

"Are you sure? Maybe he just couldn't manage to grab hold of you."

"Oh, I'm sure! And sure as my mother never birthed a fool, I'll never forget that smirk on his face."

"What matters now is that you are here and alive. I wonder what happened to the others?"

They looked up and about and saw that by this time, the rafts had rounded a slight bend in the river. They were well past the high cliffs, and the slopes on the riverbank allowed places to beach the rafts. The current slowed and they came upon a small island near the west bank of the river. The crews of the rafts maneuvered their craft to the edge of this island where they could temporarily pause and take stock of their situation.

The raft that had been struck was a complete loss. Its cargo of ore was at the bottom of the river and its logs were broken apart, splintered, and separated. Some pieces were on the banks of the river and others were floating downstream. Shivon had been rescued as had all members of the crew, except the one man who had been struck by the boulder as it hit the raft. They had pulled his body from the river and it was now laying on the island.

The crew chief and Erik knelt over the body of the dead crew man.

Erik said, "Poor soul, he never had a chance. It looks like the boulder struck his head. He must have died on the spot."

"Aye. And a good man he was. We'll load him onto one of the other rafts and give him a decent burial tonight. We're well past those bluffs, but I want to get back on the river as fast as we can. I intend to get several miles further on down the river before we stop for the night."

"A wise move," said Erik, "We may be past those beasts who threw the boulders down upon us, but there may be other threats nearby."

Brigit only had a few moments to check on her companions before the crew chief ordered them back onto the rafts. From a distant raft, Brigit had seen Wulf pull Shivon from the waters, but she had not seen what had transpired in the moments when Shivon neared Maengun's raft. Shivon had no time to tell her. They all leapt aboard their rafts and were off. Wulf and Shivon remained together on the same raft as he tended to her.

In spite of the numerous rapids they encountered over the next several miles, Wulf's attention stayed fixed upon Shivon. He may have noticed the rapids, but his thoughts were elsewhere.

Chapter 35 - Creekside

They made camp that night where the valley widened and a sizable creek entered the river from the southwest. It was a place that had obviously been used as a campsite previously, but there were no permanent inhabitants.

Wulf commented to Shivon as they landed, that this looked like a beautiful place for a village.

Shivon replied, "Aye, that it is. There is enough level land here for some good fields, fresh water a plenty, and a view that pleases the eye."

Wulf asked, "Then why aren't there any crofters here?"

Shivon chuckled, "Well, it certainly is remote. I suspect the winters can be a mite harsh. We may not be far enough from troll country. And, though I don't know for sure, I wonder how easy it is to get to. I mean, are there some low passes to go through the hills, rather than traveling on the river? It is a thrill going down the river, though I would prefer to do it in a canoe rather than a raft, but it would be nigh impossible to travel up that river."

Wulf was pleased to see that the Shivon had fully regained her talkative nature. The near brush with death had not changed her engaging personality.

They didn't talk much as they made camp, for the men were tired from their day of navigating the many rapids of the river, and they had several tasks before them: scouting the area to make sure it was safe, hunting for game to cook for the meal, making sure there was plenty of firewood, and of course, digging a grave for their fallen comrade.

Brigit's group of travelers pitched in and helped the raft crews. After the man had been buried, the venison roasted on a spit (for Brigit had shot a deer that Erik and she had stalked), and guards had been posted on the perimeter of the camp, then there was time to talk.

As they sat around the fire, the crew chief noted that he had made that ore run down the river many times, and that they had often stopped at the very spot, but never before had the trolls attacked them there.

Maengun voiced his doubt. "Yes, we were attacked, but by windigos? Maybe it was men of the Mohak who don't like you taking the ore from their land?"

The crew chief looks at him incredulously. "Are you daft, man! Those were trolls roaring as sure as my name is Shaemus."

"Perhaps. But we didn't see them. And windigos don't come out during the day."

Shaemus snorted, "Ach, sure enough these did!"

Erik gently interrupted with a long drawn out, "Well . . ." Then he continued, "I'd say that normally the beasts are night creatures. They detest the sun. But it was heavily clouded over today, and who knows what might be able to drive those beasts to act outside their normal ways. I'd say that if it sounds like a troll, and it smells like a troll, then it is a troll."

From his spot at the fire, Wulf gave a little chuckle, for that sounded like something old Master Gerhardt back in Hamburg might say. He didn't realized he had chuckled out loud until all eyes turned to him.

Maengun said, "You think that is funny. What do you know of our land?"

Wulf calmly replied, "Yes, it is amusing, and while I was not born here I am learning about it." And then he said a bit more shyly, "And I am learning to love it."

Maegun snorted. "Pale one." Then he stood up and walked away from the fire.

That comment sent Erik back into his memories for it had been years since he had heard that. It had been a comment of derision that the original inhabitants of Eirgalon had used for people coming from the Celtic and Nordic lands of Europe - people that they wanted to leave this "land beyond the sunset" and go back to Europe. The last time he had heard it was from the mouths of some of the followers of Malsum.

Shivon who was sitting next to Wulf, reached out and patted him on the knee.

"Well, 'tis good," she said, "we're coming to think right highly of you too."

Wulf blushed.

Brigit interrupted the moment, saying, "Well, enough of that. I'd like to discuss our plans."

Shaemus nodded and said, "Well, Princess Brigit, there ain't much to discuss. We don't have much choice. The river takes us onward. We're headed down toward Pig's Eye; but before we get to the falls, we beach our rafts and deliver our ore. They've got a nice smelting furnace there and they pay a good price for our ore."

Brigit nodded. "Indeed, that is the way I intended to go. But I would like to go to Chief Ayenwatha who resides at Tionnontoguen on the Mohak River. Is there any faster route than following the Mahakentuck all the way to where it meets the Mohak, and then up that river?"

"Not if you want a water route. But if you're not opposed to doing some walking, or riding of horses, there is the route up the Sacandaga River through the land of the waving grass."

"Tell me more about that way."

"Aye. You'd still travel with us for a few more days. Right before the two rivers come together, there is a ten foot waterfall. We'll portage the rafts around it. It's done often enough and there's a good chute where we can do it. Anyway, you could leave us there. There is a small village called Two Rivers at the junction. From there you could walk, or you could most likely get some horses or mules, and trek up the valley of the Sacandaga River. There is a road that goes up the valley. After a few miles you'll come to where the valley levels out. There's lots of grassland there. It's nearly a swamp in the spring, but in the summer it dies out. That's why they call it the land of the waving grass. The river takes a sharp bend and then heads northward into the mountain. But you'll want to head south through the grasslands. It's Mohak country. I'm told they've lived there for centuries. When you get to the land of the waving grass, you won't be too far from the home of Chief Ayenwatha."

Brigit looked to Erik to get his reaction. Before he could say anything, Maengun, who had returned to the fire, spoke up.

"Are you sure you want to go to Ayenwatha? Maybe he sent that ambiguous message to draw you to him. Maybe he wants to seize the necklace from you. He does have a daughter of his own now. Maybe he wants it for her. I think you were right to search on your own. If you go there, you may lose what you have and fail to find what you seek."

He said it with so much concern and sincerity that flickers of doubt danced through her thoughts. Erik could see the look of confusion come again to her face. He wonder what power the young man had that Brigit could so easily be swayed by him?

Erik forced his own face into the smile of a simpleton as he spoke, "Why the land of the waving grass, sure enough it is that I remember that land. I was there a few short years after Ayen and Skoth forged the Peace of Alba. 'Twas a delightful land. It was near mid-summer and the people, Ayen's people, were kind and generous. If you'd be wanting us to travel along that path, why I'd say it would be better than climbing these hills, or riding these rapids, or avoiding the trolls. I'd like to go that way, iffen you have a mind to."

Wulf looked a little sideways at Erik. By now he knew him well enough to sense when the elder man was purposely shifting from his normal mode of conversation to some other mode. Sometimes he did it to teach a lesson, but not this time. For a few moments, Wulf wondered why Erik was dissembling. His eyes darted from Erik to Brigit, and then to Maengun, and then back again to Erik. Suddenly he realized what Erik was doing.

Wulf cleared his throat to catch Brigit's attention and said, "I'd go along with you if you want to go through the land of the waving grass. I'd much prefer that over traveling by water, all the while wondering when I was going to fall in it again and have a beautiful woman rescue me."

Shivon interjected, "Aye, me too. As exciting as running a rapids might be. I'd like to be off of it, and stay out of it, for a wee bit."

Brigit gave her head a little shake, as if clearing the cobwebs from her mind. She smiled at the way her friends were joking about their experiences with water. With a sigh of determination, she gave her response.

"So shall it be - through the land of the waving grass we go!"

Chapter 36 - Two Rivers

When the rafts finally arrived at the portage landing above the village of Two Rivers, Wulf was more than ready to jump off and never get on a raft again.

The five travelers settled up with the crew chief and said their goodbyes to the men who had transported them down the river. Shaemus had given them directions to a hostel where they might get a meal and spend the night.

"Nothing fancy, mind you," he said, "but if it is solid fare and clean bed you desire, then you'll find it there. They will also be able to tell you where to go if you hope to find some horses for your journey."

It was a small town and they easily found their way. They found that Shaemus had described the accommodations aptly; and given their days camping as they had come down the river, they were more than agreeable. However, Brigit was disappointed that they could find no horses for sale. She had hoped to make the journey quickly, and if what Sheamus and the others had told her was accurate, then within a couple of days they could be to Ayenwatha's city of Tionnontoguen. Without the horses the trip would be more on the order of at least three or four days.

After a good night's rest and an ample breakfast, they shouldered their packs and headed up the road that paralleled the Sacandaga River. By all appearances, it was a well traveled road and they could expect to encounter numerous people as they walked it.

Wulf felt good to have his staff in hand and his feet on solid ground, with no threat of having to board any kind of craft anytime soon. However, he was a little uncomfortable with his walking companion. It was

Maengun.

When they had assembled that morning to begin their trek up the river valley that day, Erik had suggested that he take the lead, joking that since he was old and getting tired from this journey, he was afraid that if he was bringing up the rear those young legs of the rest of them would walk away from him and leave him in the dust. Wulf had chuckled at the comment, but was wise enough to figure out that Erik wanted to be the scout and wanted to be the first to encounter whomever they might meet on the road. What he didn't immediately consider is that this meant there would be a good likelihood of him accompanying Maengun as they walked.

And so it was that Erik walked by himself far ahead of the rest of the party. He was followed by Shivon and Brigit, who engaged in lively conversation as they walked. Several paces behind them walked Maengun and Wulf. Conversation between them was minimal, and the tension was palpable.

They did encounter and pass by the occasional person or small group of people heading toward Two Rivers. They would give friendly greetings as they passed, but no one seemed inclined to want to stop and visit, which was fine with Brigit. Now that she had decided to go to Ayenwatha, she wanted to get there as quickly as possible.

After a while of silently plodding along with Maengun, Wulf decided to initiate a conversation.

"That sure was an unforgettable ride, and for me an uncomfortable ride, down the river. Those rapids were terrifying. There were several times that I thought I might fall in. Weren't you scared?"

"No."

"I mean, you fell in once, didn't you think it might

happen again?"

"It could have, but it didn't."

"I sure would like to think that if it had happened to me that you would give me a hand to pull me out."

Maengun gave a brief sideways glance toward Wulf. "I'd reach out my hand to you."

Now it was Wulf's turn to give Maengun a brief glance. And he thought - yes, you might reach your hand out to me, but would it be to knock it away like you did to Shivon? Since he had Maengun talking, he decided to keep him talking.

"That's reassuring, to know that in a pinch I can depend on you. Maengun, can I ask you about something else?"

Maengun glanced toward his walking companion, but then turned his head forward again. He was curious what this pale one wanted to know.

"Yes. Go ahead."

"It seems to me that you don't like me all that much. I'd like to understand why that is so."

It was several steps before Maengun answered.

"You don't belong here."

"How do you mean that? Here with Brigit? Here in Eirgalon?"

"You and your people have no claim to this land. Perhaps it is fine for you to come and visit us here, but you are an outsider."

It was still unclear to Wulf what Maengun was saying, so he continued to ask questions.

"You mean that because I come from Hamburg, across the sea, I shouldn't be here."

"You have no ties to this land. Your people belong in their own lands. Why do they come here to take our lands away from us?"

"But, I'm not here to take any land away from you."

"So you say. But look at the history of all the men and women who have come here from across the sea and now control this land."

"But what of Brigit? You seem to like her. Doesn't she belong here?"

Maengun suddenly sensed that he might have said too much to this companion that he had considered an inept outlander. He didn't like the way this conversation was going, so it was time to change directions.

"Ahh, Brigit. What an intelligent and intriguing woman she is. And that Shivon, with the flaming red hair. She is one of a kind. I've noticed that you've been paying extra attention to her the last couple of days."

Brigit and Shivon had been walking several paces ahead of the men. Suddenly they stopped and turned about.

Brigit spoke, "I think I just heard our names mentioned. Have you two been talking about us?"

Maengun was not surprised, for he had purposely spoken louder and projected his voice in hopes that Wulf wouldn't notice, but that the women would hear him. Apparently, his plan worked. Wulf began to blush but said nothing.

Maengun, his voice full of charm, replied, "How could we but help to talk of you? This landscape is beautiful, but the two of you have been walking in front of us for a couple of hours."

As they stood there and playfully bantered back and forth, none of them noticed that far ahead of them Erik had stopped and was talking to a man on horseback.

Chapter 37 - Sacandaga River Valley

When they did resume their journey, they looked up the road to see how far Erik was ahead of them, and they observed the horseman riding away from Erik. They voiced curiosity about what had transpired, but the answer to that would have to wait. They couldn't tell if Erik had glanced back at them, although they assumed he would have. Erik simply began walking down the road the direction the horseman had gone. By this time, the horseman had rounded a corner in the road and was out of sight.

Shivon said, "Well, I wonder what that was about. Let's pick up our pace and catch up to him."

Brigit responded, "There is no need to do that. If it was something we needed to know right away, Erik would have waited for us. We'll just have to be patient. He can tell us about it when we stop for lunch."

The sun was high overhead when they stopped for lunch. The road had followed the course of the Sacandaga River as it wound its way down the valley. The bluffs on the sides of the valley were not as high as the valley of the Mahakentuck, but they seemed high because the valley was still relatively narrow at this point. Erik had found a pleasant spot to sit and watch the river while they rested for lunch. They caught up to him and joined him sitting atop the high bank of the river where the waters tumbled about several small boulders.

As Brigit sat down next to him, she said, "So are you going to tell us about the horseman?"

Erik munching away on a hard cracker and some venison jerky he had pull out of his sack, mumbled, "What horseman?"

"The horseman you talked to on the road, and who

then headed the way we are going."

"Oh, that one. I wasn't sure you had noticed."

"Well, I did notice."

"I thought you might be too busy joking around with your friends to notice him."

"I did. What was he doing? What did he have to say."

"He came up from the river right in front of me. Maybe he had been doing some fishing. Maybe had to stop and relieve himself. He didn't say what he was doing. He simply said 'what's going on?' That's his folks' way of saying 'hello'."

"I know that, Erik." Exasperation tinged her voice. "Was there more?"

"A wee bit."

Brigit reigned in her impatience with him and politely said, "Erik, you've teased me enough. Now will you please tell me what you think I need to know about that conversation."

"Well, now. That's a lot more specific. I reckon you'd like to know that Ayenwatha had a hunch you might be heading this way. He asked Sagoye, that's Waneek's son, who lives in the land of the waving grass with the Bear Clan of the Mohak people, to send a scout this way. That horseman you saw was the scout. He invited us to to come to Kwahri in the land of the waving grass."

"How did you respond?"

"Why, I told him that you were heading that direction. You still intend to do that, don't you?"

"Of course I do."

Maengun said, "So they will be expecting us. Will they be sending horses for us to make our journey faster? Are they sending people to meet us?"

"I don't rightly know. He didn't say."

Wulf said, "I, for one, don't mind walking."

Erik chuckled. "You do look more at ease on solid ground."

Shivon added her thoughts. "I don't mind walking, but I hope we find a nice place to stop for the night. After the days on the rafts, my legs will be tired by the end of the day."

Erik said, "The scout indicated that there is a longhouse after a few more bends in the river. The valley will start widening out where the bluffs are higher on the northern shore and much lower to the south. He was sure they would take us in for the night if we can make it that far."

With a touch of sarcasm Brigit said, "Sounds like that horseman did tell you a wee bit."

With a slight smile Erik responded, "Aye. I reckon he did, at that."

Maengun hemmed and hawed as if he was deciding to say something. Brigit noticed and told him to speak up. He sounded sincerely concerned.

"I know you have said you trust Ayenwatha, but I urge you to be cautious. As a young boy, growing up in the land of my people, I often was told the story about how Chief Ayenwatha had been the most trusted and loyal of the Iroquois warriors. But then in the heat of battle, he turned on his leader and betrayed him. Are you so sure he can be trusted? What if he betrays you the way he betrayed his leader? I don't want to see you hurt."

The others noticed a cloud of doubt fall over Brigit's eyes.

"But I've known him my whole life. He's been like an uncle to me."

Erik jumped back into the conversation. "Ach, lassie, remember the time he took you hunting in the hunting woods south of Tionnontoguen, and that wild boar charged you? He pushed you to the side as he speared it while the boar's tusk slashed his leg instead of you. He still bears that scar earned in the saving of your life. You can trust him as you do your own father."

Brigit's smiled at the memory and her eyes brightened.

"Of course. I remember that day. Mother thought I was too young to go hunting, but Ayen promised to watch out for me."

"And that he did. At the risk of his own life, I might add. You can be sure he harbors no ill intentions for you."

Maengun said softly, "But what if there are some around him who do?"

Brigit replied, "Well, then I have the four of you around me to protect me!"

Chapter 38 - Longhouse

Late that afternoon the five travelers approached the longhouse that Erik had spoken of. Several children came running to met them. They chattered excited greetings and escorted them to the central firepit of the community. There, seated upon one of the logs near the fire, was an elderly gentleman. He motioned them to come to him, and as they did so he used a walking staff to raise himself to a standing position. He spoke the first words of greeting.

"I am called Bear Claw. I welcome you to our longhouse."

Erik took the lead in giving the response, "I am called Erik." He motioned to Brigit and said, "And this is the daughter of High King Skoth and Queen Evlin. She is called Brigit." Then in turn he introduced Wulf, Shivon, and Maengun.

Speaking in the polygot Celtic tongue of Eirgalon, Bear Claw said, "You honor us with your visit. Would you accept the hospitality of our fire? We would provide you with food and lodging."

Wulf was struck both by fact the that this Mohak man spoke Celtic, as well as by the formality of the exchange at this habitation on the edge of the Rondax mountain wilderness. He decided that, if given the chance, he would talk to this man about how this came to be.

They spent an enjoyable evening eating and visiting with the men, women, and children of the longhouse. It was a warm early summer evening and the outdoor longhouse fire was kept burning late into the night. The others had gone to their beds for the night, but Bear Claw, Erik, and Wulf remained gazing into the fire and

195

talking.

Finally, Wulf asked, "How is it that you have come to speak the language of Eirgalon so well? You speak it better than I do."

Bear Claw laughed. "I've lived in Eirgalon longer than you have, though in my youth we called it by another name."

Wulf blushed slightly, for it was true. He was a newcomer to this land.

Bear Claw went on to tell him the story of how his people had been called upon by Malsum to assemble and to make war on the pale ones of Eirgalon. Bear Claw had been with Ayenwatha on the plain of Alba when Ayenwatha had rebelled against Malsum and forged a lasting peace with High King Skoth of Eirgalon. In the years that followed, Bear Claw had traveled about the land, but in later years had returned to the longhouse where he had spent some of his childhood years.

Bear Claw grinned at Erik and said, "And I remember you, Erik, Shield-of-the-King. I watched you on the plain of Alba, standing guard with Sagoye, as our leaders met."

Erik reminisced, "Those were interesting days. So much happened so fast."

Bear Claw mused, "Back then you were guarding the king and queen. Now you travel with a princess and a shaman. Looks like these days are also interesting."

Wulf looked puzzled. "Shaman? What shaman?"

Both Erik and Bear Claw turned and looked at Wulf. They said nothing. The fire crackled loudly and cast flickering shadows about them.

Wulf said, "What?" Then a look of incredulity spread across Wulf's face. "You mean me?"

Bear Claw smirked and said, "If that druid's staff

you carry didn't mark you as such, the way you dealt with the windigos certainly did."

"How do you know about that?"

"I sometimes travel far in my dreams. It is a gift I have. I may be getting old and feeble. But my dreams can still be strong. Now, tell me what happened as you remember it. Then I will tell you if I saw anything different about it. It may be that you can gain insight from my dream."

So Wulf told him the tale. Erik had to fill in a few spots, for Wulf was not totally aware of all that had transpired when the trolls attacked, and when he sat stunned during the aftermath.

The fire burned low and Erik tossed a couple more logs onto the fire.

When they finished their tale, Bear Claw sat silently gazing into the fire for several moments. Then he said, "That matches what I have seen, but there is more. You mentioned that young Maengun who is with you now, disappeared after the attack. I didn't see him in my vision, but I did see a wolf, holding a bow in its jaws, fleeing through the blazing trees."

Erik asked, "And you did not see Maengun being carried off by one of the beasts?"

"Not in my dream. I saw no one captured by the windigo, although I did see the Anishanaabe men fall before them."

Wulf queried, "Can you tell me more about the wolf? I remember wolves howling during the attack, but I didn't see any?"

Bear Claw answered, "I thought it most unusual that a wolf would seize a bow in its jaws. It was a huge wolf. Perhaps what I saw was symbolic. Perhaps it represented a powerful weapon."

Erik stroked his beard. "Or, perhaps there is more to Maengun than meets the eye."

Bear Claw asked, "You think this wolf I saw represents Maengun?"

Erik pursed his lips. "Or perhaps is him."

Bear Claws eye went wide as his jaw hardened and he whispered, "Limikkin."

Wulf was puzzled. "You mean a shapeshifter?"

Erik answered him, "Aye, laddie. They are an evil lot."

"If he was, wouldn't we be able to see that?"

Erik shook his head. "Sadly, no. I've had dealings with a couple of them, they pass as a normal human. They look just like one of us. In fact, at times they can make themselves mimic one of us. Why, if I didn't know better, you could be a limikkin sitting here in front of me, pretending to be my friend, Wulf."

Wulf's jaws clenched with a determination Erik hadn't noticed before, Then Wulf said to them, "Tell me everything you know about such creatures. I need to know."

Bear Claw nodded with understanding. "Spoken as a shaman true. Knowledge is power. I will begin, and Erik may add when he chooses."

Time slipped past them and Erik had to put more logs on the fire as they shared their knowledge of limikkins with Wulf. Bear Claw related stories of the legends and lore of his people and Erik shared his personal experience with the limikkins that had abducted Evlin, including the actions of the Green Man in saving her from their grasp.

When they had finished they noticed that Wulf was holding his oak staff. They couldn't remember seeing him pick it up, but now he was holding it tightly with one hand and running his other hand along the grain of its wood and touching the symbols Master Unaine had carved into it.

With his gaze intent upon the staff he said, "Thank you. Do you know where Unaine harvested the fine wood of this staff?"

Erik murmured, "No, he never told me."

Wulf looked up at him, "It was taken from a young sapling growing near the remains of an ancient oak fallen on the forest floor - Fearglas' resting-place."

"What? I never told Unaine where that was. How do you know this?"

Wulf cocked his head slightly to one side, as if in thought. "I just know it."

Bear Claw said, "A shaman true."

Erik stroked his beard again. "I think it is time to turn in for the night. We have a long walk again tomorrow."

Wulf replied, "The two of you go on in. I think I'll sit here for a while as the fire goes out and the embers cool."

The elder men looked at each other, nodded to each other, and then went to the longhouse for the night. Wulf sat for a long time by that fire, watching its glow diminish. Finally, during the hour of the wolf (the hour of deepest darkness an hour before the first light of the sun begins to brighten the skies) he too arose and went into the longhouse.

Chapter 39 - On the Road to Kwahri

When they arose in the morning, Maengun was gone. Brigit expressed surprised when Erik asked her about him.

She said, "Didn't you see him leave? He left in the middle of the night when you were still outside at the fire."

"We saw no one leaving."

She seemed puzzled. "Perhaps he went out the opposite end of the longhouse."

Erik gave her a dubious look. "And why would he do that? Where was he going? What was he doing?"

By this time Wulf and Shivon had joined them.

Brigit continued her response to Erik. "I don't know. He said he had a strong premonition that danger lay ahead of us and that he was going ahead of us. He said he hoped to rejoin us in Kwahri."

Shivon gave a questioning look and Brigit said, "That's the name of the major settlement of the Bear clan of the Mohak in the land of the waving grass. It is where Sagoye awaits us. From what Bear Claw tells me, it is two day's walk from here."

Shivon noticed that as Brigit gave this explanation to her, unspoken messages were going back and forth between Erik and Wulf in the glances they exchanged. She determined to ask them later about it.

As they made their farewells with the people who had hosted them during the night, Bear Claw extended an invitation to Wulf.

"I hope you come back some day. Mayhap, there are pieces of your learning in which I might give you aid. I would be honored to share my knowledge with you."

Wulf smiled. "I'd like that. If possible, I will come."

Then Bear Claw turned his words to Brigit, "As for you, young princess, I know not where your journey will take you, but you have three loyal companions standing here with you."

Brigit said, "Only three? What of Maengun?"

"He is not here. I cannot say about him. But in these three, who stand before us, I sense loyalty."

She politely thanked him, and then they were on their way. The road continued to follow the course of the river. The valley widened slightly and the hills that surrounded them diminished in height. Much of their day was spent traveling through woods, although there were frequent openings and many sizable glens. It was a peaceful time of walking together. They occasionally encountered travelers going the other direction and would briefly stop to ask them if they had encountered Maengun. None of them had.

It was mid-afternoon and they were walking abreast in a large open area, when Wulf asked Brigit what she knew of the shapeshifters called limikkins. Brigit's body noticeably tensed before she responded.

"I've been told about them, but I have never met one. At least that I can remember. Have you been told about the time one sought to attack me?"

When Wulf shook his head, she went on, "I was just a babe and my mother had laid me on the ground as she and her friends made supplication at a sacred grove near New Alba. A limikkin in the form of a rattlesnake coiled to strike at me. I have been told that it was frozen in mid-strike when I raised my hand in defense."

In astonishment, Wulf exclaimed, "What? You have such power?"

Brigit shook her head. "I don't know. People tell me I did it, yet I feel no such power within me, or that I can touch."

"But yet the action of the limikkin was stopped." He paused as he thought, and then spoke again. "What powers do they have? And how do you kill one?"

"I don't know that I know all their powers, but I can tell you what my teachers told me."

For the next several minutes, Brigit took on the role of teacher. She recounted the legend, lore, and knowledge about limikkins that she had been given as she grew up. Throughout the sharing, Erik would often nod his head in agreement, but added no comments. Wulf soaked it in, as did Shivon who walked with them.

Brigit asked, "Is there anything else? I think that is pretty much all I know about them."

"One more thing," Wulf briefly hesitated, "is it possible to recognize one if they walk among us?"

She slowly shook her head. "Not that I know of. I have been told that my grandfather, Fearglas, could, but if that is so, I don't know. I wish it was as easy as looking into their eyes, but I just don't know."

Wulf nodded his head in appreciation for what Brigit had shared with him. The conversation moved to other topics, and Wulf's thoughts moved inward as he considered what he had been told. The terrain shifted to a more densely wooded path wide enough for only two to walk side by side. Erik took the lead with Brigit, and Wulf dropped back. Shivon dropped back with him.

After a while she said softly to him, "So what is it that you and Erik were saying with those 'all-so-knowing' glances you were exchanging before we left this morning? Was it about limikkins or was it something else?"

Wulf motioned with his hand to slow down. They kept walking but slowed down enough so that soon they were several paces behind the others. If they kept their voices low, the others wouldn't hear them.

"Listen, Shivon, I trust you, and I trust Erik, but I worry about Brigit. Erik and I fear she seems far too trusting of Maengun and I just don't trust him at all. "

She snorted lightly and whispered back, "Well, sure enough, you know I don't trust him."

"Last night we had a conversation with Bear Claw about limikkins. A thought flashed in my mind that perhaps Maengun was such. But I can't prove anything about it. I just know there is something about him I don't like."

"I agree. If we ever see him again just tell me what to do."

"Did you see him leave last night?"

"I heard him whispering with Brigit. But then he went back to his sleeping pallet near the far end of the longhouse. I couldn't make out what they were saying and I never saw him leave."

"The way he just disappears like that, like the way he disappeared when the windigos attacked, makes me suspicious. I know it doesn't prove anything, but..." there was a long pause before Wulf continued, "I wonder what he is up to. Could he actually be a limikkin? If he was a limikkin, why would he be deceiving us, and more importantly - what is he after with Brigit?"

Just then, Brigit turned around and said, "Hey, you two sluggards - why are you lagging behind? What are you whispering about?"

Shivon reached out to touch Wulf on the arm and said, "Oh, Wulf was distracting me as he was telling me about his homeland. I'd say he is trying to practice his charms on me."

That made Wulf blush and start to protest, causing Brigit to chuckle and say, "Well don't fall so far behind. We want to make it to the next village by nightfall."

Chapter 40 - The Bend

It was late afternoon when they came to the great bend of the Sacandaga. The vista to the west opened up before them as they walked out of the canopy covered path. Before them lay the land of the waving grass. It was a wide expanse of meadows and marshland. After cutting between high slopes, the river curved away to the north. Where the river bent northward, a small creek came from the south and west out of the fascinating land of the waving grass. It was quite a change from the rugged valleys and mountains they had traversed. The road split where the creek entered the river. One path crossed the creek and followed the river northward. The other curved to the southwest and followed the southern edge of the grasslands where they met low hills.

On the south side of the river's bend the land rose to a high hill. Upon this hill was situated a log palisade. It wasn't as large as the major Mohak castles on the Mohak River, but it was the first one Wulf had seen. As they followed the road uphill to the palisade, they noticed a party coming to the palisade from the opposite direction. Three men were leading a horse, and on the horse a bundle was slung.

Erik said to the others, "This doesn't look good. That's they way they carry a dead man. And I recognize that horse. It is the scout's horse."

They picked up their pace and came to the gate of the palisade at the same time as the other party. There were no guards at the gate. During these decades of peace, the practice of posting guard during the day had been done away with, although a watch was still kept on duty during the night.

Brigit and her companions allowed the others to

enter first, and followed them into the central courtyard. The elders of the community gathered about them and the men who led the horse told their story.

They had started down the road toward Kwahri during the mid- morning. Then they had stopped for a brief rest at noon, where one of the small streams ran down from the hills into the waving grass marshlands. While they were resting, they heard the snickering of a horse in the shrubs by the river bank. When they went to investigate, they found the horse tied to a bush and the body of this man dead on the ground next to it. Some of the man's clothes had been torn, as if he had been attacked by a wild animal, and his throat had been ripped open. So they wrapped him in the sleeping roll that was in the pack on the horse, placed him over the horse's back, and made their way back to the Bend longhouse.

One of the elders asked, "Is this the man who lodged with us last night? That is his horse."

Sadly, one of the men answered, "It is."

Brigit asked, "Why would someone do this?"

All eyes turned to her. While women held a place of respect in Mohak culture - and in all of Eirgalon for this was now a part of Greater Eirgalon - it surprised the people to have a young and unknown woman speak in this situation.

The elders glanced to Erik, for as an elder warrior who accompanied this young woman they expected that he would be the one in authority. Erik returned their glance and then by a subtle head motion he redirected their gaze to Brigit.

An elder asked Brigit, "That is a good question. And who are you to be asking it?"

"I am Brigit, daughter of High King Skoth and Queen Evlin. This man was taking news of our approach to Sagoye at Kwahri."

"It is our honor to greet you, Princess Brigit. But since you know this man, perhaps you know more than we do. He did stop here last night, but he said nothing of his mission, only that he was headed to Kwahri."

"It is possible that he was attacked because of his knowledge of us, but are there other possibilities?"

"None that we know of. Our land has been at peace since your father made peace with Ayenwatha. There used to be Anishanaabe raids on our lands, but it has been many years since the last one, and this murdering of travelers is not their style."

Now Erik spoke, "You have spoken true. The Anishanaabe have a reputation for being strong adversaries, but seldom would they attack travelers. Perchance did any of you encounter a single young man, with striking appearance of comely looks? He was traveling with us, but left us and went on ahead of us."

The others looked from person to person, and all shook their heads in denial.

A different elder said, "We have not seen him. Perhaps the same tragedy that befell this young man has befallen your friend. We will keep a look out for him. But as for the four of you, please accept the hospitality of our village. Take sustenance with us and rest from your journey here for the night. In spite of who, or what, might be out there, you will be safe in our lodge."

The men of the village led the horse and its human bundle away. They would take care of the body and give it the proper respect and attention that their customs called for.

After the evening meal, Erik asked Brigit to take a walk with him that they might talk in private. They left the others and went strolling outside the palisade. They walked several paces down hill toward the waving grasses of the marshland and then sat down. It was a long conversation and the sun was setting before they returned to their host's lodge inside the log palisade. When they did, they noticed that guards were now posted at the palisade gates.

Wulf and Shivon were left alone when Erik and Brigit left, and Shivon suggested that they find a high spot on one of the palisade towers that they might watch the setting sun settle into the hills on the far side of the waving grasses.

The warm summer evening was calm and peaceful. The season was approaching the summer solstice and a near full moon was rising in the east as the sun touched the western horizon. They sat in silence for a while looking at the awe inspiring sight, although for brief moments Wulf surreptitiously glanced at Shivon. Her flaming red hair was set ablaze by the rays of the setting sun and she looked stunning. They were already sitting close to each other, but suddenly Shivon edged over until she was touching Wulf and leaned her head to the side so that it rested upon his shoulder.

"It is such a beautiful sight, isn't it, Wulf?"

"Yes, it is. This is such a wild and wonderful land. I never stop being amazed by the sights I see."

They made pleasant observations about the weather and the view for several minutes, but then Shivon ventured into personal territory.

"Wulf, I really like you. I mean, well, there is more to it than just like." She reached out and placed her hand upon his hand, and then pulled it into her lap and held it with both her hands. "When this quest is finished, assuming we live through it, will you stay here in Eirgalon, or will you go back across the sea?"

"I have thought about that. I don't know. My family is back home, but there is something about this land. I want to stay here. But I just don't know."

Shivon gave a little laugh and said, "Well, sure enough I think there are reasons for you to stay here."

She then turned her head and leaned up to kiss him. Gentle was her kiss at first, but then she held it and it grew in passion. The action took him by surprise, but he soon returned it with equal ardor.

The sun had long since set and the moon had risen high in the sky before the two of them finally descended from the parapet and made their way to their host's longhouse.

Chapter 41 - Kwahri

Brigit and her companions rose early because they were determined to get on the road early and to arrive at Kwahri by midday. They spoke but little as they walked, for each one had serious thoughts that were occupying his or her mind, as well as their watching with special vigilance for any dangers on the road. The scout had been killed on this stretch of road, and it was possible that whoever attacked him was lying in wait for them.

Shivon was thinking of how she had become enamored with the young man from across the sea and of how she was also drawn to the princess of Eirgalon. Wulf's thoughts fluctuated between the thoughts of Shivon, Brigit, and the call of his emerging druidic powers. Brigit's long discussion with Erik caused her to think about her quest, and her relationships with Shivon, Wulf, and Maengun. As for Eric, he kept the bulk of his attention on their terrain and the possible dangers about them. However, he too wondered how the relationships between his young companions would eventually work themselves out.

The road skirted the southern edge of the land of the waving grass. There were many paths that led into the tall grasses. A springtime of normal rainfall had followed a winter of more than normal snow in this valley so the grasslands were still wet and green. In fact, in many places they were more marshlands than solid ground. Later in the summer, much of the land would dry out, but it was still dangerous to enter the marshlands without an experienced guide. So the travelers kept on the main road to Kwahri.

At mid-morning they came to a place where a bridge had been built across a creek and where the grasses towered above them on both sides of the road. Soon after crossing the bridge and walking for a short distance, they could see the castle of Kwahri rising on a distant hill at the southwestern edge of the land of the waving grasses. They could see that there were several longhouses inside a large palisade of logs. It was much larger than the village they had left that morning and was the largest habitation they had seen since leaving Ticonderoga weeks ago.

There were no guards standing watch at the gates; however, there were tall watchtowers that were set high on the palisade walls. The travelers could be certain that they were observed as they approached. Indeed, as they came near to the gate, a contingent came out to greet them. One of them was none other than Sagoye.

He recognized Brigit for he had been to Tara several times during the course of her life, and he also immediately recognized his old friend, Erik. His history with Erik went back to the time of their standing guard for their respective leaders on the plain of Alba when the Peace of Eirgalon was forged. The mutual respect they had shared during those days had developed into a genuine friendship over the years. Indeed, since Waneek was Sagoye's mother, and Erik had a unique relationship with Waneek, they were family of a sort.

Sagoye greeted Princess Brigit in formal terms and then he went to Erik and greeted him in a more casual way as old friends. They clasped arms and slapped each other heartily on the back. Brigit then made introductions of Shivon and Wulf, whom Sagoye eyed over carefully.

To all of them Sagoye said, "Welcome to Kwahri. Herein lies an ancient longhouse of the Bear Clan of the Mohak people. My wife is a member of that clan, and you are welcome in our home."

They responded with appreciation, and Wulf queried him, "You said it is your wife's clan. If it is your home, then isn't it your clan?"

Sagoye smiled, "I was born in the Wolf Clan of my people, as was Ayenwatha; but when we marry, we go to the clan of our wife and live with them. Our children are members of the Bear Clan."

"So are you of the Bear, or of the Wolf, clan?"

"By birth, I am of the Wolf, and I am still considered to be of the Wolf Clan, but the line of the family runs through the mother's side. My wife's mother is one of the clan leaders of the Bear Clan in this place. You will meet her soon. I deem her to be as formidable and wise as my own mother, Waneek."

Erik added, "And that, my boy, is saying something!"

Sagoye said, "But enough talking out here. Come. Enter Kwahri. Come to our home. Enjoy our hospitality. Food and lodging are yours for the night. We will talk later. Come."

But before they could turn and enter the gate, Erik stopped them and said to Sagoye, "There is something I must let you know without delay. The scout you sent out to look for us was murdered on the way. He met us, and I sent him back to you. He apparently stayed overnight in the nearest village and then on the following day was slain on the road. We encountered the people who found his body a distance off the road. They took his body back to the village."

"This is troubling news. I will have to investigate this. But for now, come with me."

They followed Sagoye through the gates of the palisade and into the main courtyard of the castle of

Kwahri. Wulf noted to himself that it was similar to the last palisaded village they had stayed in but it was on a much larger scale. They followed Sagoye through the central courtyard, to the largest and most impressive of the longhouses. Sitting outside the door of the longhouse, and working on making some dried pemmican, were three elderly women. One of them was the mother of Sagoye's wife.

She looked up from her task as they approached and said, "Greetings, Chief Sagoye. I see you bring guests to our longhouse. Are these friends of yours?"

"They are indeed, Wise Woman Kahn-Tineta."

She spoke first to Sagoye, "An interesting group it is that you bring to lodge among us: a princess of Eirgalon, an old warrior, a young shaman, and a young female warrior. They are welcome among us, though I would hear from them concerning their intentions." Then she turned her attention to the guests, "Welcome. We give you the hospitality of our home. There is food available near the fire. Our young maidens will assist you. Go. Eat. And then return to sit in our circle and talk with us."

They did as they were instructed. Sagoye helped them find places for their gear in the longhouse and then he led them to the fire where a hearty stew was being served.

As they were eating, Wulf said to Sagoye, "The wise woman called you 'chief' - how can you be their chief if you are not from their clan?"

Sagoye smiled, "I see that your companions have not taught you all of our ways. As I told you earlier, we of the Mohak people have several clans. Most villages have longhouses from several clans within their walls. The leaders of those clans are the wise women. The wise women are the ones who choose men of good character and skill to lead the village as their chiefs. I am honored that they have chosen me to be one of our leaders."

Wulf asked another question, "And how did the wise woman know so much about us?"

Sagoye smiled. "Long ago I learned not to question how it is that wise women know so much. It is enough that she knows."

After they had eaten their fill, they returned to find Kahn-Tineta and the other two women sitting on some blankets near the longhouse.

Kahn-Tineta spoke as they approached, "Come. Join us in a circle. May our hearts be pure and our conversation be true."

The four travelers and Sagoye sat down and joined the three wise women in their circle. Then Kahn-Tineta fixed her gaze upon Brigit and said, "Daughter of the Bear-Witch. My name means 'One who makes the grasses wave' and I speak for my clan. What would you desire of the Bear Clan?"

Brigit replied, "I don't claim to speak for my mother, or even to ask a favor in her name, but I have come to seek understanding concerning this necklace I wear and concerning completion of my father's task. I don't even know what to ask; but if there is any guidance you may have for me, I would welcome it."

A slight smile curled upon Kahn-Tineta's face. This was a polite and respectful request from a young woman who wielded position and power.

"The blood of the Bear-Witch runs in your veins, young Brigit. You may not have felt its power, but as the clan leader of the Bear Clan of our people, I can assure you that I sense it."

A flicker of surprise crossed Brigit's face. She said

nothing, but nodded in acceptance of the observation.

"You are growing in wisdom, young one. Think for a moment about what it is that you value the most. While you think, I will have some words with the others."

She turned her head slightly and focused her gaze upon Wulf.

"What have we here? A shaman not from our land, yet of our land. You carry the staff of Celtic druids, yet it is unfinished. As you sit, I see your hand idly touch that divot in the wood - as if you sense its lack. Why is there no spirit stone embedded there?"

Wulf's face furrowed in thought. "I have wondered about this impression. Master Unaine bequeathed me this staff. Yet I was told little about it. This seems to be a flaw, yet it is not. What are these spirit stones of which you speak?"

"They are a gift of the earth to us. They are a power of the earth and sky to protect the world that is. Perhaps one day you will acquire one. The earth often gives as it is needed."

Then Kahn-Tineta turn her gaze upon Shivon. Kahn-Tineta smiled a knowing smile. "And here is the maiden warrior. I can see in your eyes the vigor for life and the passion in your heart. Where will your heart lead you? You may ask a question of me, but as for the answer - ah, well dear - you can only follow your heart."

Shivon, usually one for many words, said nothing. She pursed her lips slightly and sighed with resignation. Or, perhaps it was determination.

Then Kahn-Tineta looked to Erik. They talked for several minutes. Erik gave to her and Sagoye a brief summary of their trip and the difficulties that they had encountered. He asked for no advice, nor was any given.

He ended with sharing his curiosity about what had happened to Maengun, for Maengun had left word with Brigit that he hoped to rejoin them at Kwahri.

Kahn-Tineta nodded in acceptance for all that Erik had shared and then turned to one of her wise woman companions, as she responded to Erik.

"This is Genesse, clan leader of the Wolf longhouse in Kwahri. Genesse, perhaps you will share with our guests your knowledge of Maengun."

Chapter 42 - The Circle Conversation

Genesse took a long breathe and then began her tale.

"A young man by that name encountered some men from my long house who were going out hunting in the waving grass. They met the young Anishanaabe man on the road near the bridge that crosses the stream through the waving grasses. He told them that he had been attacked by an evil limikkin and that he needed to get to his people as soon as possible for healing. There is a small village of the Anishanaabe that lies about a day's walk west of here, near where the earth gives up its spirit stones. Rather than bring him here, a couple of the men took him in the direction of that village. He told the ones who returned here to look for his friends, who would be following him within a few days, and to then ask those friends to come to him at that village. We have heard nothing of him, or our men who went with him, since that time."

It probably wasn't Wulf's place to speak, but he did anyway. "You're telling us that he said HE was attacked by a limikkin? What were his injuries? How do you know he was telling you the truth?"

"My people said they saw no physical injuries, only that he seemed weak and that he asked for help." Then with a little disdain in her voice she added, "Should we not respond to people in need? We are people who give help when we are asked. If he was your friend, I would think you would be grateful for that."

"Hmmph. I'm not so sure he really is a friend."

Sitting next to him, Brigit recoiled slightly from him when he said that. "Wulf! Enough! I know you don't like him, but he IS our friend, and we have a responsibility to him." She turned back to Genesse. "Of course we will go to him. You have been most generous to give us hospitality for the night. In the morning we will leave and go to him. Believe me, I know how dangerous limikkins can be. If he needs our help, he shall have it."

"Devotion to a friend is admirable," said Kahn-Tineta, "but what of your questions and your quest?"

Brigit pursed her lips. "One day's travel to the west in order to give aid to a friend will not hinder my quest. It may even take me in the right direction, since I'm not really sure of where to go. As you said to Shivon, one must follow her heart. In the absence of specific information to guide my quest, I will follow my heart, which says to go give aid to a friend in need. Or do you have other words to guide me?"

"True friends are wealth beyond compare. You will be well served if you treasure and protect them. I have no words of direction to give you. But perhaps Sagoye does. I understand his cousin, Ayenwatha sent word to him that you might come this way. Perhaps he sent other words as well."

Sagoye nodded in affirmation. "He sent written words. Words from the hand of his wife, Enat, who is of Fada Innis."

"She is a wise woman in her own right. Would you share those words with us?"

"They are intended for Princess Brigit. I will place them in her hands and she may decided if she would share them with us."

Sagoye then reached into a pocket of his leather jerkin and pulled out a small leather pouch. He leaned over and handed it to Brigit. She took the pouch and opened it. Withdrawing a sealed parchment from it, she looked at the wax seal. Impressed in the wax was an image of the Green Man. She couldn't help but smile, for she remembered the time as a young girl when Enat had shown her the medallion of the Green Man and told her its story. It had been given to Enat by Enat's mother, and it had played an important role in the abduction and rescue of Brigit's mother, Evlin.

Then Brigit brought her mind back to the present and slipping her finger behind the wax seal, she pulled the parchment open. Silently she read the message that was scripted in fine old Ogham lines. Brigit couldn't help but smile. Enat was a scholar who knew many languages. The ordinary person couldn't read this ancient script. Few people could. But Brigit's parents had made her learn it. She knew with certainty that Enat had intended this message for her eyes. She read:

Spirit stone fills space
Young oak grows apace
Loon's call echoes forth
Wolves circle
Necklace given
Life saved
Hidden revealed
True arrow
Bound free
Quest complete
Hope

All eyes were on Brigit as she read. They waited patiently for her response. She gently re-folded the parchment and placed it inside the small leather pouch. She looked over at Sagoye and said, "Thank you for delivering this. They were indeed words of Enat for me. Perhaps I will share them later, but for now I think it is best that I keep them to myself."

The serious side of the circle conversation ended with that announcement. Kahn-Tineta asked Wulf if he would spend some time with her. He was puzzled about what she might want with him, but he was not one to say "no" to a person of her stature, so the two of them walked off together. Sagoye motioned for Erik to come with him, and they also walked away. That left Brigit and Shivon with the other two clan leaders.

Genesse said to them, "There's no need for the two of you to sit around here. Why don't the two of you run off and explore Kwahri."

With that dismissal, Brigit and Shivon excused themselves, rose, and also walked off. They ambled among the longhouses and other buildings of Kwahri, and then made their way through the gates and ventured outside the log palisade. The sky was clear and the sun was still far from setting on this summer day. As they looked to the north and east they could see the waving grasses in the foreground and the distant slopes of the Rondax mountains on the horizon. There was a peaceful quality about this valley.

There were numerous people out and about. Some were at work in the fields of the "three sisters" crops. The corn had been planted in hills of mounded soil earlier and was now several inches tall, so the workers were planting the beans and squash seeds in the hills around the corn. The beans would climb the corn as it grew and the squash would cover the ground, limiting the growth of weeds. Seeing the people working in the "three sisters" fields, Brigit recalled how she had been taught that this example from nature was an apt illustration of how people might prosper when they work together.

Brigit was brought out of her contemplations by Shivon speaking.

"Look over there." They had been walking around the edge of the palisade and Shivon pointed to the southwest, "Those folks look like they are Celtic farmers."

"Yes, and up on the hill above them there are what appears to be some crofter's houses."

"Let's go visit them. We have time before the evening meal in the castle."

Brigit hesitated. "Maybe I should go back and get my bow. Just in case we run into danger."

Shivon laughed. "We're safe enough. We have our daggers, although I can't imagine who would want to attack us here."

Brigit reluctantly agreed and they made their way toward the hills across the vale.

Chapter 43 - Druid's Staff

Wulf left the circle conversation wondering what Kahn-Tineta wanted with him. He knew so little of this land and its people, especially the Mohak people who now surrounded him. The woman who led him into the longhouse of the Bear clan was not physically imposing. She was diminutive in stature, but carried an aura about her that demanded respect. He followed her to the center fire of the longhouse, where she beckoned him to sit on one of the platforms to the side. He tried to make himself comfortable, while she reached up to a storage compartment. She rummaged about it for a bit and then pulled out a small fist-sized woven reed basket. Holding the basket in her hands, she sat down next to him.

"Wulf, walker of the woods, what is it you desire most in life?"

Wulf struggled to answer. He decided to ask for clarification.

"Do you mean what do I want to get out of life? Do you mean what to I hope to do in life? Do you mean how do I hope to live my life?"

"Yes. That is what I mean."

Wulf gave a little sigh inside himself as he thought to himself - it is never wise to try to outthink or outtalk a wise woman. He was silent for several moments as he thought. She waited patiently for him.

"I've never really thought about how to put what you ask into words, but I know that I want to do what is right. However sometimes that is hard to know. I reckon I want to be kind and generous with others and I know that I don't want to start thinking too highly of myself. I want to keep a humble heart. I guess I'd say that I'd like to help others, and that I'd like to make a difference for good."

"You have a good heart, young man."

Wulf stammered a thank you and then said, "But I'm not perfect. Sometimes I try so hard, but I don't do what is right, or I am not kind, or . . ."

Kahn-Tineta lifted one hand to stop his protest, and he stopped.

"None of us are perfect, but in you I see an honest young man with a good heart. Undoubtedly in your walks in the woods, you have seen trees whose hearts are rotten. They may look strong for a while, but eventually they fall. Those trees with a strong heart stand through wind and storm. You are like a young oak and you have a good heart. That is enough."

She reached out her hand and gave him a firm pat of assurance on his knee. Then she took the small basket she held and unfastened its clasp. She opened the cover and drew out an object that was wrapped in a small piece of cloth. It was a solid clear crystal, approximately one inch long and about one half inch in diameter. It appeared to have small flecks floating inside.

With reverence, Kahn-Tineta held the crystal in her open hand for a few moments. Then she extended her hand toward Wulf.

"Last summer, this spirit stone came into my care. After meeting you today, I believe I know to whom it belongs and where it belongs. Would you be so kind as to allow me to hold your staff for a moment?"

Wulf's eyes were wide open, both at the beauty of the spirit stone and at the request for his staff. He handed it to her without protest. She held the staff with one hand and gently positioned the crystal into the divot in the wood. It was a perfect fit.

She smiled a broad smile. "I thought so. A perfect

fit. Now, would you hold the staff and stone while I get some cord?"

He was tongue-tied, but nodded his agreement. She deftly took some strong cord and securely fastened the spirit stone to the druid staff.

After making the final knot she said, "This cord will hold it for now, but I would suggest that in the future you take some fine wire of your choice and redo this."

Finally, Wulf's tongue found some words, "I don't know what to say. Thank you. It looks beautiful. I don't know how I can repay you."

"You don't repay me. It is a gift. Use it wisely. Use it to live the way you told me you wish to live."

"May I ask you something?"

"Ask, young shaman. I will answer as I am able."

"Can you teach me how to use this spirit stone? Even the staff seems to possess powers I don't understand."

Kahn-Tineta smiled. "The power that you must learn is the power that lies within you. The true power in any totem is the power it enables you to channel within yourself. You show wisdom by asking for help. I admit that I do have some knowledge that might be of help to you. I will teach as I am able."

Wulf lost all track of time as his next hours were spent in deep concentration while he learned from the wise woman of the Bear clan of Kwahri.

Chapter 44 - Crofters

The visit of Brigit and Shivon to the nearby Celtic crofters offered numerous surprises. First, they revealed that there were numerous Celtic settlers in these lands. There were far more of them than Brigit had suspected. The Peace of Eirgalon that had been forged eighteen years ago had enabled people of different cultures to live in peace. Brigit was not surprised that they were doing so, but the degree to which those with Celtic/Norse ancestors had migrated into the Haudenoshonee lands was astonishing.

Second was the fact that although people from different cultures lived near to each other, they didn't always give up their traditional lifestyle, for the homesteads of the crofters were more like the settlements in the eastern lands than they were a mixture of the cultures.

Third, the total population of Eirgalon was obviously growing and expanding as settlements expanded into previously sparsely settled lands.

And finally, the settlers expressed a great apprehension about the Anishanaabe people. Some of them were scattered throughout this region, but others lived in much greater numbers to the north and west. The settlers had heard rumors of Malsum's influence among the Anishanaabe and they worried that Malsum might incite the Anishanaabe to violence against them.

On their way back to the castle of Kwahri, Shivon asked Brigit, "Do you think it is safe for us to try and follow Maengun to that village? The crofters seemed worried about the local Anishanaabe. What if they are followers of Malsum? We will be walking right into their hands."

"Don't worry so much, Shivon. I'm sure everything will be just fine. They didn't have any proof of any of that. All they told us was that they had heard rumors. You can't trust rumors."

"Well, usually when you see smoke, it is because there is a fire."

"We'll be safe. Maengun is there. And Erik and Wulf will be going with us."

"Maybe we should ask some of Sagoye's people to go with us. Just in case."

"I don't think that is necessary."

They continued their conversation as they made their way across the fields to the castle. When they reached the gate of the palisade, they found Erik and Sagoye sitting with their backs against the logs. The men were enjoying their conversation and the view.

Shivon interrupted them saying, "Erik, would you please tell Brigit that she should take some extra warriors when we go to the Anishanaabe village? The crofters we talked to spoke of rumors they have heard of Malsum's influence there. I think we should take extra men, but she refuses to ask for Sagoye's help. Please talk to her and convince her that this would be a wise course of action."

Sagoye spoke before Erik could respond, "I would certainly accompany your party, and would bring several of my men, if Brigit so desires. But you should know that the village you speak of may not warmly welcome us. In times past we had frequent trade and contact with them, but they have grown suspicious of all save their own kind. They no longer wish to deal with us. I fear that if I were to approach their home fire with a band of warriors, they would see us as attackers. However, if Brigit asks, I will go with her."

226

Brigit held up her hand and shook her head. "No. I don't want additional warriors. I agree that they would probably see that as a threat. Since we are friends¹ of Maengun, I am sure they will accept us into their village."

Shivon shook her head in disbelief, but said nothing.

Erik commented, "If Brigit has decided that just the four of us will go, then that's the way it shall be. Shivon, you may be right about what you say, and it is a true friend who gives counsel of caution when she senses problems, but this is Brigit's quest. The decision is for her to make."

Erik then turned his words to Brigit, "Do you anticipate leaving in the morning? Or will you delay for a day or two?"

Brigit replied, "I think I'd like to leave early in the morning. If it is a day's walk from here, we need to get an early start. It would be better to make it all the way to the village in one day rather than to have to camp overnight in the woods. I'll be ready at dawn, if the three of you will. And by the way, where is Wulf? Has he been with Kahn-Tineta this whole time?"

Erik and Sagoye looked at each other and then Erik answered, "He was with her inside the castle for a long time, but then they came out and went into the woods to the northeast."

"Didn't anyone go with them? I mean, doesn't Kahn-Tineta need protection?"

Sagoye chuckled, "You don't know Kahn-Tineta well enough yet. That woman needs no protection!"

Erik laughed out loud, and Brigit and Shivon just looked at each other wondering what the two men knew that they didn't.

Erik said, "Oh, don't stand there looking like that. You know full well that many wise women aren't just intelligent. Often they have powers which touch the spirit realm. Brigit, you've seen that in your mother, and you've even seen it in your aunties - the daughters of Unaine. Not to mention, Waneek - Sagoye's mother. Did you think a wise woman of Kwahri, the ancestral home of the Bear clan of the Mohak, would be any less formidable?"

Brigit smiled. "Of course you are right. With the talk of dangers and warriors, the attack on the messenger, and all that we have been through in the Rondax mountains, I just grew concerned for her safety in the woods away from the protection of the castle."

Erik added, "Not to mention forgetting about Wulf. If the trolls couldn't stand up to him, then I'd not be too overly worried about him traipsing through the woods only a few steps from the castle."

The four of them enjoyed the sight of the sun approaching the horizon for a few more minutes and then they went inside the palisade to enjoy the evening meal and the hospitality of the people. They were well into enjoying the evening meal when Kahn-Tineta and Wulf rejoined them. Wulf said nothing to them about what had transpired, but they noticed an expression of contentment on his face. Both Brigit and Shivon were wondering what that might mean, but neither one said anything to the other, and each one determined that at some point during the coming day's walk, she would broach the subject with him.

Chapter 45 - Coming Storm

It was a beautiful sunny summer morning on the southern edges of the Rondax Mountains. The party of four had risen at first light, consumed a light breakfast of cornmeal and black bean porridge, and had assembled their gear. They bid farewell to their hosts and headed out the western gate of the palisade just as the rays of the rising sun were striking the hills which lay westward beyond the waving grasses and woodlands.

After leaving the tilled fields and grasslands around the environs of Kwahri, the first half of the westward path to the Anishanaabe village wound its way through peaceful woods and clearings. Their experiences in the rugged terrain of the Rondax Mountains made it seem to the travelers that this was a land that was almost level. The path was narrow, and they walked in single file. Sagoye had instructed them that if they followed the main path, and didn't turn off onto any of the deer paths that crossed the road, then they would end up at their intended destination. Wulf led the way, which seemed natural since the others now recognized he possessed a special affinity for - and deep connection to - the woodlands. Brigit and Shivon followed, and Erik brought up the rear.

By late morning they had come to where a spur of the foothills extended out of the mountains. They continued to move through heavily wooded areas, but encountered steeper hills and ridgelines. The sun was straight overhead when they stopped for lunch. It was at a high spot with a view that allowed them to look back over the terrain they had traveled through. Far in the distance they could make out the castle of Kwahri.

As they enjoyed the view, and the few moments of

229

rest and nourishment, Brigit said to Wulf, "Well, are you going to tell us about your time with Kahn-Tineta? You were with her much of the afternoon and evening. What did you talk about?"

Wulf smiled as he recalled the conversations and the education. "She had a few surprises in store for me." He held out his druid's staff so they could clearly see the spirit stone that was now embedded in it.

Shivon gave a light giggle and teased, "So she gave you a pretty piece of rock to tie to your walking staff. I am supposed to be impressed?"

Wulf didn't take the bait and replied, "It is pretty. I didn't ask for it, but she seemed to think it would look nice attached right here. It does. Don't you think so?"

Brigit responded, "Aye, pretty it is. Do you know what that is?"

"Indeed, I do. Kahn-Tineta was kind enough to tell me about it."

"Including how you can use it?"

"She did give me a few pointers."

Brigit fingered her necklace. "Did she happen to tell you any pointers that would also apply to these moonstones?"

Wulf reflected a moment and said, "She taught me that the true power of the totem is the power that comes from within the wielder. Does that help?" That comment made Brigit frown, and Wulf went on, "The totem is sort of like a channel that can help focus the energy within the person. Does that make sense to you?"

"It should. I've been told that before, but nothing seems to help." She sighed and went quietly into inner reflection.

Shivon said to Wulf, "And do you now feel that you can control those fires you hurled at the trolls?"

"More now than I did then. At the time it was more of a gut reaction than anything else."

"Well, it was a good gut reaction."

Erik interrupted the conversation by pointing to the western sky. "It looks like we have a storm rolling in. We've got miles to go yet. I think we better get moving."

Wulf stood up, looked at the sky in all directions, and then replied, "I think we only have a couple of hours before the front is upon us. I agree, let's get moving. And be sure to have your rain gear at hand."

They quickly shouldered their gear and hurried down the trail, with Wulf again in the lead. The path turned northward as it wound into the hills. They could see a high bluff rising in the west. They crossed several small streams and passed by several ponds as they made their way. The sky completely clouded over and true to Wulf's prediction after a couple of hours the wind shifted to the east. Wulf stopped and turned toward the others.

"The rain will soon be upon us. It's time to have our rain gear on. Do we look for shelter, or do you want to keep going?"

"Do you have any idea of how far we have left to go to reach the village?"

"From what Sagoye told us, I suspect it is still a couple of miles. I'm sure the rain won't hold off that long."

Bridgit contemplated the choice for a few moments before saying, "I think we must go on. If we take cover and wait out the storm, we may be stuck out here overnight."

Erik gave his thought, "That might be better than rushing into an unknown situation in the middle of bad weather."

By this time the travelers were bundled as best they could for the coming rain.

Brigit said, "You may be right, Erik, but I say to move on.

They hurried up the path and within minutes the gusting east wind carried droplets of water. The temperature dropped, and soon the rain began pelting them.

As Erik plodded along behind the others he thought, "I'm getting too old to be doing this."

Chapter 46 - The Village

The rain continued unabated. They were soggy and tired when they stumbled across a small stream and into the village an hour later. The village consisted of several Anishanaabe style wigwams scattered throughout a grove of trees area near a couple of small lakes. The The driving rain limited their vision, but they could still see that the forest-covered hills of the southern Rondax mountains embraced the lakes on three sides.

Apparently, all the residents were inside their lodgings for no one hailed them as they approached the wigwams. Wulf had become accustomed to seeing the longhouses of the Mohak people and none of his fellow travelers had told him that the Anishanaabe used a different type of construction for their homes. These structures were a number of smaller round-roofed huts made by bent saplings tied together and covered with bark and woven reed mats. Whereas the Mohak longhouses were more substantial and had also started to use some of the carpentry techniques of the Celtic settlers, these buildings used only the traditional ways of their people.

The four travelers huddled together for a few moments deciding what to do, and then Erik bellowed out a greeting. Heads appeared at the doorways to some of the lodges. Then an elderly man holding a bearskin over himself came out of the largest of the lodges. They couldn't read any expression on his face. He said nothing to them. He looked them over, and then motioned for them to follow him into his lodge.

They shook the rain off of their clothing as best they could and entered the lodge. There was a fire burning in the center firepit of the lodge and light from the open smoke vent in the roof helped to give minor illumination to the dwelling. Seated at the fire and looking at at the visitors were an elderly woman and a teenage woman. Their expressions were hard to read, but seemed to emote apprehension.

The old man muttered something in his tongue to the young woman and she got up and left the lodge.

Shivon, who understood the language, whispered to the others, "He told her to go get the boss."

The elderly woman arose and helped the travelers take off their wet coats and hang them to dry. The man then motioned them to sit around the fire. Even though it was a summer storm, it felt good to have the fire take the chill off their bones after walking through the cool rain.

After several minutes, the door flap swung open and Maengun entered the lodge, followed by a young warrior.

Maengun joined them in their circle around the fire and as he did so he began speaking, "I hoped you would come. Once the storm hit I was sure you wouldn't arrive today. I thought that if you had left Kwahri this morning, you would have taken shelter when the rain began."

Brigit replied, "We thought about it, but I wanted to make it here today. The folks at Kwahri said that you had been hurt. Are you alright?"

Maengun gave a strange little smile and answered, "Ahh, why yes I am. My people have taken good care of me. And what about the four of you? You had no problems on the trail?"

Shivon answered with a hint of sarcasm, "O, we are just fine. We love walking on a slippery path through a rainstorm." Then she added, "I don't suppose your friends would have anything warm for us to drink, to take the chill off.

Maengun gave a big smile, "Why, of course. I have already thought of that. I instructed my friends in my wigwam to make you some fresh raspberry tea. It should be here soon. See, Shivon, I do have your best interests in mind."

At that moments the door flap to the wigwam was pulled open and the young women who had left earlier to get Maengun returned. In her hands she carried a steaming pot, from which wafted the scent of raspberry tea.

The elderly woman in the wigwam retrieved four pottery cups from a basket near the back of the dwelling and handed them to the four travelers. The young woman began to pour the tea into the cups.

Shivon said to Maengun, "Aren't you going to have some?"

"No, no. Guests first. You have your fill. I had just finished a cup before I was told of your arrival. Drink up. It will warm you. It is one of the traditional drinks of my people. Isn't it good?"

All of them, except Wulf, had enjoyed such drinks before and immediately drank some. Since the drink was new to Wulf, he inhaled the fumes of the drink deeply before taking a small sip. His brow wrinkled slightly.

He looked up from his drink and looked at Maengun, "It has a slight bitter taste to it. Is it supposed to?"

Maengun reassured him, "Yes, it is fine, the raspberries used are very fresh. Perhaps they could have ripened a bit more, but they are still good. No?"

Brigit said, "Don't worry, Wulf. You're just not used to it. I'm sure it is as Maengun says. Just slightly unripened berries. But the heat of it feels good."

Erik had a puzzled look on his face. It was as if he

was trying to focus on something. After her first sip, Shivon had drunk the rest of it with relish. Being from Hochelaga in the north, where such a drink was common, she enjoyed the freshly brewed tea.

Wulf took another sip, and then drank deeply. Then he shook his head, and muttered, "I don't mean to be rude, but there seems to be something wrong with this."

Maengun, with that strange smile on his face, said, "Why, what ever could be wrong?"

Brigit and Shivon were already slumping over into unconsciousness.

Erik, with his last remnant of alertness, mumbled, "Poison," and then he too slid into unconsciousness.

Wulf groggily reached for his staff, but Maengun pulled it away before he could grasp it.

"You won't be needing this," said Maengun, as Wulf slumped to the ground. Then Maengun's face broke out into a huge smile and he laughed.

The elderly man and woman in the wigwam looked at each other with expressionless faces, the young woman had an expressions that hinted of fear.

Chapter 47 - Mysterious Shaman

Maengun turned to the young woman who had brought in the tea, and harshly said, "Go get Megissogwon."

She hurried out the door and ran to a far wigwam. The travelers were slumped over in various positions on the floor, and Maengun looked from one to another and laughed again.

"They were so easily drugged. How trusting. How foolish. They walked right into my trap."

Maengun instructed the young warrior that had accompanied him to go out and find some strong cords to bind the captives. The elderly man and woman had not moved. Now Maengun told them to check the visitors and make sure they were completely unconscious. As they did so, they re-arranged the supine forms so that they were laying on the sleeping pallets.

Several minutes later, the young woman re-entered the wigwam. She was followed by a man who appeared to be in his early sixties. He walked with a slight limp and his shoulders were hunched over. He had once been strong and imposing, but the last years had been hard on him.

Megissogwon's eyes went immediately to the form of Brigit and his gaze focused on the white and black moonstone necklace lying across her throat. He smiled in satisfaction.

He glanced at the others and said dismissively, "Bind her and dispose of the others."

Maengun replied, "We may need the others to get her to willingly hand over the necklace. I say we keep them drugged while I persuade her to give it up. I may need them as leverage to convince her."

Megissogwon grunted, "Do it your way, only get me the Loon's Necklace." He turned to leave the wigwam, leered briefly at the young Anishanaabe woman who had brought him to the wigwam and said to her, "You, come with me." Looking back at Maengun, he said with a tone of disgust, "And get rid of that iron amulet the girl is wearing!"

Then he departed. With a look of dread on her face, the young woman followed him.

Maengun said to the old man and old woman, "You heard the shaman. Remove that piece of iron from her hair."

Shivon had carefully woven the iron hammer-shaped amulet into a braid of Brigit's hair. Rather than undoing the woven braid, the woman took a small cooking knife and cut off the braid. She then held it out in her hand toward Maengun, but he shook his head.

"Throw it away. I don't want anything to do with it."

Holding it in her hand, she walked out of the wigwam.

The young man who had been sent to fetch cords to bind the captives returned with some sturdy deer-hide cords. They then bound the hands and feet of Shivon, Wulf, and Erik. One by one they carried the still unconscious travelers and all their gear out of the wigwam and took them to a wigwam on the far side of the village.

They left Brigit lying on her pallet, but Maengun took care to move her bow and gear to the opposite side of the dwelling. While Maengun was busy helping the young warrior move the travelers, the old woman returned. She surreptitiously showed the old man that she had removed Brigit's hair from the iron amulet and then she glanced at the closed doorway and quickly pushed the amulet into a pocket of Brigit's leather jerkin.

The old man's eyes had widened in alarm, for they were disobeying Maengun's command, but he nodded his head to signal his agreement with her action.

In the far wigwam, the travelers were guarded by two women, the young warrior, and a frail looking old man. Maengun gave them his instructions. They were to make sure that none of the three captives were unbound before Maengun gave the order to free them. If any of the three started to regain consciousness, they were to give them another dose of the sleeping drug.

Maengun then made his way back to the dwelling where Brigit lay. He sat down next to her and watched her as she slept. There was a moment when his hand lifted and moved slowly toward the moonstone necklace, but before he touched the glistening stones he jerked it back.

The rains stopped and the cloud cover started to lighten, but then dusk descended upon the land and the village fell into semi-darkness. Summer night sounds from the woods and waters surrounding the village echoed about the wigwams. A few villagers left their dwellings to retrieve dry wood from their covered woodpiles. Most of them returned with it to their wigwams to feed their cook-fires, but a few men started a fire at their central fire pit. They gathered about it. Normally this would be a time of boisterous talk and friendship. Today their conversations were subdued. Frequently their glances went toward the wigwams where Brigit was being held, where the other travelers were captive, and to where Megissogwon had gone.

There was a second fire in the woods near

Megissogwon's wigwam, where a number of his men had gathered. Their conversation was louder and filled with laughter. There was a sense of revelry and success as they bantered about. They didn't care to mingle with the local villagers, but occasionally a man would wander over to check on the wigwams that held the captives. They set up a spit and began roasting a haunch of venison over the fire.

Chapter 48 - Awake

The dose of drugged tea was so strong that none of the prisoners re-gained consciousness until the next morning. Erik stirred first, for he had consumed less of the tea than the others. The women forced another dose of sleeping potion down his throat as the young warrior carefully looked on. Shortly thereafter, they gave additional doses to Wulf and Shivon. They would sleep the day away.

Back in the first wigwam, Brigit stirred to consciousness. She blinked her eyes several times as she struggled to bring her vision into focus. Gradually the form of her friend, Maengun, became clear to her. Maengun had dozed intermittently during the night, but now he was fully awake and attentive, as he knelt before her.

Brigit remained lying down and her voice croaked as she tried to speak. "What? What happened?"

Maengun shushed her. "Don't speak. Here, drink this water."

He put one hand under her head and gently lifted her so that her lips might touch the cup of clear water that he held before her.

"Take little sips. The water will help sooth your throat and clear your mind."

She wanted to gulp it down but he only allowed her to sip a small amount at a time. After drinking, she lay her head back on the ground and was still for several moments.

Finally she said, "My head hurts so much. What happened?"

"Don't move. Lie as still as you can for a while. If the water stays down, then I'll get you a few bites of food."

"I am hungry, but what happened?"

Maengun smiled as he responded, "It must have been the cold rain that caused your body to take a chill. And then you broke out into a fever. You've been in a delirium for two and a half days. Your fever just broke this morning. You need to stay quiet and rest."

Brigit smiled at his reassurance, then a frown of puzzlement settled upon her face.

"Two days? But the others? Where are they? Why aren't they here?"

"Relax. Don't worry. They are fine. They have been worried sick for you. They spent all of the last two days huddled about your sickbed. When your fever broke this morning, and you were resting peacefully, they decided to go to the other side of the lake and check out one of the local legends."

"What? Why?"

"Shhh. Quiet now. Rest some more. Your mind will clear. I'll explain it all later. Now, no more talking. Sleep again."

Brigit didn't argue. She closed her eyes and relaxed. Maengun's voice was so calm and reassuring. He was right. All could be explained later. Her breathing slowed and the comfort of sleep again overtook her.

Maengun's expression was one of satisfaction. She was falling under his spell. He looked over at the old woman and old man who sat on the other side of the dwelling. He motioned for them to stay quiet and to keep an eye on her while he went out.

Upon leaving the wigwam, Maengun stopped briefly to check on the condition of the other captives, and then made his way to Megissogwon's wigwam. Shortly after he entered, the young maiden who had accompanied Megissogwon into his wigwam left in a hurry. Maengun remained in the dwelling for some time before he left to return to Brigit. On his way, he stopped to poke his head through the door of the other captives' wigwam and to give some orders to the guards.

When he re-entered Brigit's wigwam, his face was all smiles. He started to speak to the old man and old woman; and as he spoke, Brigit's eyes fluttered open. He smiled at her and she returned his smile.

"So you awaken," he said with a chuckle.

She took a deep breath and said, "Yes. How long did I sleep?"

"Since we last talked. Only about an hour. How do you feel?"

"Only a slight ache in my head. And I am hungry."

"We'll get you something," he said, and motioned to the old woman to bring some food, "and as you eat, I will give you an update on what has been happening."

As she ate he proceeded to tell her that that while she had been unconscious the villagers had told her companions about the legend of the cave which lay on the other side of the lake.

"It is said that in this cave, one can commune with the gods. The day of the summer solstice will soon be upon us. The legends say that if a worthy supplicant enters the cave before dawn on that day, and if the sun would chance to break the eastern horizon on a cloudless dawn on that day, then the first rays of the sun will burst through the opening of the cave and reveal the secrets of the gods on the back wall of the cave. Your friends decided that while you recover here, they would go to the far side of the lake, and see if they can find the cave of legend."

Brigit's forehead wrinkled in thought. "That doesn't

sound like them. They would wait for me," she paused and then questioned, "wouldn't they?"

Maengun shrugged his shoulders. "I don't know what to say. They are gone."

Brigit unconsciously lifted her hand to touch her hair. With a start she noticed that her braid had been cut off.

"What? My braid? What happened to my hair?"

Maengun thought quickly and responded, "Your braid must have become undone by the rain. Your hair was matted and bothering you in your delirium. We cut it off so that you might rest more comfortably. Besides, that braid was in your way. Even tied up, your hair must have occasionally gotten in the way when you shot your bow."

Brigit squeezed her eyes shut as if trying to focus and remember what had transpired. She sighed in exasperation.

"Erik's iron amulet of protection was woven into my hair. Erik wanted me to keep it."

"You will be fine without it. There was no real power in it. I lost mine long ago. I think it may have slipped out of my pocket when I fell in the river. But look, I'm still fine. The limikkin attacked me but I escaped it."

Brigit's visage lit up in interest at that comment. "Yes. I've been wondering about that. Tell me what happened."

Maengun gulped, and thought for a moment. "I'd rather not speak of it yet. The memory is still painful for me. But you should know I survived, though I feel I am still regaining my strength. My people here helped nurse me back to health. As they will for you. You should rest some more. Stay here in the wigwam." He motioned toward the old couple. "These folk will get you whatever you need. Rest. I will be back soon."

He then got up and quickly departed.

Brigit looked at the old couple and tried to speak with them, but quickly realized they spoke only the Anishanaabe tongue, of which she knew but few words.

After several moments of confused looks, the old woman glanced apprehensively toward the door. When she determined that no one was by the door or about to enter, she mimed to Brigit the action of cutting her hair. Then she mimed taking an object from the hair and putting it in her pocket. Next she pointed to Brigit's pocket.

Brigit reached her hand into her pocket. Her eyes flared wide as she felt the iron Thor's hammer amulet. The old woman gave a slight smile, and then held a finger to her lips as she warned Brigit to say nothing about the amulet. Brigit returned the smile and nodded in understanding. She left the amulet safely in her pocket as she withdrew her hand. Her mind was filled with doubt and unanswered questions, but she sensed she must be cautious in how she pursued them. For now, it was enough to get her strength back.

Chapter 49 - A Day in the Village

Maengun returned to Brigit a couple of hours later. She was ready to be up and about when he came for her. She had brushed through her hair, and with the help of the old woman had trimmed it so that it fell in a neat frame of curls about her face.

As they left the lodging of the old couple, Brigit noticed a mixture of expressions upon their faces that could only be description as a combination of relief and apprehension. Brigit looked back toward the wigwam after they had walked several paces away from it. She noticed the young woman who had served them the tea came from behind the dwelling and had quickly slipped inside. Brigit considered how she would like to talk to the girl, but Maengun was leading her away and as he did so he pointed to the lake that she could see shimmering in the distance.

"These waters are sometimes called by my people the Lake of the Loons. Let us walk to the water's edge. Shall we?"

Brigit couldn't refuse his request. She felt drawn by the sight of the sparkling waters, as well as by the name Maengun had given. She, unconsciously reached to her neck and fingered the necklace that she wore. To her side, but out of view from her direction, Maengun smirked.

They made their way through the village and came to the shore. She could see bluffs rising on the far side of the lake and she wondered if that was where her friends had gone. She raised her hand and pointed to the bluffs.

"Is that where the legendary cave is?"

"I believe so. But I have never been there."

"Perhaps we can go there. Why don't we get a

canoe, paddle across the lake, and see if we can find the others?"

Maengun gave her the appearance of being deep in thought, then he answered. "I think we should. But you are still recovering from your ordeal. And we are several hours behind them. We wouldn't be able to catch up with them. If they don't return tonight, then we will go to them in the morning. No doubt they would have camped by a source of fresh water, and we will be able to find their camp."

That sounded reasonable to Brigit. They spent the afternoon walking among the pine and oak trees of the woods that neighbored the lake. Occasionally, they stopped to sit and rest. Brigit was surprised at how rested she felt. She thought that she should feel more exhausted after her couple days of fever and delirium. Maengun would often draw her into light conversation about what seemed to be meaningless topics. She found herself enjoying his company more and more. It reminded her of their first days of travel together, when it was just the two of them. She began to wonder how she could ever have doubted him.

She normally would have been very aware of her surroundings, and given the events of her journey, wary of hidden dangers, but the gentle and charming nature of Maengun's presence lulled her into complacency. She never noticed that from distant vantage points the eyes of the mysterious shaman, Megissogwon, were upon her.

When Maengun escorted her back into the village, she did feel that everyone one was watching her. But that was to be expected. After all, how many of them had ever seen the Princess of Eirgalon before? Brigit was curious about the village and would have liked to explore it, but Maengun insisted that they return to the original wigwam because they would have a meal ready for her.

He was right, for when they entered, the old woman had a savory smelling stew warming over the fire. The young maiden was there with the old couple, but when Brigit entered she rose as if to leave.

Brigit said to her, "Please stay. I'd like to talk."

Her eyes took on a look of alarm, but she said nothing.

Maengun intervened. "Brigit, she doesn't speak your tongue. Besides, she has an errand to run."

Maengun spoke a few words to the maiden in the language of her people and she hurried out of the dwelling.

Brigit asked, "What did you say to her? I could make out the word 'shaman' but I didn't understand anything else."

"Oh. I was just reminding her of a task she needed to complete for the local shaman before the sun sets."

"Perhaps you could act as a translator between us, when she gets back. I'd like to ask her a few questions."

"Perhaps," Maengun smirked slightly as he continued, "but I doubt she will be back this evening. You'll just have to make do talking to me."

Brigit motioned to the old man and old woman who sat on the opposite side of the fire. "Maybe you can translate for them."

"Certainly, but they won't have much to say. After we eat we can try."

They did try to engage the couple in conversation, but as Maengun had warned, the elder Anishanaabe folks were reluctant to say much. Perhaps it was their natural way, or perhaps it was something that Maengun had said to them, but they said little.

Suddenly Brigit had a thought. "What happened to the Mohak men from Kwahri who brought you to the village? I haven't seen them."

Maengun hesitated before he responded. "You didn't pass them on the path while you were coming here?"

"No. We encountered no one."

"That's strange. They hoped to return to their homes before the storm. Perhaps they took shelter when the storm broke. They may have ventured off the path for shelter, and then you missed them."

Brigit's face showed her puzzlement as she stammered out, "Perhaps."

Maengun shrugged. "It's too bad you missed them, but they are not here. They are gone."

They continued to talk as night fell, and finally Brigit felt herself ready to sleep. As she drifted off, she felt a sense of comfort at the strong presence of Maengun, but also had a vague sense of uneasiness about her.

Chapter 50 - The Captives

Late that evening Maengun's men allowed the other captives to regain consciousness. First they made sure the captives were securely bound - hands tied before them and feet shackled so they could only take short, shuffling steps - then they gave them water to drink and gagged their mouths to keep them quiet. In the deepening darkness of the summer evening they took them from the wigwam and led them on a path around the lake until they came to a lean-to shelter they had built. A fire was already blazing in front of the lean-to and the captives were pushed into the lean-to.

When they removed the prisoners' gags, Shivon spoke to them in their tongue, "Why are you doing this to us? Where is Brigit?"

The men seemed startled that she spoke their tongue and muttered amongst themselves about the red-haired pale-skinned witch.

She again asked, "Why do you do this?"

One the the men, who appeared to be a leader of the group of men, responded, "We do what the shaman tells us."

Shivon replied, "We have done nothing against you or against your shaman. We only came to your village to find a friend."

This caused the men to laugh.

The leader chuckled as he said, "That was not our village. They are nothing. We follow the great Megissogwon."

Erik cursed some unintelligible words under his breath and spat.

The leader turned his attention to Erik. "So you recognize the name."

Erik glanced at Shivon who translated the comment for him.

Erik grimaced as he tilted his head toward the leader, "You can tell him that if he follows that worthless piece of horse manure, then he can go with him to hell, iffen that is, his kind have such a place."

Shivon said, "I can't exactly tell him it the way you said, but I'll try to make him understand your idea."

She then spoke a few sentences in the Anishanaabe tongue to the leader of their captors.

He listened intently, and then laughed for several moments before he replied.

"You fool. He is from the spirit realm. That is why we follow him. He has great power. If we should die in service to him, then we will have great power in the spirit realm."

After Shivon had translated that for Erik (and Wulf, who was listening closely), she asked the man what they intended to do to them. She listened to his response and then relayed the message to her companions.

"He said that the shaman wanted to kill us when we were drugged, but that Maengun persuaded the shaman to let us live, because we might be of some use to him. Then he said he'd like to kill us all as soon as possible, and that if we give him any trouble he will. At the end he added that if we cause him problems we will never see Brigit again."

Erik replied with a grunt and then said, "Tell 'em that if he needs us around for Maengun then he better feed us something. That, or let us eat some of the traveling food in our packs."

Shivon relayed that message and to her surprize the leader nodded. He glanced at the captives' gear that the men had thrown into a pile near the lean-to, thought

251

about it for a moment, then gave a slight shake to his head. However, he soon gave instructions to his men to give the prisoners some of the bread they had brought from the village and pieces of meat they had roasted over their fire.

They were given the food and water. The fare, though simple, replenished their bodies. When it looked as though the guards were getting comfortable for the night, Wulf whispered softly, hoping the guards wouldn't hear.

"Erik, what do we do now?"

Erik whispered back, "First, don't think they can't hear you. They're listening. Second, we may think they can't understand our language, but don't bet your life on it. Third, now that you started whispering like this - don't change. Keep whispering."

The guards did nothing to stop them from communicating with each other, so Wulf continued.

"Do either of you know what they have done with Brigit?"

Erik responded, "She was drugged like the rest of us. I saw her passing out as we did. I don't know what they have done with her, or where they have taken her."

Shivon whispered, "I don't think Maengun would hurt her. Not yet. At least not until he gets what he wants from her."

They talked for a long time, without interruption from the guards, but they came to no decision about any course of action they might attempt. While they surreptitiously tested their bonds, they found them secure, and they couldn't risk making overt efforts to loosen them. They sat and contemplated what they might do.

Chapter 51 - Revelation

Late into the night, when the fire had grown dim but the alert eyes of the guards still watched them, Megissogwan strolled into view. The young Anishanaabe woman followed meekly behind him. When they reached the fire the shaman grabbed her by the arm and pushed her toward the sitting captives. Then he gave orders to the guards.

"I have no more use for this one. Don't let her escape, and when the time comes for you to dispose of the others, dispose of her as well."

A light flickered in Wulf's eyes, or maybe it was just a reflection of the flickering fire, as he watched the man. He was about to speak, but Shivon spoke first. Her words were polite, yet her tone bordered on disrespectful.

"And who would you be?"

"I am the nightmare of your people, pale woman. What a weak lot your leaders have sent to confront me: the toothless whelp of the Bear-witch; a simple girl of the north; a buffoon of a man-child from over the waters; and a tired, white-bearded, old warrior. Fools and weaklings, all of you."

Shivon was not one to back down, and she let her sarcasm have full rein. "Oh, and that's a fine greeting, to be sure. I don't suppose an old man who pushes young women around in the dark of night, and who greets people with such respect, would have a name?"

The shaman sneered. "Oh, I have a name. Or several of them. Your people of the north have heard me called Megissogwon." Then he looked at Erik. "But the pale ones to the east call me, Malsum. I have no love for any of you with pale skin and the sooner you are vanquished from our land the better."

Erik whistled through his teeth and said, "So you're the one."

That made the shaman smile. "Yes, I am the one. And though my plans were thwarted many years ago, they are coming to fruition now. I will succeed. And your people will be vanquished."

Wulf spoke for the first time, "I don't understand. Yes, you have us as your captives, but you are in the wilderness of this land, and you only lead but a few men."

"You know nothing, boy-from-beyond-the-sunrise. I lead many more men than you think. And soon I will have in my grasp an object of great power. It is a talisman that, when joined to my natural powers, will make me invincible. With it, I will destroy the pale ones and make this land great again."

"Do you mean the Loon's Necklace?"

"Indeed! And tomorrow, it will be mine!"

"But I know that you can't just take it from Brigit. It has no power if it is taken from its guardian by force. You must know that."

Malsum smiled a wicked smile. "Oh, I know that very well. But, you see, I won't need to take it from her, she will willingly give it to me."

Shivon blurted out, "She would never do that. She would die first!"

Malsum gave an evil chuckle. "Oh she will give it to me. She loves her friends so much that, in order to save them, she will willingly hand it over. Perhaps then I will allow her to die. Or perhaps I shall torment her a while before she dies."

Erik said, "You don't know her. She is a stubborn one. She knows who you are and what you can do. As

Shivon says, she will die before she hands it to you."

Malsum was obviously enjoying himself. He almost rubbed his hands in glee as he responded.

"I know her kind, but she doesn't really understand me. She is so easily deceived. She has believed lie after lie from my servant, Maengun. I have used him to cloud her judgement. She will hand it to him and he will deliver it to me. Such a weak fool she is. What a disappointment she must be to her parents." Then he gave a vicious laugh.

Erik responded with anger, "You won't get away with this. I swear I'll kill you, and Maengun, before I allow either of you to harm her."

Malsum laughed even louder. "Blustering old fool. There you sit trussed up like a pig to be butchered. You overestimate your power, and you underestimate me and my pet limikkin."

Wulf muttered, "I knew it."

Again Malsum laughed, "And knowing did you so much good, didn't it? The three of you are such fools. I almost think I should let you live, just to amuse me. But, no, I think not. I would tire of your stupidity soon enough."

Shivon bravely declared, "You're not going to get away with this."

"But I already have. You can't stop me." He then gave her a long look that became a leer. "If I had more time I would take pleasure in your flesh," he glanced at the Anishanaabe maiden, "but, unfortunately I need to go and make preparations for the morning."

Shivon felt the bile rise in her throat at the thought of what Malsum was suggesting. She looked at the face of the young maiden and saw an expression of revulsion on her face.

With a final spiteful laugh Malsum turned from them, muttered a few words to the guards, and disappeared into the darkness.

Chapter 52 - Final Morning

Brigit stirred to wakefulness before the sun rose. The air carried the promise of a fine sunny summer day. Maengun was sitting and watching her as she opened her eyes.

She stretched, and asked, "Don't you ever sleep?"

He chuckled in a friendly manner, "Oh, I sleep, but just not as much as others. It looks to be a beautiful day. Do you think you are strong enough and ready to cross the lake so that we might find your friends?"

"Of course. You saw me yesterday. You know I am back to normal."

"Then let's grab a quick mouthful, and be on our way."

The quickly prepared themselves and the elderly couple provided each of them with a handful of nuts and berries, as well as a waterskin. Brigit grabbed her gear and her bow and then they were on their way to the lakeshore.

Maengun had a small canoe waiting for them. The lake was close to a mile wide and perhaps two miles long. Maengun pointed to a wisp of smoke that rose from the opposite shore of the lake.

"That is probably their campsite. We'll head there."

They settled into the canoe and pushed off. Brigit sat in the front and Maengun sat in the back. When they were near the center of the lake, Maengun directed Brigit's gaze to some activity on the distant shoreline.

"It looks like there is someone putting out from shore. Perhaps they are returning across the lake."

Brigit replied without turning around, "Yes. Perhaps." Several moments later, she added, "But I thought you said they walked around the lake to the bluffs? Why would they have a canoe?"

"I did? I wasn't with them, so I don't know, but there certainly looks to be a canoe coming this way."

The quiet sounds of the early morning on the lake were suddenly punctuated by the laughing cry of a loon. Brigit looked up and could seeing the arrow-like flight of a loon coming towards them. Within moments it had circled them, and then descended and skimmed to a landing on the lake.

They continued to paddle in the direction of the campsite and the oncoming canoe. That canoe was moving slower because there was only one person paddling.The front person in the canoe was obviously just a passenger, since he dipped no paddle into the calm waters of the lake.

As they closed the distance between them, the expression on Brigit's face turned from curiosity to concern. See could see that the passenger in the other canoe was Wulf. She didn't recognize the other man. At a distance of approximately thirty yards, the other man in the man in the canoe yelled out for them to stop.

Maengun held his paddle in the water to bring the canoe to a halt in the waters.

Brigit could see that there was a gag in Wulf's mouth, but she yelled out, "Wulf, what is going on?"

Wulf shook his head and the man behind Wulf shouted something in Anishanaabe.

Brigit turned to Maengun and asked what the man had said.

Maengun replied, "He said to take off your necklace and to give it to me.

"To you? Why should I give it to you."

"He said to give it to me or he will shove a knife into Wulf's back. Then we can move closer and I can hand it over to him."

"But I can't just give it away. It is the Loon's Necklace."

"Listen, Brigit," pleaded Maengun persuasively, "you'd be doing it to save the life of a friend. And after all, you can't use it. It doesn't really have any power. It's just some pretty rocks."

Brigit could see that Wulf in the other canoe was vigorously shaking his head.

Maengun added, "Brigit, please. Do it. You have to do it, or he will die with a knife in his back."

Brigit gave her head and little shake and squeezed her eyes shut for a moment as if trying to clear her head and focus her thoughts. Then she opened them and looked at the man seated behind Wulf. She slowly raised her hand toward the necklace. She lifted it over her neck. She could see a smile creep across the face of the man in the other canoe.

Then a look of determination came upon Brigit's face and she murmured to herself, "I will save my friend."

She dropped the necklace to the floor of the canoe and as she quickly reached down into the canoe and grabbed her bow. Pulling an arrow from the quiver, she fluidly lifted her bow, nocked the arrow, pulled the bow taunt, and released the arrow. The others were frozen in surprise as the arrow flew through the air and plunged into the chest of the man behind Wulf.

The man's eyes went wide with shock, and then with pain. He tumbled out of the canoe, capsizing it. Wulf, with his hands bound and his mouth gagged, was plunged into the water.

Maengun said to Brigit, "Quick, hand me the necklace now and I will save him for you."

It didn't make sense to her. Why did Maengun want the necklace now? Why didn't he just dive into the lake to save Wulf?

At that moment, the loon that had been swimming near the canoes started making the clucking sound that loons will make when giving warning of impending danger.

Out of the fog of memory flashed the story of the the boy and the loon's necklace. She recalled the message sent from Ayenwatha, "In time of need. Remember the necklace." She saw in her mind the image of the young boy of the story, tossing the necklace about the head of the loon, Medawisla.

With no more hesitation, she reached down and grabbed the black and white moonstone necklace. She heard again Maengun begging for it. She looked at it one more time and then she flung it out the canoe toward the loon as it plunged under the water.

Maengun screamed, "No," and threw himself out of the canoe in pursuit of the necklace.

As Maengun's dove into the water Brigit saw his body appear to morph into the shape of a large otter. She looked around. The man from the other canoe had splashed about briefly, but was now under the water. Wulf and Maengun were gone. The other canoe was capsized, yet floating on the water. Silence descended over the scene.

Chapter 53 - Struggle on Shore

The scene on the shore became hectic as they saw what was transpiring out on the lake. Malsum had arranged it so that Erik and Shivon where situated behind some thin foliage and could see what was happening on the lake, yet not be easily observed from the lake. Their hands were still bound and next to them was the young Anishanaabe maiden who was to share their fate. The leader of the guards had taken Wulf out in the canoe, but his men remained as guards surrounding the captives.

As the action on the lake began, Malsum stepped out from the brush and stepped to the very edge of the water. He spread his hands wide, and in a soft, undulating rhythm he began to chant a spell. Erik had no idea what was being chanted, but he knew it couldn't be anything good.

In his loudest voice, Erik shouted, "Beware, Malsum!"

Immediately, the guards struck him from behind, and knocked him unconscious to the ground.

The shout and the resulting commotion was enough to draw Brigit's attention away from the rippling waters and to the shoreline. There was only one moment of hesitation, and then she acted.

She reached down to pick up again her bow. She touched the iron amulet that Erik that fastened to the bow, then drew another arrow. She nocked it to the linen bowstring. As she drew the bowstring back and focused on her target, a surprising event occurred. She had always had good vision and with practice had developed outstanding accuracy, but it was as if in this moment she could see the finest detail on her target as if she were standing mere steps away from it. There was more at work than practiced skill - there was latent power sprung to life.

Seated in the canoe, she aimed for the heart of the chanting shaman standing more than a hundred yards away. As she released her arrow she willed its flight to pierce his heart. With a gasp, he grabbed at the arrow in his chest and crumpled to the ground.

The guards rushed forward to kneel at his side and give him aide. All to no avail. The broadhead arrow had struck dead center, slicing wide wounds through the heart. Malsum tried to whisper some words, but his eyes glazed over and his body went limp. Within moments, death was his reality.

The guards looked at each other. They had watched as their leader had been shot in the canoe and disappeared into the water, to be followed by Maengun, who had not reappeared. They had just witnessed the death of their shaman, Megissogwon, who the pales ones called Malsum. There was nothing for them here. They gave brief glances toward the captives, but stalked past them, picked up their gear, and walked off into the woods.

After they departed, the maiden rushed to the dead shaman and pulled a knife from his belt. She didn't hesitate, but plunged it through his eye and into his brain. She pulled it out and then rinsed it off in the waters of the lake.

She looked out on the lake, and saw Brigit paddling her canoe. She was circling it around the capsized canoe and looking into the water for any sign of the others. There was still no sign of Wulf or Meangun.

The maiden stood up and went to Shivon and Erik. As she passed the dead form of the shaman, she spat upon him. The maiden quickly freed the captives by slicing the leather cords that bound them, and slipped the knife into a pouch she carried.

Then she said, "I am called Shania."

Shivon gave her a look of surprise. "You speak our tongue."

"A little."

"Why didn't you speak it before?"

"They," she motioned to where the others had disappeared, "didn't need to know."

Shivon nodded in understanding. Erik was struggling back to alertness and they helped him to a sitting position.

He asked, "What happened?"

Shivon quickly said, "Brigit put an arrow through the shaman's heart, and the others have run away. She is searching the waters for the Wulf. Shania, here, has freed us from our bonds."

They heard a loon's laughter from a distance down the shoreline. When they looked, they saw the form of Wulf lying on the shore. They could see him raise his head. Shivon quickly grabbed Wulf's staff from their gear that the guards had piled near a tree, and she started to move towards him.

Only a few seconds passed before they heard the splashing of water from the opposite direction and quickly turned their heads in time to see an otter emerging from the water and then morphing into the form of Maengun.

Shania hissed, "Limikkin!"

Erik shakily arose from his sitting position and grabbed a broken branch lying on the ground to swing at Maengun. Maengun laughed as he easily avoided the blow and then wrested the branch from a still unsteady

Erik.

Maengun couldn't resist a momentary pause to taunt Erik. "And now old man, it is time for you to finally get what you deserve."

Swinging the branch over his head Maengun laughed as he brought it crashing down. But it never reached its intended target. Shivon had rushed forward with Wulf's staff and swung it in a counter-parry to Maengun's blow.

There was a flash of light as the branch and the staff connected. Maengun's strength far surpassed that of Shivon, but perhaps the power of Wulf's will was channeled to Shivon by the spirit stone in the staff. The two adversaries were held for a moment in a frozen tableau.

The momentary pause was enough time for Shania to step forward with the shaman's knife she had retrieved from her pouch.

Maengun cried out in pain and surprise as she thrust the blade into his side.

Erik, trying to stagger to his feet, gasped, "Does anyone know his true name?"

Shania answered, "I heard the shaman call him, 'Shining Forked Tongue'."

Erik, remembering how he saw Fearglas kill the limikkin Gakko so many years ago, yelled out, "I call you by name, Shining Forked Tongue. Now die." Then he directed his words to Shania. "Twist the knife, and stab him again. Repeat what I said. Do it till he drops."

Moments later, Maengun fell to the ground. He looked up briefly. He spat blood from his mouth and tried to speak, but was unable to say anything before he lay still and died.

Shania, stood over him. Blood dripping from the

knife she still held. She looked up, and looked to Erik for direction.

"What do we do now?"

Erik took a deep breath, and said, "We breathe. And thank the gods we are still able to do so."

Brigit ran her canoe up on the shore, jumped out of it, and ran to them. She stood with them as they stood looking at the fallen bodies of Malsum and his servant, Maengun.

Wulf was the last to join them as he made his way down the shoreline to them.

A puzzled Shivon looked at him and asked, "What happened to your bonds?"

A grin crossed his face as he said, "Now that's a tale that will take some telling. But right now I think we have some work to do. Right, Erik?"

"Aye, my boy. Right you are. We need to get enough dry wood to make a pyre. We'll be needing to burn these monsters - and the sooner that is done, the better!"

Chapter 54 - After the Ashes

The five of them, for Shania acted as if she was one of them, went to work dragging deadwood from the surrounding area and making a large pile of it on the very edge of the lake. When they assembled an amount that satisfied Erik, they situated the bodies of Malsum and Maengun upon it.

Brigit then turned to Wulf. "I could show you my fire-making skills, but I imagine you can do the job a little better and faster than I can. Would you do the honors?"

Wulf nodded in grim satisfaction. He reached out and picked up his druid's staff. He held it out toward the pyre. Without a word said, the spirit stone in the staff started to glow, and then a flash of fire shot out from the end of the staff to the pile of wood. The pyre erupted into a huge bonfire. The immediate, intense heat caused the watchers to quickly step backward several steps.

Erik whistled and said, "Still learning your own strength, young Wulf?"

Wulf gave a sheepish grin, but said nothing.

After a few minutes of silence among them as they watched the roaring fire, Erik asked Shania, "How is it that you came to know our language? And why did you help us?"

Brigit added, "Yes, tell us your story. We have time."

Shania sighed. "Where do I begin?"

Erik chuckled. "At the beginning."

"The village on this lake is where I was born and raised. However, I spent a couple of summers living in the land of the waving grass, near Kwahri. My parents thought it was important to learn the ways of the Mohak and Celtic folk of Eirgalon, so they made an arrangement for me to live with people they knew at Kwahri. I enjoyed my time there, but my heart lies with my village. It was a good and peaceful village. At least it was until Megissogwon and his men came among us last fall."

Brigit asked, "Why did they come here?"

"They came to lay a trap for you, Princess, and to acquire the Loon's Necklace."

"What? How do you know that?"

"Many were the times I was forced to be with them and to serve them. They talked amongst themselves as if I was but a dog at their feet and couldn't understand what they said."

"That must have been a terrible time for you."

"It was. But I lived through. Many did not. My parents lost their lives because they opposed the evil shaman."

"So you helped us because of the evil Malsum visited upon your village and family?"

"Yes, and because of the Four Fires Prophecy."

Brigit looked startled. "But the Fires Prophecy warns your people against trusting us and living with us. Maengun told me so."

Shivon muttered, "You can't believe anything he told you. He was Malsum's limikkin. He lied. He tried to steal the necklace. He tried to kill us."

Brigit's jaw noticeably tightened as she thought of how she had been deceived.

"You are right, Shivon. Shania, would you tell us of the Four Fires Prophecy as you know it?"

Shania told them the tale in words similar to what Maengun had told it to Brigit several weeks ago.

The first fire was for the people to rise up and move

to the turtle shaped island - Hochelaga. We were told that if we did not leave our homes on the eastern shores, we would cease to be. We left our villages and traveled to the place of purification. We settled and made our hearth fires at Hochelaga.

The second fire was when the people prospered and grew in numbers. We were told some would move to live by the great waters. The people expanded from the first fire to the second fire and then going beyond to the furthest reaches of those great waters. Our people were to scatter about the shores of those great waters. However, with so many clans, and so many villages, so far apart, the people would struggle to be united as one.

The third fire prophecy spoke of a time of calling together of the people who had scattered from Hochelaga to those scattered about the waters. The clans and villages would unite as one by sending leaders to meet. Our people do this now. Our numbers are great, and yet though we live scattered about the great waters, we are as one. There would be threat and opportunity before us.

The fourth fire was a fire with two prophecies. It is a prophecy with a choice. Both prophecies foretold the coming of the new people from the lands of the sunrise. People with light skin would come among us.

If they were to come wearing the face of peace and brotherhood, then there would be a future of bountiful times for generations of our people. They would bring new knowledge and wonders that could be joined to our knowledge and ways. Together the people from beyond the sunrise and the people of the great waters would form a mighty nation. We were told that if they come with knowledge and a handshake, they come to build a life together with us. Then we should build of fire of cooperation with them.

The second part of the prophecy was a warning that there is danger for us. We are warned that the light skinned ones entering our lands may wear the face of death for us and our ways. We are told that if they come with weapons and promises of peaceful brotherhood, but with greed for our land, we should not trust them. If so, then we should rise up against them and build a fire against them.

Brigit interrupted Shania to say, "Maengun only told me the second prophecy of the fourth fire."

Shania responded, "It is what Megissogwon, whom you called, Malsum, taught him. The evil shaman took our prophecies and twisted them to suit his desires. He hurt all he touched." She spat with a vengeance as she thought of how he had touched her. Then she went on, "I know the goodness of your people. I saw it as I lived with the people of Kwahri. The light-skinned ones who live among them are good people."

Brigit tried to reassure her. "I have visited some of those people on our journey here. They are good. They live in harmony with the good people of Kwahri. I promise you I will do all I can to bring the prophecy of the the fourth fire's handshake and peace among people into reality."

Shania nodded. "That is how it should be."

Chapter 55 - Under the Water

The pyre was still burning with intensity when Shania finished sharing about the Four Fires. Their conversation subsided for several moments into silence. They listened to the crackling of the fire as its smoke rose to the heavens. From the far side of the lake they heard the wailing call of a loon.

The sound triggered a thought and Erik wondered aloud, "This water is called The Lake of the Loons. I'm wondering if our young druid will ever be telling us what happened to him when he fell into the water. I know he can't swim." He looked at Wulf and asked, "How did you end up alive, and on shore, and free from your bonds?"

Wulf gave a little shake of his head. "I'm not sure. It is sort of blurred in my mind. I was sitting there in the canoe with my mouth gagged and my hands tied. I do remember seeing Brigit shoot the arrow and heard it hit the guard. And I remember the canoe capsizing and falling out of it. Then I was underwater. I remember thinking that I was going to die. But I didn't." Then he wrinkled his forehead in thought. "Or did I?"

Several heads turned toward him in unison, and Shivon said, "What did you say?"

"I'm not sure I didn't die. I can't explain it. There are flashes in my mind. I remember the events of my life were flashing through my mind. There are images of a loon and an otter struggling. I remember something pulling me through the water. But I have no idea how I ended up on shore, and I have no idea how it came to be that my gag was removed and my bonds undone."

Wulf paused in his narration, deep in silent thought, and then asked, "How long was I under the water?"

Brigit was the one to answer. "It seemed like ages. After you went in, and I tossed the necklace to the loon . . ."

Wulf interrupted, "You did what?"

"I did what the boy in the legend of the necklace did. I threw it to the loon, to lie about its neck."

From out on the lake there came the wailing sound of a loon.

Then Brigit continued. "Then Maengun jumped in the water."

"To save me?"

"No. It was for the necklace. To me it was obvious he was chasing the necklace. I searched for any sign of you. Then I heard the commotion on the shore, and I shot Malsum. I watched as the guards left, and I saw Shania stab Malsum." She paused, and looked in wonder at Wulf. "Wulf, you were gone for far longer than I, or anyone I know, could hold their breath under water."

When Wulf said nothing, Shivon asked, "Wulf, do you remember anything else?"

Wulf shook his head again, as if trying to clear it, "There was a voice. As I was taking my first breaths on the shore. I heard a voice."

Shivon impatiently said, "And? What did it say?"

"It seemed to be calling me by name, yet it wasn't calling me 'Wulf'."

They all looked at him and waited for him to continue. He looked each one of them in the eye before he continued.

"Green Man - find the cave." Then he added, "The voice kept repeating that. Green Man - find the cave. Like a heartbeat."

Brigit said, "That was probably your mind remembering the cave that the three of you were searching for yesterday. Did you find it?"

Shivon looked askance at Brigit. "What are you talking about? We were held in captivity since we arrived in the village and were drugged. We've been tied up and pushed around from the time we were knocked out until the action this morning."

"That can't be. Maengun told me that after two days of watching over me in my delirium, you went searching for a legendary cave where the secrets of the gods are revealed."

"More of that scum's lies," declared Shivon, "this is only the second day since we were drugged. There is no cave."

Shania meekly said, "But there is."

Now all turned to her. She continued.

"There is such a cave. Our elders have passed on the legend that on the day of the summer solstice if a worthy supplicant enters the cave before dawn breaks on a cloudless day, then the first rays of the sun will burst through the opening of the cave and reveal the secrets of the gods on the back wall of the cave."

Wulf asked, "Do you know the way to this cave?"

"I think so. I have never entered it, but my grandfather, who was the village shaman before Megissogwon murdered him, pointed it out to me when I was a young girl."

Brigit spoke, "I'm still confused as to what day it is, and to how long I was drugged. When is the the summer solstice?"

Shania answered, "It is tomorrow."

"Then we must find the cave. How far away is it?"

Shania pointed to the steep hills rising above them to the northwest.

"It lies above us in those hills. It is perhaps a half

hour walk from here."

Wulf said, "Then take me there. We will go and find it today. The fire will burn itself out as the rest of you watch over it. There is nothing more for me to do here. Shania and I will find it today, so that tomorrow we may make a pilgrimage to it before dawn."

The others gave their assent and soon the two of them were on their way.

Shania led Wulf up a wooded ravine. True to her word, it was almost a half hour later, and the sun was past its zenith, when Shania stopped and pointed toward the ridgeline of a hill.

"On this side of that ridge there is a crack in the rocks. That break is entrance to the cave."

Wulf smiled at her. "Come on then. Follow me, and let's see if my insights lead us to the cave."

He tapped his staff on the rocky soil. An even wider smile spread across his face as he began clambering up the slope. Shania followed close behind.

It wasn't long before they stood at the narrow opening of a cave. They could look back through a break in the trees and see the glistening waters of the lake to the east.

Wulf smiled again. He found it easy to smile again now that his foes were vanquished and now that he was again in the woods. He turned to Shania.

"Well, here we are. Shall we go in?"

Shania quickly shook her head. "Not I. It is not my place."

"I'm not so sure about that, but for now I'll let that be."

Then Wulf tapped his staff to the ground and the spirit stone began to glow. Holding the staff before him, he slowly and carefully walked through the crevice and into the cave. A few minutes later he returned.

Shania asked, "Is this the right cave?"

"I believe it is. Tomorrow we will have the others here before the sun breaks the horizon. Then we'll find out for sure."

Chapter 56 - The Cave

The night was short, both because of the summer solstice, and because of the high level of anticipation among them. The sky was devoid of clouds and beginning to brighten in promise of the sunrise as they made their way through the woods to the cave. Wulf confidently led them, halting only when they could see the entrance to the cave.

There he turned and faced the others. "I believe it is almost time. Shall we go inside?"

Erik cleared his throat, and they turned to look at him.

Erik said, "I reckon I'll just find a nice spot to sit and watch the sunrise from here."

Brigit reassured him, "Erik, it is okay. You can join us."

"Ah, well, I thank you for the invitation. But my place is out here. You young ones have the responsibility for what happens now. And besides, the legend mentioned worthy supplicants. I might not be all that worthy. As you might have heard, I was rather wild in my younger days. No. I think it best if I stay out here. I see a nice niche in the rocks over there," he pointed to a place several paces away, "I'll just go make myself comfortable and wait over there."

Brigit knew it was useless to argue with Erik when he had made up his mind. "As you wish, dear friend."

Shania timidly said, "I, too, will wait out here."

Shivon added, "As will I."

At first Brigit was going to protest, but she could tell their minds were made up. She said to Wulf, "Well, then - it looks like it is just the two of us. Lead on."

Wulf held his staff before him and the glowing

spirit stone lit their way. After walking several yards through the straight and narrow crevice, they came to a circular open area. It was approximately twenty feet in diameter and perhaps fifteen feet in height. They could see there was a small fire pit in the center of the area, and a couple of small boulders along the perimeter where people might sit.

Brigit asked, "Should we start a fire?"

"No. It's not necessary. My staff gives enough light. But I think I should extinguish it, and allow the natural light of the sun be the only light to brighten this room."

So saying, the light of the spirit stone grew dim and then vanished entirely. They sat quietly in the near darkness of the cave, as the pre-dawn light shining through the crevice grew with the moment of dawnbreak approaching.

Their eyes were focused on the far wall of the cave as they waited. Suddenly a voice behind them spoke. "Don't turn around yet. Wait for the sun."

They did as they were told. Their eyes remained on the far wall.

Brigit asked, "Who are you? Why did our friends let you in?"

The voice chuckled. "I am the voice behind you, and your friends didn't let me in. I am here because I choose to be here."

Wulf said, "Shall we just sit here and ask questions of you, or shall we wait for you to tell us what you wish to tell us?"

The voice chuckled again. "You are a delight. Why, of course you may question, or you may listen. The choice is yours."

Both Brigit and Wulf decided to wait silently. But they didn't have to wait long.

The voice voice spoke again just at the sun broke the horizon illuminating the cave in a brilliant golden light that bathed them in its glory.

"Feast your vision upon the wall. Brigit, What do you see?"

"I'm sorry, but I can't see anything but an empty wall."

"Not even any shadows playing upon the wall?"

"No, nothing."

"So what you see is that the future of your people is yet to be written. You have brought the quest of your father to its completion. The future of all inhabitants in this land lies open to the great possibilities of this land. Your task as a leader of your people is to guide them in filling this blank scene with images of all people living in peace and harmony. There are no shadows of the past that will change what is. The future is yours to build."

"Was the necklace the key to all this?"

"In a way."

"Would you explain it to me, please?"

"The necklace gave you the power of choice."

"But I, or we, have always had the power of choice."

"Hmmm. Perhaps I say it better if I tell you it placed you in a situation and gave you the responsibility to choose. Would you choose personal power, or would you choose to sacrifice for another? Do your people choose power over others, or do you choose to live in peace with others?"

"And so, by giving away the necklace to the loon, as the boy did in the legend, I made the choice for sacrifice and peace."

"Simply stated. Yes. Now you, Brigit, may go. However, I would like Wulf to stay. I have some words for him."

Brigit didn't argue, but she turned to go out of the cave. In a small crevice, to the side of the entry, she could see a hooded figure. She couldn't make out details of his face because of the shadows of the hood and because at that very moment the sun passed beyond the opening of the cave, and the brilliant light within the cave gave way to a much dimmer illumination

She didn't know how for sure, but whether by a woman's insight or some unknown power within her, she suddenly who it must be. It must be the benevolent spirit of legend. She ventured to speak his name.

"Gluskabi, thank you. I ask no favor of you, for you have already favored me, as well as the many people of this great land. I would simply let you know, that, if in the future, you wish to visit or speak with me again, I would be honored."

She didn't wait for a response. She simply stepped past him and exited through the opening.

Gluskabi smiled as she passed, and then he stepped forward and went to sit down facing Wulf.

Wulf looked up and made eye contact with the being of legend. When Gluskabi said nothing, Wulf swallowed deeply and spoke.

"I saw shadows."

"So you did."

"How was it that I could see them, and Brigit did not."

"Your situation is different."

"How?"

Gluskabi gave a mirth-filled chuckle. "When you entered this cave, did you feel you had been here before?"

Wulf replied, "Certainly. I was here yesterday.

When I found it with Shania."

"You don't need to play games with me. I mean when you entered it yesterday, did you feel you had been here before?"

Wulf sighed in resignation. "Yes. I did. The moment I took my first step into the crevice I knew exactly what I would see within the cave."

"It is as I thought and hoped. You saw shadows, because the shadows of the past touch your life."

"What do you mean?"

"I'll answer you with a question. When you came up out of the waters of the lake - what was your first thought?"

Wulf gave a little chuckle. "I wondered if I was dead or alive."

"Perhaps symbolically, or perhaps in actuality, but certainly in truth, as you passed through the waters, you passed through death to life. You have been reborn. You are more than what you were before."

"I'm not sure what that means."

Gluskabi gave a hearty laugh. "That's good!" Then after a short pause he went on. "There is more to you than there was before. Consider. Who are you? Are you young Wulf from beyond the great waters? Or are you the one who is the protector of the fields and forests of Eirgalon?"

Wulf answered, "I'm not sure."

"I am." declared Gluskabi. And the choice that lies before you today is the choice of being who you are, or denying who you are."

Wulf sat for a moment in silence, thinking. Then he said, "You want to know if I accept being the Green Man of Eirgalon."

Gluskabi nodded. "I would probably have said,

'The Green Man of the Fields and Forest', but yes, that is what I want to know."

"I know that this is where I belong, and that this is where I want to be. I have no desire to go back to Europe. I love this land, and I love these people. But how can I be the Green Man? The Green Man died before Brigit was born? I'm a simple man. I am no god. How can I be who you ask me to be?"

"Life and death and rebirth - this is the cycle of life. Who is the Green Man, if not the very embodiment of this. You may think yourself lesser than the gods, but who is to say what makes one a god, or how a god knows itself? Perhaps the gods come to know themselves through the lives of the humans they touch."

"If I am to be the Green Man, how will I know what to do? How will I learn the skill and power I need to do the job of serving field and forest?"

"I trust you will learn as the need arises. You will find tutors and wise people who can give you guidance. No doubt you have already found this to be true, have you not?"

Wulf smiled. "Yes, I have." He paused, and then asked, "One more question: Can I still be called 'Wulf'?"

Gluskabi laughed a hearty laugh. "You will probably be called by many names, but consider - was Fearglas not called Fearglas? Why should you lose a name that belongs to you? Now go, before your friends wonder what has become of you."

When Wulf walked out of the cave, Erik was waiting for him, with Brigit, Shivon, and Shania standing behind him.

Erik asked a question, which was more a statement of fact than a true question. "It is time to move on, isn't it?"

Wulf nodded in affirmation and they started to walk away. Then Wulf said softly to Erik, "Do you have any idea what happened in there?"

"Specifically, no. But if I had to guess, I'd say that by look on your face and the color of your eyes that you've been given a job."

"What? The color of my eyes?"

"Aye. For as long as I have known you, which, granted, isn't all that long, you've had brown eyes. Now your eyes are about as green as green can be."

Wulf hesitated for a moment before he asked, "Have you ever known anyone with a similar eye color?"

Erik thought for several moments. "Well, I've known a fair number of people with green eyes, but only one that truly resembled yours, and he passed from from this life more than eighteen years ago."

Wulf gave a little chuckle. "Erik, you've got the gist of it. No need to say more. Let's get back to Shania's village. We have a little work to do there. We must help the villagers before we move on.'

"Sure enough, young Wulf. Let's get moving."

Chapter 57 - Farewells

They made their way back down to the lake, and from there they took the canoes across the lake to Shania's village.

The villagers initially greeted them with suspicion. However, when they learned from Shania that Megissogwon and Maengun were dead, and that the other men had run off, then the villagers welcomed them with open arms.

Shania and Shivon acted as interpreters for Brigit. Since the events of the fateful morning when Brigit had given away the necklace, she had felt a sense of herself that she had never experienced before. It had started with the way she had directed the flight of her arrow into the heart of Malsum. Now it was expanding itself into other areas. Her mother and others had tried to teach her arts of healing, but while she had the knowledge, the actual skill had eluded her. Now she seemed to sense what illnesses others suffered, and she had a sense of what to do for them. In her heart she knew she was a healer. So she set about listening to the villagers and healing them as she was able.

Meanwhile, Erik and Wulf noticed the lack of men in the village. People that would normally be providers of game for the villagers were absent. The villagers explained that Megissogwon and his men had killed or driven off the able-bodied men, and that only the old men and young boys remained.

Erik took some of the boys to hunt and Wulf walked with some of the old men to the lake. Within an hour Erik's crew returned with a deer. Shortly thereafter Wulf and the old men returned with baskets full of fish. The old men were chattering about how the fish seemed to jump into their nets. Wulf just smiled. They set up a spit and started a fire to begin roasting the venison and fish.

That evening, the villagers enjoyed a feast, the like of which they had not experienced in many months. During the course of the evening, Brigit promised to send men from Kwahri that would help the village recover from the damage that Megissogwon had inflicted upon them. The old woman who had tended Brigit expressed concern that the people of Kwahri might want to take revenge on the village for the death of the two young men that had escorted Maengun to the village. She was unsure of how they had died, but knew that in some manner Maengun was responsible for their deaths.

Brigit promised to explain the situation, and that no revenge would be taken. All slept well that night. With their full bellies and hopeful hearts the villagers were ready to meet their future.

Shania said her good-byes to the travelers in the morning.

Brigit asked her, "Why don't you come with us?"

Shania shook her head. "Perhaps one day I will visit you at Tara, or perhaps one day you will return here, but for now my place is with my people here."

Brigit and the others nodding with understanding. Again they thanked her, for her assistance had been instrumental in defeating Malsum. But they understood her determination to stand with her people and they again promised to send help to the village and to re-establish the former relationship the village had with Kwahri.

The walk away from the village was decidedly different from their journey to the village. The weather was now bright and sunny, with a soft summer breeze.

They had walked for about an hour when they came a place where the road split and a lesser path went to the right. Wulf called for the party to stop and they gathered around him.

"As you know, Gluskabi spoke with me in the cave. Our discussion led me to understand that Eirgalon is my home, and that I will not be returning to Europe. Brigit, I ask that you would communicate this to my Uncle Walter." He handed her a letter. "I suspect that he may have departed by the time you return to Tara, if so, then send this onward to him by another trading vessel to Hamburg."

Brigit showed her surprise. "What? Are you leaving me right now? Can't you go further with us?"

Wulf sadly shook his head. "I am now a guardian of this land. I wish to learn more of it. Shivon has told me of the Thundering Waters that lie at the western end of the first of the great waters." He pointed to the path leading west. "This path takes us in that direction. We must say our farewells here."

"We?"

Shivon took a deep breath. "Yes, we. I am going with him."

"What? Why?"

"Brigit, you know I love you. And I always will. But I love him too. I can't really explain it, but in some way I think he needs me. I know I want him. I hope this isn't good-bye forever. I believe we will cross paths again."

Wulf added, "I know the two of you have a special relationship, and I really don't want to stop that, but I know our paths must part for a time, and I do love her. I promise to protect her." And then he chuckled. "And to let her protect me when I need it."

Brigit could see that they had made their decisions, and she would respect them. She gave each one a long embrace, as did Erik, and then they watched as the couple walked away, down the path to the west.

As Wulf and Shivon turned a corner and walked out of their sight, Erik proclaimed, "The fields and forests of Eirgalon are blessed to have such guardians. May their lives be long and prosperous."

Brigit echoed the thought as she whispered in a soft voice. "You will always have my love, my friends. May you live long and prosper. And I promise, I will make sure we meet again."

They stood for a moment longer, and then Erik said, "It looks like it just the two of us now, lassie."

They turned and resumed their walk to Kwahri. As they walked, they enjoyed the beauty of the summer countryside and they talked.

Erik asked, "And how does it feel to finally come into your own.?"

Brigit smiled broadly. "It feels so good. You always believed in me, Erik. You don't know how much that means to me. Even when it felt like others doubted me, and even when you saw how Maengun swayed me, you believed in me."

"Awe, lassie, I may not be as smart as some of the wise folks about you, but I have some common sense, and I know talent and potential when I see it. You've always had an abundance of those. You just had times when you doubted yourself. In the future trust yourself. I suspect that you are going to have an interesting life as a leader of Eirgalon."

There was a long pause in the conversation.

"Erik. I'm going to need good people around me. I don't begrudge Wulf and Shivon for following their own path, or Shania for staying with her village, but I'm going to have to have people I can trust. Will you be by my side?"

There was a painful pause.

"Awe, lassie, I don't know what to say. I'm a simple warrior, and an aging one at that! I imagine you'll be traipsing all about this beautiful land. I don't reckon my old bones will be up to doing what I see you doing. Not that I wouldn't want to. However, I can promise to give you my advice on who to trust."

"Erik, I need you. If I'm to prevent wars and establish peace in a growing Eirgalon, I will need people like you."

"Aye, you do. And you'll have me as long as I have breath, but I'll only be able to help you as I am able."

"So be it."

She smiled, but then her face turned quizzical as he added, "And one more thing."

"What?"

"It's about the idea of establishing peace."

"Yes?"

"Peace is not the absence of war. It is the building of cooperation among people and working for the well-being of all. Peace is a never-ending process."

She smiled even more broadly, "My faithful Erik. Sometimes a warrior, but always the teacher."

He returned the smile and they walked down the road together into the future.

THE END (or perhaps, just the beginning)

Erik's Map - by his own hand
(Source: Academy Archives)

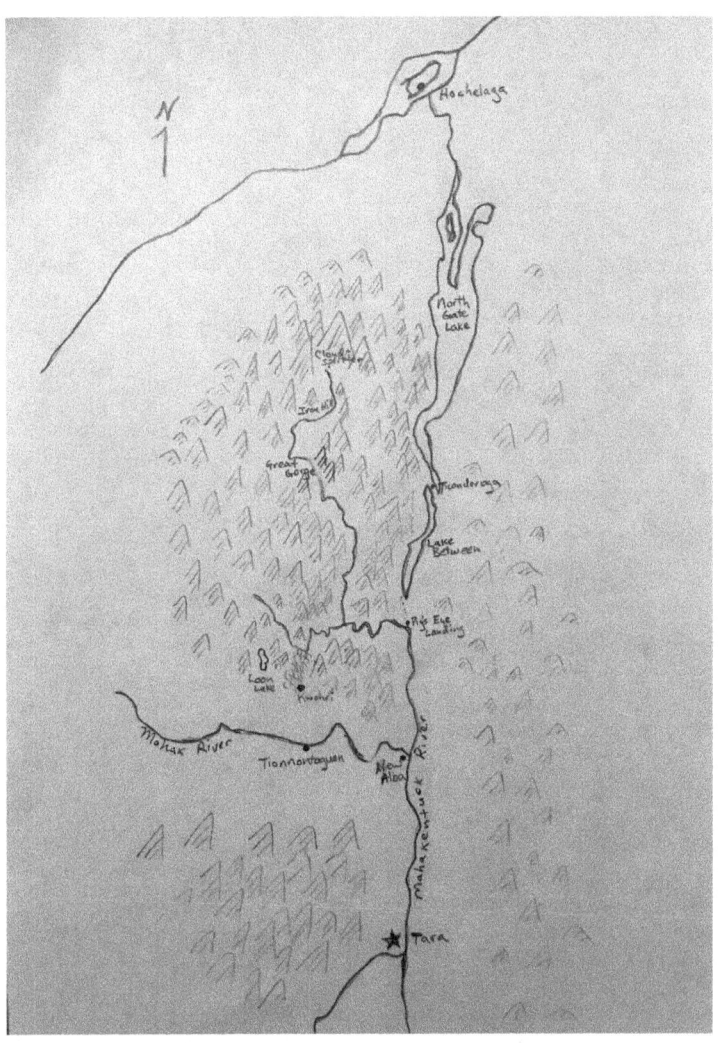

List of people in the Chronicles of Eirgalon series:

Akonni - Mohak warrior
Angnus Mulerider - operator of Ironhill mine
Asin, Mikom, and Noodin - Anishanaabe warriors
Ayenwatha - warchief of the Haudenoshonee
Bjorn - captain of a Glesga longship
Claire - wife of the ruler of Drogheda
Duncan - King of Glesga
Enat - daughter of Unaine of Fadis Innis
Erik - warrior and advisor to Skoth
Evlin - daughter of the Fearglas, partner of Skoth
Finn - Erik's nephew, Chief shipwright of Tara
Gakko - Senadondo's mate
Gela - wise woman of the Lenape
Genesse - leader of the Wolf Clan in Kwahri
Jake - one of Erik's men
Kahn-Tineta - Wise Woman of the Mohak,
Sagoye's mother-in-law
Keith - Chief of Dundee
Kenda and Tekaya - Oneida warriors
Lil - Duncan's wife
MacGregor - leader at New Alba
Maeve - mother of Tkaden
Maengun - young man of the north
(Anishanaabe for "wolf")
Malsum - incarnation of the evil god, Lox
Marilla - wife of Finn, proprietor of Tante's Table
McLean - ruler of Drogheda
Megissogwon - mysterious shaman of the north

Moran Doyin - Many People Land of the Powhatan
Notaku - protege of Keith
Olaf, Lars, Finn - sons of Rolf
Rolf - one of Erik's men
Sagoye - Waneek's son, Mohak warrior
Senadondo - limikkin (shapeshifter)
Shaemus - chief of the ore raft crews
Shaina - Anishanaabe maiden
Shivon - young Celtic Woman from Hochelaga
Skoth - High King (Ard Ri) of Eirgalon
Talli - sachem of the Esepus village of the Lenape
Teite - daughter of Unaine of Fadis Innis
Theofinn - druid master at Dunsheelin
Turla - war captain from Heilsand
Unaine - former king of Fada Innis
Waneek - wise woman of the Mohak
Walter - Captain of the Hamburg cog
Wulf - young German man, nephew of Walter

Novels in the Chronicles of Eirgalon

The Land Beyond the Sunset:
A Celtic America Called Eirgalon - Book 1

Search for the Loon's Necklace:
Chronicles of Eirgalon - Book 2

Brigit's Bow: Chronicles of Eirgalon - Book 3

Author's Page: amazon.com/author/joelkreger

www.ingramcontent.com/pod-product-compliance
Lightning Source LLC
Chambersburg PA
CBHW061946170626
46813CB00006B/2551